I0583966

TRUST

TRUST

AZOPHI ACADEMY™ BOOK TWO

TR CAMERON   MICHAEL ANDERLE   MARTHA CARR

DISRUPTIVE IMAGINATION

This book is a work of fiction. All of the characters, organizations, and events portrayed in this novel are either products of the author's imagination or are used fictitiously. Sometimes both.

Copyright © LMBPN Publishing
Cover by Mihaela Voicu http://www.mihaelavoicu.com/
Cover copyright © LMBPN Publishing
A Michael Anderle Production

LMBPN Publishing supports the right to free expression and the value of copyright. The purpose of copyright is to encourage writers and artists to produce the creative works that enrich our culture.

The distribution of this book without permission is a theft of the author's intellectual property. If you would like permission to use material from the book (other than for review purposes), please contact support@lmbpn.com. Thank you for your support of the author's rights.

LMBPN Publishing
PMB 196, 2540 South Maryland Pkwy
Las Vegas, NV 89109

First US edition, August, 2020
ebook ISBN: 978-1-64971-114-4
Print ISBN: 978-1-64971-115-1

For those who seek wonder around every corner and in each turning page. And, as always, for Dylan and Laurel.

— T.R. Cameron

THE TRUST TEAM

Thanks to our JIT Readers

Veronica Stephan-Miller
Dave Hicks
James Caplan
Diane L. Smith
Misty Roa
Deb Mader
Heidi Bauer
Kelly O'Donnell
Paul Westman

Editor

SkyHunter Editing Team

CHAPTER ONE

Special Forces Captain Jackson Reese's status as one of Major Anika Stephenson's three subordinates got him access to the bridge of the *Cronus* on a pretty regular basis.

Today, though, he would have been just as happy to be below decks with his crew, who knew the ship was in for a fight but didn't realize quite how poor the odds were.

The bridge was an oval, wider side to side than front to back. White bulkheads contrasted with colorful displays mounted on them, small ones along the periphery and a mammoth one set on the forward bulkhead. Control stations marched around the outside of the space, some occupied, others empty. He'd never quite figured out whether they were dedicated to specific tasks or not, since the singular uniform style of the *Cronus's* crew made it impossible to guess their area of expertise.

Near the display was a long, curved control surface with two chairs. The helm operator sat in one, with the weapons control operator positioned beside her. The captain's chair occupied the middle of the space. Jax and

Stephenson stood behind the other curved control panel, a mirror of the one below, which was slightly above and a few feet to the rear of the seat of authority. Captain Jensen spun her chair to face them. The combination of piercing eyes and long black hair restrained tightly in a bun gave her a stern look.

"Pretty bleak picture, wouldn't you say?" Her voice was more amused than worried, which meant she knew something he wasn't aware of or was posturing for her crew. He would respect either, but hoped for the first.

Stephenson nodded. She was almost a decade older than him, with short-cropped blonde hair, a bodybuilder's physique, and a strong face that was a little on the wide side compared to the rest of her. No wrinkles showed yet on her pale skin, except for some laugh lines here and there. "Indeed. Looks bad for us." She gestured up at the screen. "That's a lot of enemy ships." She also didn't seem particularly perturbed, increasing Jax's sense that he missed some vital piece of knowledge. *As usual, lately. I wonder if the captain was part of the Academy at some point too.*

He followed his superior's motion and took stock of the situation yet again. A sextet of alien vessels hung in space like a wall separating them from their objective. They were strangely organic, with spikes and bulbous projections utterly unlike the smooth lines of his ship. The *Cronus* had jumped into a system held by the Dhelear, a member of the Alien Coalition, who had recently stolen it from the Confederacy. The Coalition claimed it was an independent act and wrung their hands in false sympathy while carefully doing absolutely nothing to rectify the planets' theft.

This left an opening for the United Constitutional

Corporate Alliance. The transitional moment when a planet or system changed possession was a perfect opportunity to make it happen again. Sometimes, three or four capture and recapture cycles would occur before someone with the ability to take it also proved able to hold it. The *Cronus* had been tasked with arriving ahead of the invasion to drop its contingent of Special Forces soldiers—all three teams, this time—to prepare the battlefield on the lone inhabited world.

What they hadn't expected was the blockade waiting to greet them. The intelligence communicated by their spy drones had apparently been manipulated. *Wonder what other surprises they have up their alien-sleeve-equivalents.* "A lot of enemy ships who knew we were coming."

The Captain swiveled her chair to face forward. "Or they decided to throw up a blockade on the most likely entry route, and we stumbled into it. Either way, it's true: six-on-one are pretty bad odds." Her voice changed from musing to command, a sharp-edged decisiveness replacing the former amusement. "Sensors, any useful information yet?"

Jax had never managed to put names to faces among the bridge crew, as Jensen rarely referred to them by anything other than position. He supposed it made things easier, especially if she worked with multiple shifts of different personnel. Still, his sense of the woman was that she'd know each of those she led as completely as he did his team, so he judged it a conscious simplification. *I wonder if it changes under times of stress?* He looked up at the screen. *I guess I might be about to find out.*

A tall black-haired man at a station on the left replied,

3

"Nothing new, Captain. Our scans aren't permeating their hulls. They continue to emit trace elements consistent with engines ready and have shields raised."

The senior officer grunted. "Tactical?"

A woman standing a few feet in front of Jax and Stephenson at the curved control panel answered quickly, her tones confident and bright. The back of her head showed long hair precisely restrained in a braid that coiled upon itself and was held in place with a metal clip that looked like it might double as a throwing weapon, to judge by the sharp edges. *My kind of person.* "Openings in the ship's hulls could be torpedo tubes. External cannons are aimed at us. No clear data on whether they're projectile, energy, plasma, or other. Their shields are positioned in our direction."

Captain Jensen drummed the fingers of her left hand on the arm of her chair, an inch or two away from the control panels set into the front end of each. "Science, what do we know about them?"

A tall woman with red hair turned to face the Captain from a station on the right side of the room while lacing her hands behind her back. Her face was covered with freckles, giving her an almost innocent look that contrasted with her words, which were delivered with a slight accent he couldn't identify. "They're wicked bastards, pardon my language. The Dhelear are considered to be among the most aggressive species in the Coalition, likely because they tend to strike out on their own as they've done here. Their physiology is similar to ours in the most basic ways: bipedal, two arms, two eyes, nose, and mouth all pretty much where ours are. They have three biological sexes, the first changing into one of the others at their equivalent of puberty. However, that's where the similarity ends. Sharp teeth and claws are standard, and leathery skin with strategically placed bone plates beneath add to their martial prowess." She shrugged. "Their culture embraces personal combat as the deciding factor in most disputes, probably an evolutionary result of their physical natures."

Captain Jensen nodded as a small smile crept onto her face. "So, are these combats usually one-to-one? Dhelear to Dhelear, as it were?" The redhead answered with a single nod of assent. "Well, that screams opportunity, doesn't it?" She swiveled again to face Jax and Stephenson. "Major, are your teams ready to go?"

His superior officer nodded. "Whenever and wherever, as always, Captain."

Jensen rose to her feet. "Communications, hail the nearest ship. Put me on screen." She pulled down on her tunic and ran a quick hand over her hair, which was as disciplined and pristine as the rest of her.

A male voice from somewhere on the bridge responded, "Aye, Captain. We're connected."

An alien appeared on the main display, to one side of the view of all the enemy ships. The science officer had neglected to mention that the Dhelear had turquoise skin, a strangely soothing shade given their martial nature. It said, "You are in our system. If you encroach any further, you shall be destroyed. Go back where you came from, human." Its voice as rendered by the translation software was smooth and deep.

Jensen shook her head. "I'm afraid we can't do that. We intend to take possession of the planet and the system.

Soon our ships will outnumber yours, and we'll do as we please. However, in recognition of your prowess in liberating the area from the Confederacy, we will honor you with a single challenge. Your ship versus the *Cronus* for the right of passage beyond your blockade. You win, we call off our reinforcements and leave you to it. We win, you and your ships depart."

Jax turned away from the screen and murmured, "I don't think the fleet is going to like that."

Stephenson raised a hand as if she was scratching her nose and whispered, "Nor will they likely adhere to it. This is about survival."

He rotated back without responding. It made sense. They weren't going to be able to defeat all six with anything short of a miracle. The other ships would doubtless have an estimate of when the *Cronus* could jump again and would act before she could escape. That left stalling for time as the only real option.

The creature on the screen didn't look fooled. Nonetheless, it nodded. "Very well. We shall begin in six minutes." Jax assumed that some sort of temporal conversion happened in there that the translator took care of.

Captain Jensen replied, "Acknowledged. *Cronus* out." She stalked back to her chair and punched a button to activate the whole-ship intercom. "All hands, we are now at Condition One." Around them, the bridge personnel acted quickly but calmly to take seats, and the tactical officer pointed for him and Stephenson to do the same. They complied, pushing the chair's arms inward to keep them from floating away if gravity was lost or being hurled across the room if the ship took a hit. Similar actions would be taking place throughout the vessel as her crew moved from Condition Two, preparing for battle, to the actual waging of it.

The communications officer rerouted signals, and the Captain's voice emerged from the comm in his ear. "Tactical, confirm the other ships are retreating at a proper rate?"

The woman replied, "Confirmed. They will be out of range when the timer runs out." He noted that a set of numbers was counting down on the main display, showing just over four minutes remaining.

Jensen nodded. "Good. Shields eighty percent front to begin. They're likely to try an all-out punch in the mouth if our research on them proves true." The UCCA hadn't personally gone up against the Dhelear before, but their spies had retrieved information from the Confederacy, which had. "Then, watch out for sneaky stuff. Probably torpedoes set to loop and hit from an unexpected direction."

Cronus's tactical officer replied, "Aye, Captain."

The captain drummed her fingers again. "Weapons, half-strength lasers and particle cannons at first. Torpedoes to strike from the sides. If they shift any power away from their front shields, hit them with everything except the railgun. We'll hold that in reserve." A man's voice acknowledged the order. "Helm, evasive at your discretion. Don't position us between them and the rest of their ships, though."

She paused for almost a minute as the clock ticked down. Over his comm, reports from various sections of the ship came one after the other to confirm that the vessel was ready for combat. Then she asked, "Science, any evidence the bastards are likely to cheat?"

The woman's voice held a note of amusement. "They're rather like us in that respect, too, Captain."

At that instant, with a minute and eleven seconds remaining on the timer, the Dhelear ship fired.

CHAPTER TWO

Captain Jensen's guess had been correct. Their enemy opened up with everything it had, which turned out to be a mix of lasers and projectiles. The shields dispersed the former and slowed the latter to the point where they bounced from the hull without damaging it, transmitting a sound like a light rain through the ship.

The tactical officer announced, "Defenses holding. Torpedoes launched, heading port and starboard. Balancing shields."

Jensen nodded and ordered, "Weapons, let's test their three-dimensional thinking. Four torpedoes, one top, one bottom, one to each side. Continue the underpowered lasers and particle cannons." On the display, a quartet of small blue dots matched the two green ones already present, marking the powered projectiles as they traveled toward the ships.

The enemy's missiles struck first, detonating as they met the energy of the *Cronus's* shields. The sound of rain became a rattle as the powerful explosions were partially dissipated and the remainder spread across a wide section of hull, reducing its ability to penetrate in any single place. Stephenson grunted. "Scoured some paint off with that one." Jax nodded. His experience with ship-to-ship combat was primarily theoretical, the practical portion limited to moments like these.

Their missiles slammed into the enemy vessel, causing blossoms of brightness to appear on each side. Jensen asked, "Tactical?"

"No penetration, Captain."

"Well, if it were easy, they wouldn't have sent us, right?" She tapped the control panel on her display. "Weapons, I want torpedoes to look like they're going to the sides, then converge on this point. When they do, lasers and particle cannons simultaneously. Wait a moment, then give them a shot from the railgun."

"Aye, Captain." His voice signaled an eagerness to comply with that particular order. In his place, Jax would feel the same.

They weathered another pair of torpedo impacts from the enemy while the weapons officer put the plan into action. Jax leaned forward unconsciously to watch the torpedoes near their target. A few seconds before they were to hit, Jensen shouted, "Evasive pattern Zulu, execute." The ship heeled to port, and she continued, "Hold fire." A moment after, a flash of light on the other vessel sparked an incandescent trail that reached for the *Cronus* but passed to their side. Had the Captain not maneuvered, they would have been hit. She growled, "That's a big laser."

The tactical officer agreed. "At least three times as large

as any we've got. On the scale of the ones our biggest ships have. They must have some amazing energy throughput."

"Let's save the analysis for later. Hopefully, it'll take them a while to charge it up again. Clever not using it right out of the box." She shook her head. "Smart ship. Weapons, set up that attack again."

The helm officer moved them back into proper alignment, and another pair of torpedoes shot out at their foe. As they struck, a barrage from the lasers and particle cannons peppered the spot. He understood the theory behind the strike, weakening the shields with the guns and putting major stress on that location with the torpedoes to drain it further. Alone, the attacks wouldn't have penetrated. Even together, they probably only had a minimal likelihood of damaging the enemy vessel.

But the railgun was the real attack. A long barrel ran the entire length of the ship, completely hidden from view. Few ships the *Cronus's* size would carry such a heavy weapon, but since she'd been designed from the outset to ferry Special Forces troops, the decision had been made to put a little extra iron in the glove. Electromagnetic force from oppositely charged rails on either side of the barrel pushed an inert spear of metal down the long tube. A panel in the forward hull opened in time for the projectile to fly out, pass through the weakened portion of the shield that might have slowed it, and slam into the enemy ship's skin.

Pieces floated free as their foe's vessel maneuvered, and the sensors officer announced, "Seeing inside now. Thanks for the hole. We have explosions happening. Vibrations like compartments sealing up."

The Captain grinned. "Excellent. Weapons, set up a

barrage to keep them busy. Stephenson, we have until their big cannon is ready to fire again before we need to destroy them. Can't risk that thing hitting us if we can avoid it. Your people have that much time to break in, steal anything worth taking, and get back out. Coordinate with Tactical for shield penetration."

She slapped her restraints free and rose, striding for the door that led to the main part of the bridge. "You got it, Captain." Jax followed. *Now the real fun begins.*

A lift ride, a quick stop for gear, and a run through half the ship later, Jax bolted into the *Cronus's* hangar bay. The cavernous rectangular space was four decks high, with catwalks at each level ringing the outside. It was empty in the center, where the interior doors that led to the small airlock were located. In non-combat situations, the huge hangar was left pressurized so crews could work without vacuum suits on the array of ships positioned around the perimeter.

The light cruiser had four undistinguished rectangular shuttles, each configured for space jumps. They also served the mundane function of ferrying passengers. They were parked in pairs at the ends of the rectangle, with three always ready to go and one on a maintenance rotation. On the left side from where he'd entered at the bow end of the chamber was an array of smaller ships. Tugs, repair skiffs, and the torpedo-like vessel the SF teams referred to as the "lovers' coffin," designed to send two people and a copy of all the ship's data away from the *Cronus* as fast as possible before jumping to safety. No one ever expected it to be used, but Jax approved of its presence. *Even backup plans need backup plans.*

He slowed as he neared the breaching craft. It was another rectangle, rendered in featureless black except for the opening that faced the middle of the area. His team members were seated inside, with a spot beside the entrance left vacant for him. Identical ships on either side of his sat closed and quiet, only the slight vibration rising through his boots signaling that all three were prepared for flight. He jumped in and gave a voice command to join the shuttle's comm network. He'd already been talking with his squad on the way down, so the team was battle-ready. "Close her up, Stick."

"Affirmative, Captain." Panels slid in from the left and right to seal the passenger compartment. Outside, heavier metal blocks would be creating a second seal for the short trip to the enemy ship.

He toggled his connection to Anika Stephenson. "Major, my team is good to go. Request permission to fly."

She replied, "Affirmative. Permission granted. Hangar will open in ten seconds." His commander was located somewhere near the middle of the *Cronus*, in an auxiliary command center that could be configured to oversee any type of operation, including taking over all essential functions of the vessel in case of damage to the bridge.

Jax cut his feed to her and gestured to his people. "So, everyone ready for this?" They were featureless in their combat suits' dark helmets, but their voices were clear, calm, and energized. Although they were all the same rank, a pecking order existed among them. First to speak was

Beatrice "Wasp" O'Leary. "About time we got some action. All this training to get Newbie up to speed and no ops to seal the deal. Finally, we'll get to see what he's made of."

Jax laughed. She was right. They'd been doing an extensive amount of drilling, a requirement whenever a new member was added to the team. The loss of Kyle Drent on their last mission still hurt, but they all knew "Kansas" wouldn't want them to grieve overly much. This op would seal the transition from their former complement to their present one, and they were all definitely ready for the sense of solidity that would accompany it.

Kyra "Books" Venn, the unquestioned superior intellect among the group, asked, "So, the aliens like to fight, huh? Anything in particular we need to watch out for?"

Chatter between the pilot and the control center encroached upon the edge of his hearing, and the ship surged smoothly underneath them. He called up a view from the bow camera on his display and watched as the hangar swung around them, and their ride descended through the open hatch. "I can't imagine the teeth will be a factor unless we're already seriously screwed. But they've got claws, and I think we can expect that they'll use them if we get in close."

Darius "Dare" Lyton patted his suit. "Good thing this works against blades and ballistics." They were all adorned in matching outfits, black everything with overlapping armor plates strapped onto it. They did indeed protect against the two attack types Dare had mentioned, in addition to collecting and dissipating energy attacks. When pristine, they were capable of shunting off almost any incoming damage. *They won't be pristine for long, I'm guess-*

ing. In his display, the *Cronus* disappeared from the camera view, and their craft sidled into line with the pair that held Major Stephenson's other Special Forces contingents.

Things were about to get busy, but he had a moment left to speak to their newest addition. Sebastian Welker didn't rate a customized call sign with the team yet. That was another step that lay on the other side of the impending action. All new members held the mantle of "newbie" until their formal initiation through a shared mission. His file said that he'd had "Strings" hung on him at some point, and that would work well with his people's existing call signs, so it would probably carry forward. "Newbie, you good?"

Welker's voice was always softer than you expected it to be. "Perfect, boss."

Major Stephenson took over the channel. "All right, people. We're thirty seconds out. Team One is aft top, Team Two center bottom, and Team Three forward top." Jax had asked for the front of the ship, and Stephenson had indulged him. "You know the drill. One, engines, Two aux command, Three bridge." The other two captains, one in each of the ships to their left, acknowledged, and he did as well. She continued, "If the opportunity presents itself, test the stun setting. However, don't jeopardize yourself or the mission to do it. They're hardly innocent bystanders. Chuckleheads."

His team laughed at that, and he grinned. Her delivery was perfect, calculated to reduce their tension. Not for the first time, he thought about how good she was at her job, which involved understanding people down to their very core. *Like knowing to send me to the Academy, although that was only partly about me.* His thoughts wandered to his adventures with Cia and his other unit, who while not military had represented themselves well.

Then the time for thinking was over. The three ships hurtled forward toward the alien vessel. Fire from the *Cronus* slammed into its shields along their path, allowing their reinforced crafts to penetrate it without losing much speed. They shifted directions as soon as they were inside, heading for their targets.

Jax rolled his shoulders and his neck, wincing at the crack that sounded in his helmet. *Too young to be this old. Maybe I need to give in and commit to being a full robot, instead of just having a cyborg arm and leg.* "All right, people. Here we go. Remember, I don't want to look like a jerk in front of the other captains, so try not to screw up." They laughed, and he nodded. *Right. Let's do this.*

CHAPTER THREE

His ship spun at the last minute to point the opening he'd come in by toward the enemy vessel, then rammed into it. He couldn't see the operation but knew a seal would be created between their hull and the enemy's. Then a series of explosive and incendiary charges would blow a hole in the other one.

Before the back panels retracted, Jax slapped the release for his restraints, rose, and grabbed the rifle mounted on the bulkhead above where he'd been seated. When the expected opening gaped before them, he led the way into the Dhelear vessel and turned to face the bow as soon as he was inside the large corridor. His team fell in line behind him, Newbie in the second position followed by Books, Dare, and Wasp. A wireframe schematic of the ship's interior was drawing itself into existence in one corner of his display as information was fed from the other teams' sensors and theirs. "Team Three, on station." The other two groups reported in shortly thereafter.

Major Stephenson replied, "Continue to primary objectives. Pick up anything interesting you see along the way."

Jax selected team-only communication and ordered, "Forward, people. It looks like we need to get two levels down and a decent distance ahead. Books, move up behind me. Newbie, keep your eye on the sensors and especially look for data accesses. If we're lucky, they'll have something hackable here."

"On it," Kyra Venn replied, and Welker acknowledged, "Affirmative." The Special Forces, at least under Stephenson's command, operated on the principle of "Mission first, intel always." That meant gathering information was a priority on any assignment, in addition to their primary objective. Ships tried to invade one another's computers as a fundamental part of any battle, but it was rare to succeed with only wireless access. Each member of his team carried multiple devices that could either pull intelligence directly or, better, act as a bridge to the *Cronus* so her crew could infiltrate the systems if they could find a data port.

Their path ended at a closed bulkhead door. "Everybody to the left," he ordered, stepping in that direction. "Books, see what you can do with it." Venn strode forward to examine what looked like an oversized palm reader on the side of the barrier. She poked the rectangle with her finger, then with a small tool, but the unit failed to respond. He shrugged. "Okay, blow it, and let's hope there aren't too many of these between here and there."

She attached four fist-sized shaped charges in a diamond shape on the surface, and they all turned away as the explosives detonated. The metal was tougher than it looked, but a few kicks with the sole of his boot buckled the sections that had refused to give way, sending the center part crashing into the area beyond.

His first sight of a Dhelear in the flesh was as it fired the rifle it carried. The weapon itself was overly large, about half again as big proportionately as their own. It spat a series of projectiles, one of which caught the armor plate on his right arm as he pulled back out of the way and deflected into the hull. *Oh, sure, shoot at my human arm. Jerk.* He leaned into the passage and depressed the trigger, sending a stun beam out at the enemy.

The alien wore what must have been its version of battle armor, a thick leathery-looking garment that clung to it like a second skin. He wouldn't have known it was wearing anything, except for the suit's scarlet coloring. The fabric—or whatever it was—lit up with something that resembled printed circuits as the stun beam struck, the energy blast spreading out from the point of impact with a brilliant intensity that faded as it moved further from the source. By the time the glow had reached the being's shoulders, it was almost gone.

Jax activated the wide channel and announced, "Stun ineffective against red armor. Switching to projectiles." The other groups didn't reply but would use the knowledge to inform their progress. He leaned out again and sent a triple burst at the alien, ducking back as it returned fire. He pulled a fiber optic camera out of his sleeve and stuck it around the corner. An image of the enemy down on one knee appeared on his display. No blood or open wound was visible, but apparently, the concussive force of the bullets had done something. "Wasp, with me." He moved through the doorway and stepped to the left so O'Leary could go to the right as she followed. He flicked on his external speakers and said, "Put down your weapon and lay on the deck."

The alien shifted, but not in the direction indicated. He and O'Leary fired at the same time, and the Dhelear fell backward. Jax ran ahead and kicked its weapon to the side, then raised his gun and pointed it down the corridor ahead of them. "Wasp, bind him. Newbie, sling his rifle so our people can check it out later. Team, forward behind me." In moments they were at his heels, and he crept forward down the long hallway, his boots soft on the metal floor beneath them.

Captain Catherine Lorenzo, leader of Team Two, reported in over the wide channel. "We've tapped into their computer system. Tell the *Cronus* hacks to have fun." They passed doors on the interior side of the corridor, and each one left uninvestigated was one more itch at the back of his brain. His preference would have been to clear them in sequence, but that didn't align with their objective. They needed speed, which meant leaving potential threats behind them and hoping Lyton would be up to dealing with anything from his rearguard position.

They reached the elevator they'd been heading for. "Major, do we have control of their systems yet?"

Her response was immediate. "Negative, Axe."

"That's okay. Team Three loves a challenge." He switched to the team-only channel. "All right, we can't rely on the lift. So, we're going to have to go down the shaft without it." He pointed at the indentation in the left wall ahead. "Books, get us in there. Wasp and I will watch forward. The rest of you guard behind."

In addition to being the smartest of them, Kyra Venn was also the most proficient with subtle explosives. If he needed a big boom, he'd turn to Beatrice O'Leary for that, or do it himself. But precision jobs he left to Books. She pulled the demolitions bag off her belt and withdrew a spool of what appeared to be black string. She used the material to outline the lift doors, the sticky substance bonding instantly as she pressed it against the metal. Then she ran a small tool over the top to nullify the outermost layer, ensuring it would blow forward rather than back at them. When she finished, she stepped to the side and put her spine against the wall next to it. She said, "Ready."

Jax replied, "Do it," and a sharp sizzling noise sounded behind him that ended with a flat crack. Again, the alien metal had provided more resistance than expected, and it required three of his team working together to get the doors free. When they announced the task was complete, he faded back to examine the shaft.

The lift itself wasn't obviously visible below their position, giving him hope that they might be able to manage the two decks down they needed to go without it flying up to smash into them. As he'd expected, doors were positioned on either side of the shaft on their target level. It only made sense that the ship's main areas would have better access to the interior. The vertical tunnel itself was a solid cylinder except for the doors, which would make the next part difficult.

"Books. Look two levels down, across the shaft. Think we can be subtle?"

She stepped beside him and peered down. "Nope. It

would take at least a couple of minutes to get down there, set up the explosives, and blow it."

He nodded. "Okay, then. Newbie, guard front. Wasp, we need a sticky bomb."

O'Leary's athletic skills were the best on the team, so she always handled sticky bombs. The small grapefruit-sized spheres had a cylindrical handle sticking out of a side, making their casting a matter of some finesse due to the irregular balance. She pulled one out of her pack and pressed the button on the top, which retracted the sheath covering the main part of the ball. Now it would adhere to whatever it touched. As long as the throw was good and the handle didn't strike first, the device would likely be sufficient to blast open the doors two decks below.

Wasp stepped forward, took a moment to judge the angles, and gently swung the object to prepare for the toss. She shifted her weight and threw in one smooth motion, and the sticky bomb obediently sailed directly to the target and stuck to it with a *clang*. A tap of a button on her wrist comm detonated the explosive.

Jax let his rifle fall on its sling to hang down from his chest. "Let's do it, people." He leapt forward, activating his magnetic boots and gauntlets in midair. His hands and feet struck the far wall, and he clung there for a moment before shimmying down the wall feet-first, his toes sliding down in turn as he released and reapplied the power to the magnets. He was halfway to his objective when O'Leary hit the surface above him. Belatedly, he warned, "Be sure to check for the lift before you jump."

He stopped above the opening, put his gauntlets on the wall near his feet, then used them as a rotation point to kick his legs out and swing feet-first through the shattered doorway. He hit the floor awkwardly and fell backward, which turned out to be a lifesaving moment of clumsiness as weapons fire ripped through the air over his head, laser and projectiles both. "Contact," he yelled and scrambled to twist and bring his rifle into shooting position.

O'Leary landed beside him, and the 270-degree view in his display showed that she did so with more agility than he'd managed. His initial shots were better, though, knocking the enemy on the right-hand side backward with two successive triple-bursts of bullets to the chest. Wasp had selected energy, and while the alien's armor dissipated it, whatever feedback or spillover made it through the suit caused it to stand upright in what looked like pain. Jax shifted his aim and put three rounds through its head, dropping it. O'Leary strode toward the one he'd first downed, repeatedly blasting it with energy. She knelt to bind it as the rest of his team entered the passageway behind them, and he climbed to his feet.

"Okay. We have another section of corridor on the other side of that bulkhead door," he pointed at the barrier ahead, "and then we should be at the bridge. Books, go set the charges." They blasted through and dropped a trio of enemies with synchronized fire. The captain of Team One, Hugo Frangilo, reported over the comm that engineering was secure moments before they reached the hatch blocking the way to their objective. Jax growled softly at not having been the first unit to accomplish their goal, then pushed the concern away.

He considered essentially knocking and asking the enemy to surrender, although in a more technologically involved manner. But with what they knew about the enemy's mindset, he'd be giving up a strategic advantage for nothing, since his enemies weren't likely to accept. Instead, he waited while Books wired the door, then took the forward position as she blew it inward.

Jax stepped onto the bridge with his rifle held ready but didn't fire. The crew members stationed there stood at attention but carried no weapons, and only the captain who they'd seen before had his claws visibly extended. The alien's hands flexed as he locked eyes with Jax. Stillness filled the space for several breaths, then Jax ordered, "Everyone have a seat." The aliens looked at the captain for permission, and he nodded but did not himself obey the command as the rest of his people did.

He asked, "Perhaps you would be willing to face me one-on-one for the pride of victory?" Jax's helmet translated the words almost instantly after the being made the sounds that must have represented them in his language.

Jax shook his head. "My boss won't let me. And besides, you cheat." He and Stephenson had discussed the possibility after leaving the bridge and before they'd separated to attend to their responsibilities. "Now, do I have to shoot you, or are you willing to call it a day and get the hell out of our way?"

CHAPTER FOUR

Jax and the other captains had been invited to Major Stephenson's quarters for an after-action discussion. They'd left the enemy vessel about four hours before, and their ship was now in transit toward the inhabited planet in the system. The blockade had illustrated the loss of the element of surprise, so the *Cronus* was going in as part of the main fleet, and the Special Forces teams would all have downtime until the actual fighting finished. Then they'd have their chance to do an intel sweep, assuming Stephenson found a convenient excuse to get them down there. *She's never failed at it yet, can't imagine this will be the first time.*

He arrived a good ten minutes early. Special Forces training taught the ideal that on time was late, and early was on time. Normally he'd have been a little closer to the mark, but he hoped for a few words with his superior before the others turned up and was pleased to see her cabin empty as she ushered him inside.

Stephenson's short blonde hair was in unexpected

disarray as if she'd let it fall naturally after showering. She was in uniform, and as usual wore no makeup, seemingly unconcerned with a blemish that might pop up here or there on her otherwise fair skin. When she moved, it was with the economy of a jungle cat. He'd seen her in a tank top and shorts in the gym, and it was fair to say that she had the musculature of one as well.

The room was about five times the size of his quarters, which were about as small as individual lodging could be without qualifying as a prison cell. A pair of closed doors to the left doubtless led to a modest bedroom and bathroom. He'd never seen them open. A desk with a broad curved display mounted on the bulkhead above it took up most of the back wall, and a round table just large enough to seat four occupied most of the rest of the chamber. The only personal touches were a comfortable-looking armchair in the corner with a tablet resting on it and images from Stephenson's career hanging on the walls.

She pointed him to a chair and sat across from him, taking the place farthest from the door. "You're notably early, Jackson. I presume there's a reason."

He grinned. "And you were ready for me to be notably early, Major, so I presume you have some idea as to what that might be."

She chuckled and nodded. He appreciated the level of informality she accepted from her subordinates during non-mission times; he'd worked for others who always insisted on following every rule, regulation, and recommendation. Even in a job as precise and demanding as his, that level of precision was downright annoying. "Could be

I do. How about you tell me anyway, rather than making me guess?"

"I wondered if any of the data that we pulled from the ship or the planet gives us any more information about the Academy investigation."

She lifted an eyebrow. "Eager to get back to Earth? Or is it that you're eager to get back to a particular Earth person?"

He scowled. "One would imagine that people in positions of such responsibility as you and the Professor would have something better to do than gossip." She laughed, and he turned the frown into a smile. "And it's possible, just *possible*, mind you, that it's a little of both."

Stephenson nodded. "Fair enough. So, I'll be discussing the data broadly when the others get here. But to answer your question, yes, some pieces had a connection to that inquiry. I've spoken with Maarsen about them, and we think we have a path forward. It's going to be a challenging one though."

Her face remained completely neutral, which was a message all of its own. "You'd already planned to send me back. You played me. Again."

Stephenson laughed, but it held no mockery, only enjoyment of the ongoing game. "It's possible. Just *possible*, mind you."

A signal from the door announcing the arrival of the others cut off his retort. He rose as they entered and shook hands with each of them in turn. First was Catherine Lorenzo, who had joined the *Cronus* shortly after he did. She occupied the lowest end of the acceptable height range for Special Forces personnel, a hint over five feet.

Her skin was a couple of shades tanner than his and was stretched tight over the hard muscles displayed by the quarter sleeve black uniform she wore. Short but stylish dark hair fell over her forehead, and her eyes were the same shade of deep brown. Their intensity frequently intimidated those foolish enough to challenge her authority.

Hugo Frangilo occupied the opposite end of the spectrum. He stood at least six feet tall, more if you counted the spiky blond hair that terminated in a perfect flattop plane. His face was long and strong, with hard cheekbones and striking blue eyes. You wouldn't know that his skin had ever been touched by sunlight. Smiles came easy to him, but one got the sense that they didn't go very deep, whereas Lorenzo wore her emotions openly and proudly. *And me, I'm somewhere in the middle of it all, I guess. We make a pretty complete package.*

Their skills were complementary as well. Every squad could handle any kind of assignment, but intrigue and subtlety were his strength, Lorenzo was the most accomplished tactician and wrecker-of-things among them, and Frangilo had the smooth patter of an experienced negotiator always ready to spill from his mouth.

He retook his seat as they sat, Lorenzo on his right and Frangilo on his left. Major Stephenson smacked her hands gently on the table. "Okay, first, well done all of you. The *Cronus* is safe because of your actions. Pass that along to your teams." Stephenson had already shared her congratulations during their return flights from the alien ship, but she could always be counted on to ensure the presentation of formal accolades. "Second, I'm putting Team Three into rest rotation. Team One is back in front, and Team Two is training."

They nodded, as that announcement was expected, the cycle their standard practice. "I'll be on detached detail for a short time. There should be no missions for us while I'm gone, as our ride is en route to its maintenance slot. That'll mean a week of downtime." She gestured. "Jackson, hand me that tablet." He complied, and she hit a few buttons then projected a holographic representation of the planet they'd liberated over the table. "So, the Dhelear were allegedly acting on their own volition here. But it would be foolish to ignore the possibility that they're lying, especially since the data we pulled shows that they had access to several seemingly confidential sources inside the Coalition."

Lorenzo asked, "Which ones?"

Stephenson shook her head. "Unknown. The trail leads back to the central network, and we can't follow it further. I'd sure like to get one of our teams in there." The Alien Coalition's headquarters was a massive station deep within their territory, positioned roughly in the middle of a triangle comprised of three of its earliest and most powerful members. They only knew of it from references found in ships they'd fought. No human had ever set eyes on it and lived to tell the tale, according to all the information they had. "In any case, there's no way to be certain this wasn't part of a bigger scheme."

Frangilo grunted, sounding annoyed. "I don't suppose we can do anything about it at this point, though, right?" He grinned suddenly. "I know. Let's go grab one of their other worlds and see what we find."

They all chuckled at that, but Stephenson shook her head. "You're not wrong. We're not instructed to take action at this time. That'll be decided by those above." She pointed at the ceiling.

Jax quipped, "On the hull?"

The Major sighed. "Jackson, you should visit medical and make sure that your intelligence quotient wasn't reduced during the last mission. Now, let's all discuss what the next few weeks are going to look like."

The meeting had been typically brief, and he'd spent a few minutes after talking shop with the other captains. However, another ritual beckoned. He wandered back to his quarters and changed into civilian clothes and departed for Space Street, where his team was scheduled to meet in a quarter hour.

The *Cronus's* primary recreation hub rose through multiple decks and was designed to give the illusion of being on-planet rather than in the middle of a hunk of metal floating in a deadly vacuum. The main thoroughfare looked a lot like a sidewalk you'd find in any city, and the bars, restaurants, and shops that decorated both sides of it emulated different flavors of Earth businesses. He exchanged nods with a pair of plainclothes security officers, ship's crew, and headed into one of his favorite spots, the Queen and Rook tavern.

The bar was modeled after an Irish pub and had wooden chairs, wooden tables, and a large wooden bar with a stripe of frosted metal to keep one's drink cold running along it. The popular spot boasted a boisterous clientele. Recorded soccer games from Earth played on the screens mounted above the bar, and people cheered as if they were real-time and deeply meaningful. Jax had reserved a table for them, which had required a not-insignificant tip to the bartender in advance, and as he sat, a server sauntered by and deposited a cider in front of him. The drinks were limited by type since the place offered only beer, cider, or whiskey, but had several options available in each category. What he'd been given was a mystery, but it was sweet, tart, and hit his nerves like a gentle hand stroking his hair.

He sighed and grinned up at his team as they arrived in a bunch. They had traded in their uniforms for casual clothes as well, simple shirts and black trousers the unwritten rule for them all. He'd chosen the middle spot in a curved booth, and they climbed in on either side, Darius Lyton and Kyra Venn on his right, Beatrice O'Leary and their newest addition, Sebastian Welker, on his left. The server swung back, took their orders—Irish Whiskey, Lager, Stout, and Cider, respectively—and vanished into the hubbub a moment later. In the time he'd been there they'd gone from two deep to three deep at the bar, and half the tables had someone standing next to them talking to the occupants. *I love it here.*

Lyton asked, "Why do you always choose the loudest places on the street?"

Jax laughed. "Consider it training in how to focus among distractions."

O'Leary shook her head. "You're full of it, Axe. You only like it because you dig the servers' skimpy outfits."

He shrugged. "Well, not *only*. The cider's top rate, too." They had the kind of bond that permitted any sort of insults to fly, within reason. In truth, both the male and female employees of the place dressed to impress and were more attractive than he'd ever be. They were also *Cronus* crew members, something he never forgot no matter how many drinks his evening revelry might entail. But his people liked teasing him about his love life, or rather his lack of it, more than almost anything else.

He countered, "And we can all see you sneaking looks at that guy's ass, Wasp, so maybe you shouldn't be the one throwing stones." Her gaze snapped back to him, startled because that's exactly what she'd been doing. Everyone laughed again.

Venn bumped him with her shoulder. "Show Newbie the thing."

Jax shook his head, spotting the server inbound with their drinks. "First, business." When they each had one, he raised his in a toast. "To another successful mission for Team Three." They all clinked glasses and sipped. He lifted it again. "And Welker, who reclaims his call sign. Here's to Strings, now officially part of our particular group of miscreants."

They laughed and completed the toast, then Venn smacked him on the arm. "Quit stalling and show *Strings* the thing."

Jax grinned. "Right." He pulled a coin from his pocket, an oversized half-dollar he'd received as change his first day on the *Cronus*. It had become a good luck charm; although he wasn't particularly superstitious, he didn't feel comfortable with the idea of giving the item away, either.

He handed it to Venn with a nod as she finished clearing the area between them of glasses he might damage.

Books put the coin in the palm of her hand and said, "Watch this." She threw it upward, and his left arm snapped out and snatched it before it could get more than a few inches into the air, the enhanced speed of his prosthetic now more or less totally under control. *Until the time comes to kick it up again, anyway.* He'd been practicing daily, slowly getting faster and faster with the limb. Unfortunately, even if the new leg the Academy had provided could handle it, speeding up only one part of one of his legs wasn't a practical idea. *More like a comical one, I'm guessing.*

Welker's eyes went wide, and he said, "Whoa. Nice. Cyborg?"

Jax chuckled. "As if someone didn't tell you already."

The other man nodded with a smile. "Still, impressive."

He shrugged. "Yeah, except for the part where an alien ripped my arm off and beat me with it."

Lyton laughed. "That's exactly how we told him the story, too. You running away while he smacked you was really the most pivotal moment."

Jax flashed an obscene gesture at the other man, and the table erupted again. He waved for another round, ready to make sure his team enjoyed their last evening together for a while before informing them he was headed off-ship again.

CHAPTER FIVE

The trip to Azophi Academy was different the second time around because he knew what awaited him, more or less, and because he was traveling with a companion. Although Anika Stephenson had been his boss for many years, he'd never had the pleasure of her company for such a long stretch. As they made the hop to the moon, then shuttled to Edinburgh to catch the maglev train, he'd learned about her past and shared his. They'd grown up on the same continent, her in the northern part of North America, and him in the middle.

She'd arranged a car to pick them up in Inverness, so he was denied the joy of riding a motorcycle northeast to Dunrobin Castle, the Academy's home. They'd more or less run out of things to chat about, so he watched the green hills pass by outside the window while she attended to work on her ever-present tablet. She had a box identical to the one he'd been given the last time he was on Earth to connect her to the Special Forces network hub in Edinburgh. He could have piggybacked the signal and checked in on his team, but he didn't want to undermine Beatrice O'Leary, who he'd left nominally in charge in his absence. She'd handle mundane matters, and Captains Lorenzo and Frangilo would assist with anything bigger. His squad wouldn't deploy without him or another SF captain under any circumstances, not that there would be any with the *Cronus* docked for repairs and upgrades.

His first sight of the castle hit him with the same powerful sense of awe that it had on his last visit. The notion that a family had lived in that giant house in the past boggled the mind. *Sure, it was the ruling family, but still. How much room does one multi-generational conglomeration of nobles need?* The answer was apparently "a lot." Their driver dropped them near the sidewalk that led to the side door, and it opened at their approach, the matching portal on the far wall of the "airlock" entry also open.

He gestured ahead at the vacant chamber and empty area beyond it. "I had a personal greeting when I got here last time. I guess you don't rate."

Stephenson snorted. "That's how they treat all the newbies. I haven't had to deal with it in ages."

Solidly and amusingly put in his place, he strode a half step behind her as she led the way into the maze of large halls and long corridors that made up the structure. She seemed to know where she was going, and it only took him a few seconds to realize they were headed toward the Professor's office. However, before they arrived, a staff member in the distinct orange and yellow accented uniform of the Academy blocked their path. He was tall and thin, older than Jax by at least fifteen years, and carried a sense of aloof formality. *Which is appropriate for someone who works in a bloody castle, I suppose.* "Professor Maarsen is occupied at the moment, Major, Captain." He nodded at them each in turn. "If you'll allow me to escort you to your rooms, he will be with you within the hour."

Stephenson looked annoyed briefly, then shrugged. "Okay, lead on."

He changed into his Academy clothes, as he thought of them, which weren't all that much different from his off-duty uniform. The black top was a little less rigid, and the matching trousers a little less creased, but otherwise they were quite familiar. He strapped the school's custom comm on his right wrist and immediately felt silly with one on each arm. He paced the room for fifteen minutes, trying to talk himself out of going to seek Dr. Juno Cray, who had suggested that she might be open to a date when he returned. *If I go now, I'll look desperate,* part of his mind said. Another part replied, *or interested. Interested is good.* He shook his head to force both parts to shut up and was freed from having to decide by a vibration signaling a message.

He strode with purpose to the Professor's office, mostly confident in the path but still checking the map on his wrist now and again. The door was open when he arrived, and he headed for the right-hand chair only to find it occupied by the Major. He frowned and sat in the other one, realizing that there'd been a pre-meeting he hadn't been invited to. *I wonder if Maarsen is doing it to screw with me. I wouldn't put it past him. Probably considers it a "teaching moment."*

Nikolai Maarsen smiled up from behind his desk. He wore a tan suit with a white shirt and no tie, a shade lighter than the longish hair on his head and face, but with less grey. His thin mustache and beard were better sculpted than when Jax had seen the man last, as were his sideburns. *Maybe yesterday was barber day or something.* "Captain Reese, wonderful to see you again."

Jax managed a thin smile that he was sure the other man saw right through. "Wonderful to be back. So what's up?" He was saddened to discover the Professor wasn't offering his guests any of the amazing whiskey held captive in the decanter on the corner of his desk. *Ah well. After the long trip, it might put me straight to sleep.* He was consistently good at managing time zone changes, but it usually required a night's rest to get himself set onto a new schedule.

Major Stephenson shook her head. "I told you he'd be annoyed."

Maarsen laughed and beamed at them both. "Of course. But what sort of teacher would I be if I didn't remind Jackson of his control concerns right off the bat?"

He sighed inwardly. The Academy's purpose, as it had been explained to him, was to identify something hindering a person and endeavor to fix it. Usually, that thing wasn't something the subject was aware of. In his case, Maarsen had theorized that he had issues around control, specifically the "wanting to be in" part. Under the guise of helping him with his malfunctioning prosthetics—

which was connected to the issue, apparently—the Professor had sent Jax on a couple of missions that pushed him to trust others, rather than relying mainly on himself. In the month or so that had followed his last trip to Earth, he'd put those lessons into practice during training and action with his team. And, reluctantly, Jax had admitted to himself that the Professor might have been onto something. *Maybe.*

The older man's mirth faded, and he wiped his eyes. "So, to business, then. Major, the information you sent was an invaluable piece of the puzzle, allowing us to drop several other things we knew into their proper places. The picture is beginning to come into clarity."

She nodded. "And the next move?"

He turned his attention to Jax. "Will involve the captain, to be sure, since we already know that he's talented at blending into Confederacy worlds."

Stephenson asked, "So I guess offering money didn't work?"

The Professor shook his head. "No, I'm afraid not. The one official we thought might be amenable resisted the bait. It was a longshot at best, anyway."

She frowned. "Your people didn't give the game away, I hope."

He offered her a dour look. "Anika, please. Of course not."

She grinned. "Gotcha."

Maarsen laughed again and rapped a knuckle on the surface of the desk. "So you did. Well done. Since that's out of the way, maybe we should give Jackson some context." He pulled a tablet out of a lower drawer, activated it, and slid it across. Jax caught it and reviewed the display.

It showed a block of nondescript buildings on a street he didn't recognize. They were each at least ten stories tall, with some reaching as many as twenty, and their seemingly random arrangement reminded him of a mouthful of perfectly vertical chipped teeth. The coloring was right too, some of them pure white, some a little yellow, and others a dirty grey in need of brushing. "What am I looking at?"

Stephenson answered, "Planet Ezora, home to the closest sector headquarters of the Confederacy government. Since it's relatively nearby, there's a decent presence from them, the Coalition, and the UCCA. That should allow you to get close without generating too much suspicion."

He nodded. "What's the objective?"

Maarsen replied, "Find a way into the admin building, grab every bit of evidence you can find about the connection between the Confederacy and aliens, in or out of the Coalition, and get out. Kind of like your other tasks for us."

Jax chuckled darkly. "Let's hope this one goes more smoothly than those did."

Stephenson looked at him with a raised eyebrow. "I meant to ask you about that. What was it, something about having lost your clothes at the resort while drunk?"

He shook his head. "A strategy. Playing a role. And playing it *well*, I might add. What's important is that it worked." He turned back to the Professor. "This sounds like it has significantly more potential disaster on the downside than the last one though, sneaking into a government building."

The other man nodded. "Yes. Your cover identities will be as pirates, and we'll have you outfitted so that nothing can be traced to here, or to the UCCA. We've acquired such things over the years and stored them against such a need."

"So you'll be sending me in with a team again? Same one as before?"

Maarsen smiled. "They're all conveniently in residence at the moment, and none of them has shown an unwillingness to work with you again."

Jax laughed. "That's quite the vote of confidence, there, Professor."

Stephenson grunted. "Well, to be fair, they've only had the one experience, and you did get naked."

He closed his eyes and controlled his tone. "I did not. Get. Naked." The others shared a laugh at his expense while he shook his head in defeat. "Fine, whatever. Timetable?"

Maarsen looked at Jax's superior. "Any reason on your end to wait?"

She shrugged. "Give our people another day to sift the data. If they find something, great. If they don't, we start this, but hold off on executing it until we're certain they've gotten all there is to get."

"Sounds like a plan." He addressed Jax. "Okay with you?"

"Sure. I need some sleep in any case." He checked his watch and grinned. "And some food. Time to hit the dining hall."

Stephenson laughed. "Best idea you've had all day. Professor, join us?"

Maarsen shook his head. "Some final things to set into motion. I'll catch up with you later, Major. Jackson, have a good rest. If I know Cia, and I like to think I do, she'll want to get started early tomorrow."

CHAPTER SIX

Jax was up before dawn the following morning, as always, and completed his preparations in record time. He threw on civilian clothing and headed for breakfast. He was digging into his pile of pancakes when a familiar voice sounded from behind him. "Hey stranger, welcome back." Cia dropped a plate of food onto the square table in front of the seat beside his, then casually strode toward the magnificent coffee urn in the corner. When she returned with two full mugs and put one next to him, he grinned.

"Okay. Clearly, you want something. What is it?"

She laughed and sat in her chair, grabbed her utensils, and dove into her meal rather than answering. After a minute, she sighed and wiped her mouth with a napkin. "Damn. I was starving. I think it's your manliness. It makes me insatiable." The sarcasm in her tone was thick and heavy, and it was like they'd been apart for hours instead of a month.

Jax shook his head with a look of false concern. "Well,

that does happen. You could probably go see the doctor, get some sort of libido-suppressing drug or something."

She nodded. "Or maybe I could up my standards a bit from the sub-basement where they must be living for me to find *you* appealing." She speared a piece of sausage and chewed it loudly. "So, have you returned for the mission, or is it a random coincidence?"

"Do you think anything here is ever really coincidence?"

"No. You're learning. That's good." She grinned. "The rest of the team is already on the *Grace*. I came back to grab some food and pick you up. While you were sleeping, we've been working. Slacker. With the resting and the laziness."

Jax shook his head and lifted his mug in a toast. "Thank heavens that I can always rely on some things never to change, like the fact the Professor is inscrutable, the coffee is delicious, and you're an idiot."

Cia chortled. "Good comeback. I think you may have gotten smarter while you were away. Another few years, and you'll hit the 'average' marker. Don't give up."

They traded insults for the rest of the meal, Jax enjoying every second of it and Cia feeling the same, to judge by the happy grin she displayed in between trying to gross him out by showing him her half-chewed food. The drive up to the airfield was uneventful, the driver the same one that had ferried him up from Inverness.

The *Grace* waited in her hangar, buttoned up and ready to go. Even the stairs had been pulled away, requiring them to use the retractable ladder to climb up to the midship hatch. He followed the pilot toward the compartment at the front of the ship, only to stop in surprise at the sight of someone he didn't recognize in the second chair. He tilted his head and said, "Hello." It came off sounding like the question it was.

Cia laughed as she maneuvered into the left-hand seat. "Copilot for this trip, and the only other person I trust to fly my girl. This is Trianna." The unexpected woman was older than her, probably his age. She had brown skin that glowed with health, dark black hair that fell in spirals to the middle of her back, and from the profile visible as she turned slightly and nodded in his direction, a pointed nose, sharp cheekbones, and at least one dark eye. What she didn't have was a desire to speak to him, as she returned her gaze to her instruments without further engagement. She was dressed in the all-black standard uniform of an Academy student and spoke almost inaudibly to the control tower.

Jax looked at Cia, and she grinned at him. "No, you haven't lost your status, don't let your masculinity get bruised. We're switching ships along the way, and there was no chance that I'd leave my *Grace* sitting out in the middle of nowhere on autopilot. Trianna will watch over her and, if needed, come in and rescue us, too."

He nodded. "She doesn't talk much."

Again, the pilot barked a laugh. "She's not as nice as I am. You'll have to convince her you're not as enormous a chucklehead as you appear to be before she'll invest any time in you."

He raised his hands in surrender. "I'll head to the back and make sure everyone's strapped in, then, shall I?"

"Good plan. Looking like about five minutes until we're

on the runway." The *Grace* could take off and land the same as a terrestrial airplane, which allowed it to use the small airfield near the Academy that lacked a VTOL rating. Something about the depth of the concrete. She'd explained it once, but he'd put it in the part of his mind where things he didn't need to remember went. He turned and headed for the rear of the ship.

It wasn't the biggest vessel, and since they had no particular reason to be hanging out in engineering or the cargo bay, and hopefully no cause for anyone to be in medical already, that left the galley and rec areas on the top deck for those who'd chosen to congregate rather than sleep through the flight. He took the metal stairs two at a time and broke into a smile at the sight of the other three members of his Academy team.

They were playing cards around the dining table, some sort of game that involved fast draws and discards and the clink of metallic chips slapping against the magnetized surface. Ethan Kimmel was nearest, the youngest of their team except for Cia. The piercings in his ears and right eyebrow added to his youthful look, as did the shock of blond hair that fell over one side of his face. The rest of his head was close-shorn, almost down to his overly pale skin.

Clockwise from him was Maria Verrand, dark of skin, eye, and hair. The latter was in thin braids today, rather than the long thick one she normally preferred, and gathered together in a tie at the nape of her neck. Even in loose clothing, her strong muscles were evident with each shift of her body.

Anton Sirenno, tanned and freckled, held the last position. Something always looked off about the man, as if he'd been put together from parts that didn't quite align properly. Large ears, a slightly small nose, and the classic square jaw sat uncomfortably with one another. However, his sarcastic personality and deep confidence made his looks mostly irrelevant. He looked up at Jax's entrance and called, "Hey, sit in for a hand."

Jax stopped beside the table and frowned down at them. "What the hell are you playing?"

"Quickstop," Kimmel explained. "The cards keep moving until someone gets a pair. They slam it down, and whoever else has one of those cards lays it on the table. Pairs are worth twice as much, and you bet each time one goes down. The game ends when the last pair drops. It's fun once you get the hang of it. Just an honor round, no money involved. Take a seat."

Jax shook his head. "I'll take a seat, but it won't be here. We're lifting off soon. Time to strap in." They didn't react with as much panic as they had the first time he'd said that to them, during his last visit to the Academy, but they still moved with speed. Kimmel packed the cards, Sirenno deactivated the table and swept the chips into a box, and Verrand walked a circle around the room to make sure that nothing was out of place that might become a missile when the ship accelerated.

He nodded in approval, then followed them as they headed to their quarters to buckle in. He called up the view from the bow camera on his wrist comm and watched as they took off, wishing he was up in the front with Cia. Co-piloting with her was the only time he'd gotten the feel of flying firsthand. Usually, he was trapped back in a passenger compartment of one kind or another, all too frequently as a prelude to jumping out of it into space, atmosphere, or both.

The launch was as smooth as high-end whiskey after a long day, and the announcement that they were free to move around for a while as the ship moved to its jump point came at the expected moment. He made his way back to the galley, arriving just after Cia and with Kimmel on his heels.

Jax said, "Okay, have you been briefed on our objective?"

The others offered sounds of negation and ridicule, and Cia replied, "Of course not. That's not how the Academy works. How about you?"

He grinned. "Well, well, well, suddenly I'm the one in the know. What a glorious feeling." After rolling his eyes, he continued, "Let's see if we can put the pieces together. We're going to a Confederacy world to break into a government building and retrieve something."

Sirenno asked, "What are we after?"

Jax shrugged. "Apparently, we don't yet need that information, unless someone else has been told?" No one answered. "Okay, that's me. Cia, how about you?"

She crossed her arms and imitated his tone. "Well, well, well, it appears that I *do* know more than you, as usual, although it's not much. We're heading to a neutral point for a ship change, then continuing to Ezora. We'll land at the main spaceport and meet a local contact of some kind in the city. They'll be waiting for us."

Verrand added, "I was told that there will be some solid security involved in whatever we're doing."

Kimmel nodded. "Me too. I have some extra hacking tools with me."

Sirenno laughed darkly. "All the instruction I received was to get on the ship, and all would be revealed."

Cia grinned widely. "Now that sounds like the Professor we all adore."

Jax sighed. "I'm usually on the other side of the need-to-know equation. It's not as much fun from this perspective." Cia gave him a pointed look, and he tapped his hand lightly on his chest to acknowledge the touch. He'd deeply offended her by not sharing information during their last mission, and while she'd forgiven him, more or less, he was still on what she'd called a "Prove it probation."

He clapped his hands. "Okay, as my commanding officer likes to say, when you have nothing else to do, train. Who's up for some hand-to-hand?"

The training session lasted until they needed to secure for the jump to their waypoint. Afterward, he and the rest of the non-pilots watched a display in the galley that showed their approach to a small moon in an otherwise dead system. The ship landed beside another, smaller by about a third. Kimmel observed, "That doesn't look like it's going to be a comfortable home." The others agreed, and when they passed through the temporary tube connecting airlocks, Jax was forced to admit they had a point.

They'd entered via the midship hatch, and a few steps inside revealed that it was definitely light on creature comforts. A wide central corridor stretched the entire length of the ship, showing the pilot compartment to the front and a cargo compartment to the rear. Doors were set into the passageway at intervals, which he hoped led to less dilapidated-looking rooms than their entry area. "What scrapyard did the Professor pick this up at?"

Cia laughed. "That's not far from the truth. She's been rebuilt from parts of a bunch of other ships and christened the *Jigsaw*. Some folks from home have been seeding disinformation about the ship and her crew since we acquired her almost a year ago. She has more power than you'd think, strong shields, and a turret that packs more of a wallop than it strictly should."

Sirenno asked, "How does that happen?"

She shrugged. "They get all kinds at the Academy, right? Some folks were apparently good at modifying weapons. Now, I'm going to preflight this baby while you all arrange to have the cargo containers on the *Grace* moved over here. They should be small enough to fit through the tube, but if not, someone will have to take a walk. Don't forget your tethers, since there's not much gravity to speak of. Or, if it's you, Jax, wing it. I'm sure you'll be fine." Cia gave him a sweet smile and headed forward.

Jax shook his head and pointed at Sirenno. "You're with me. Let's get the stuff. You two, go ahead and figure out where the important things are, and find out if the turret is automatic or run by an operator. If it's the latter, you can draw straws to decide who gets to shoot it."

CHAPTER SEVEN

Ethan Kimmel twisted his face up and breathed, "Arrrrrr." The others at the table laughed, and Cia wiped away tears of mirth.

"You are absolutely the worst pirate ever."

He scowled. "Okay, let's hear yours."

She straightened, lifted her chin, and growled, "You scallywags better get in line, or it's the plank for ye."

Jax rolled his eyes. "It figures that you'd be the best at impersonating a dirty, unethical, probably smelly sea thief."

She pointed at him. "You're first into the ocean, fancy boy."

The others laughed again, and he was forced to join in. The *Jigsaw* had been visited by officials from the planet below and given permission to land, but the busy spaceport had a queue, and they hadn't paid extra to jump the line. Getting ready for that inspection had involved changing into the clothes and gear that the Academy had packed for them and securing their stuff in a smuggler's hold cunningly concealed in the cargo bay. Jax wasn't a particular fan of the outfits and equally disliked and distrusted the pistol strapped to his thigh, which had seen better days.

He hoped their contact would have a more impressive selection of equipment for them, including more appropriate clothes to move about the city, or it would be exceedingly difficult to accomplish their mission. *A fact that Maarsen is doubtless aware of, so I'm sure we'll have what we need. Mostly sure. Okay, pretty sure.* One never knew if a given situation was going to turn into some sort of learning opportunity, and it would be like the man to think that they'd gain valuable experience by having to improvise with substandard gear.

Jax cut that train of thought short since it was neither immediately relevant nor something he could do anything about. *What will be, will be, and we'll roll with it, whatever it is.* He'd gotten some hours in the right-hand seat on the flight and happily discovered that their separation hadn't damaged his rapport with the pilot. He liked having colleagues with whom he could pick up after a gap as if it had never happened.

Cia looked sharply down at her wrist and said the words he'd been waiting to hear. "We have our slot. Time to head down."

The planet the Confederacy had selected for its regional governmental hub was primarily desert. Not the sand-covered deserts of Earth, but rather a huge expanse of cracked brown stuff that made up the surface. The ship's database had informed them it had a significant amount of clay in it, and also a ton of minerals he'd never heard of before. In his judgment, it qualified as "not a particularly hospitable place."

The city of Grefta was a literal oasis right in the middle of all that barren scorching aridity. He'd stared at it as they landed, the energy dome glimmering in the suffocating warmth, revealing lush greenery under its transparent canopy. Unfortunately, the spaceport sat outside the sheltered portion, and they had to wait a full five minutes for the dust stirred up by their landing to settle before they left the ship.

The heat hit like a right cross from a heavyweight boxer as soon as he climbed onto the ladder attached to the hatch. His breath stopped, and it felt as if his heart had as well. Both kicked back into gear after only a moment but did so at a significantly increased rate. He muttered, "One more planet I'm so glad not to live on."

Verrand, a few rungs above him, replied with a grunt and a question. "Seen many of those?"

He chuckled, then coughed as he accidentally swallowed some air thick with dust, or dust loosely encompassed by something that pretended to be oxygen, he wasn't sure which. "More than I can count." Most of the planets he'd encountered during his time in the Special Forces met that criteria for one reason or another. To be fair, their mandate didn't involve visiting resort worlds, generally speaking.

When they all reached the ground, Sirenno commented, "No car to greet us? I thought the life of a pirate is supposed to be all wine, women, and song. Or men," he added, nodding at Verrand, "or livestock." He nodded at Jax, and the group managed a weak laugh.

Jax shook his head. "The sun has evidently baked all the talent for humor out of this crowd. I think we can grab a tube into town over there." He pointed to a building more or less in the center of the landing pads. "Let's get moving."

They walked between the bright orange lines demarcating the safe zone until they reached a terminal. Double doors whooshed open in front of them, and they stepped into shade and conditioned air. As one, they all breathed a loud sigh of relief. Jax wiped the sweat from the back of his neck. "Well, that was refreshing, right?"

He got looks ranging from incredulity to a clear concern for his sanity and laughed. "No point in whining. Doesn't change anything. Hop to it."

The tube was a half-cylinder that stretched from the spaceport into the city itself. The cars were semiprivate and frequent, and they only had to wait a few minutes before climbing into one. Sirenno scowled at the people who tried to follow him in, and they wound up having the eight-seat vehicle to themselves. The sun had also baked away any real desire for conversation in the others. Despite his long experience functioning in varied climates, Jax found himself fighting to keep his relaxation from turning into sleep during the four-minute, high-velocity ride.

At the end of the line lay another terminal building, this one opulent and cavernous, decorated with greenery and polished stone. Restaurants, bars, and shops filled the concourse, and visitors milled about taking it all in while the city's residents hurried by, intent on their destinations. His group did a little of the former but mainly stayed on track. They'd reviewed their path to their contact's location during the long wait to descend to the planet, and the others seemed as eager as he was to get to it.

Or, maybe it was the promise of showers and rest that drove them. Either way, the group headed in a loose line toward the less elegant part of the city referred to by its denizens as Spacers' Gutter. The name suggested a lack of polish that didn't exist in reality. As the home to the local Confederacy officials, no serious crime would be permitted for long. The mix of terrestrial authorities in their green outfits and sidearms and the frequently occurring sight of soldiers in full uniforms sporting rifles and grenades were sufficient to keep outrages both big and small in check.

They arrived at their destination after a short walk, a casino with the entirely unoriginal moniker "The Lady's Luck." It sat between a restaurant emitting an amazing smell of cooked meat and a crowded bar with noise penetrating through every crack in its worn facade. The gambling hall's exterior was all glitz and glamour. A red marquee surrounded by winking lights announced the club's identity, and below it, doors that looked like they might be solid gold were imprinted with images—a high heel, a pair of lips pursed in a kiss, and a sketched hourglass figure. Cia snorted. "Subtle."

Verrand echoed her. "They're trying to go for a certain clientele. Kimmel, stop staring." They all laughed, Ethan Kimmel the hardest, and Jax pulled open the door. Crossing the threshold was like stepping into an alternate dimension where the brutal heat of the planet had never existed. The interior featured constant recurrences of red and black styling with golden accents, in wood, metal, and fabric. Slot machines, one of Earth's ubiquitous exports, lined the walkway that led deeper into the space.

He sauntered, taking the lead position with Cia beside him, her shorter legs leaving her always a half step behind. When she increased her speed, he matched it to be irritating. It took her a while to notice. Then she slapped his arm hard enough to echo from the nearby machines, drawing surprised looks in their direction. He repeated her earlier observation. "Subtle."

"Bite me. Do you know where we're going?"

Jax nodded. "See those two women standing by the elevator up there?"

In his peripheral vision, Cia did a nice job of checking them out without appearing to. *She's learning. Or maybe she's always been good at that sort of thing, with her trader background.* "Guards?"

"Definitely. Our contact occupies the top level and works the casino floor in the evening when the high rollers are playing. Of course, they wouldn't want us to be seen heading up there, so I'm guessing that before we reach the lift—" He was interrupted by the arrival of several muscular people in house security uniforms, three men and a woman. The males were all of a piece and fell under his mental classification of "goon." The female had sharp eyes, and her lips wore a slight sneering twist. She was nondescript, easily forgettable, which was probably a good thing for a casino security person. Their outfits were black with red trim.

She said, "We're going to have to ask you to come along."

"Says who?"

The guard answered, "A friend of yours. A teacher, I believe."

Jax nodded. "Okay, point the way." She did and led them through a side door into the backstage part of the gambling den. It looked to be the opposite of the outer portion, sterile white on all sides, cold and businesslike with no sense of comfort to it. Some trepidation accompanied the sight of the security post ahead, likely complete with cells for holding troublemakers, and he let out a breath of relief as they passed it without stopping.

They surrendered their weapons and stepped through a scanning device when they reached the end of the corridor, the surroundings making it clear that they had no choice but to comply. Once through, the elevator was the same clean perfection, with only a palm reader instead of buttons or a control panel. The guard put her hand on it, and they shot upward. Verrand asked, "Not afraid we'll knock you out and go after the VIP? Or is it that your other guards wouldn't fit in here?"

The other woman turned and regarded Maria Verrand with a smile. "First, I think the odds of me taking all of you are a little better than fifty-fifty, since you're weaponless and I'm not. But even if you did, there's always someone watching, and they'd trap you between floors and fill the car with gas."

Cia asked, "Knockout? Pepper?"

The woman's lips stretched into a thin line. "Nerve toxin. You'd be dead in minutes."

Sirenno replied, "So would you."

She shrugged. "Obviously. If it came to that, I'm either

already dead or seriously messed up. Plus, there's an antidote, so if the timing worked out, I could probably be saved."

Jax shook his head. "You people play hard."

She grinned up at him. "Count on it, bud."

The doors opened to reveal another set of burly men completely blocking their advance. Their guard said, "We're good." The pair locked eyes with each of his team members before moving out of the way, offering an unmistakable promise that any mayhem would be met with immediate and debilitating pain. The sunken living room beyond them echoed the styles they'd seen below. Soft off-white walls wrapped around windows that tinted the sunlight coming in to a gentler shade. Picture frames and lamps were gold, and the furniture was scarlet and black.

Jax walked slowly down the three wide steps onto the plush ivory carpet that covered the area. A trio of couches in a U shape bounded a glass and gold coffee table, pristinely empty. A beautiful woman sat in the center of the sofa that faced the elevators. *No, that doesn't capture her. Glamorous. Stunning. Striking.* If asked to describe her, he would have used the words "classic beauty." Dark hair fell in soft waves to her shoulders, offsetting her pale skin. Her makeup was simple and flawless, emphasizing her cheekbones, sculpted eyebrows, and in particular her deep red lips. Her face had a hint of roundness to it, a fullness that made her seem somehow pampered, or luxurious.

She wore a black dress that stretched over her right shoulder but left the other bare, extending down to her thighs where it met black stockings. A gold and ruby pin in the shape of a coiled dragon barely avoided crossing the line from opulent to ostentatious at her right collarbone. Her shoes echoed the color scheme, shining scarlet with ebon whorls and tall, pointed heels.

His gaze made it back to her face to find her wearing a small smile that acknowledged her cognizance of the effect she had on people and her enjoyment of the results. Her voice was strong and direct when she said, "Normally I'd say something clever and flirty like 'enjoying the view?' But since you're here on business, we should probably get right to the fun stuff, Captain Reese."

CHAPTER EIGHT

Despite the flirty, almost seductive way the woman had said "get to the fun stuff," the actual stuff that they got to wasn't all that much fun. Their host, Lady Elle, was the owner and proprietor of the casino in her public role. In her private life, she'd explained, she was someone who made things happen for people willing to pay for it.

Cia had frowned and inquired, "What sort of things?"

The woman had obviously been asked before since her purred response was perfectly delivered, throaty and enticing. "Anything you desire, darling." Her ability to shift in and out of seductress mode was unsettling, and he'd dealt with enough intelligence personnel in the past to be certain it was a deliberate move on her part.

He said, "So, since we made it up here, clearly, the ones who sent us have been in touch with you."

She nodded and rose from the couch. "Indeed. Professor Maarsen and I have quite the history together. He's one of the few people who I never say no to." The idea of Maarsen having a romantic life popped into his mind, and he vigorously kicked it away into a dark corner where it could be safely ignored. Her walk was as calculated as the rest of her, and he saw Ethan Kimmel's flush creep up his neck. He was about to ask her to knock it off when Verrand beat him to it.

She said, "Lady Elle, if you'd be so kind as to put the routine aside for a while, we'd all appreciate it. We're not here for titillation." The growled delivery suggested she'd likely withheld a number of choice synonyms for the good of the team.

Their host threw a pouty glance over her shoulder, then smiled. "Of course. However, if you've an urge to fulfill before you go, I have no shortage of willing partners for any of you. On the house."

Jax shook his head. "We'll stick to the essentials, thanks. It's work time. Playtime later. Maybe some of us will be back, assuming we're not chased off the planet."

She beckoned for them to follow, and they left the lush living room behind and entered a much more modern area. The walls and ceiling were still white, but brighter. There were paintings in less ornate but no less expensive-looking frames, and the furniture was mostly scarlet and black, but that was where the similarities ended. A large display table took up the middle of the chamber, and cabinets and shelves dotted the periphery. Only a single seat was available, a tall one that would serve the display table well, resting beside a low credenza. On it were four bottles of different colored liquids and an array of tumblers.

She tapped the table as she walked to the far end of it. The rectangular surface lit up with an image of the city as seen from above. Anton Sirenno asked, "Satellite?"

Lady Elle shook her head. "Computer model, updated ten times an hour from satellites. Gives us more control than simply a view from above would." She opened a small case and slipped two silver rings onto her index fingers, then put her palm parallel to the table and lifted her arm. The picture rose out of the flat surface to become a fully three-dimensional representation of the city.

Kimmel gave a low whistle. "Nice tech." Cia nodded her agreement.

Their host looked pleased by the compliment. "Sometimes I'm called upon for complex tasks. Laying out the cash for good equipment is a fundamental requirement."

Jax asked, "More complex than what we're here for?"

She laughed, and it was a pleasure to hear her do so without the sensuality she'd projected in the living room. *Makes her seem much more real and much more trustworthy. Might be an act, too, of course.* Working on intelligence-related matters caused a person to become suspicious of everything and carried the risk of throwing them into a loop of conspiracy theories at any moment. He refocused as she said, "This is probably in the top twenty percent, given the target."

She motioned with her hands and the display changed, summoning a view of the building they intended to break into. The perspective was as if they were standing on the street outside it, and the holographic image reached almost to the high ceiling. "The Confederacy Administration Building. Allegedly a bunch of offices for harried workers to keep the government running. Far more interesting to your average individual is the Security Center a block away. It pretends to be simply a base for the terrestrial authorities and the military, but it's an open secret that intelligence agencies are hiding in there as well."

Maria Verrand nodded. "A perfect distraction."

"Exactly. And if you examine the blueprints for the buildings or really any public document at all, you'd find nothing to indicate that appearance is anything other than true. Fortunately, even Confederacy officials have vices." Elle looked up and grinned, showing flawless teeth and confirming that she was, in fact, the accomplished predator he'd concluded she was. "And from them, we have all sorts of interesting information. It's amazing what some people will do to protect their families and careers."

Cia frowned. "So, you deliberately target and exploit them? That doesn't sound like something the Professor would be okay with."

The other woman shook her head. "You might be surprised at what goes on inside Maarsen's elegant skull. But there's no need to target anyone. I simply take what's offered and turn it to my advantage. No honey traps, no rigged games. But once they've done the damage to themselves, yes, I exploit it when circumstances require and sleep perfectly at night, guilt-free. Wouldn't you agree that the flaw is in the choices, not the consequences?"

The pilot nodded, but Jax could tell she wasn't completely convinced. *She walks a purer path than some of us. Have to admire her ability not to compromise herself.* He'd long ago decided that some ends justified stepping across some lines, although he wouldn't call himself a universalist about the idea by any means. He asked, "So, what have your little birds told you?"

"That all is not as it seems, here in Grefta." She fluttered her finger, and the exterior view was replaced by an image of the building as if it had no walls. From the outside, it looked quite normal, and he said so. She replied, "And I would agree, if not for this interesting feature." She snapped, and a shaft appeared on the back wall's interior, terminating at the highest floor on one end and disappearing into the ground on the other.

Jax frowned. "A lift?"

Elle nodded. "According to an administrator who has a particular affinity for roulette and an ongoing streak of questionable luck, yes. She says that it's only open on the top floor, not visible on any of the others she's been to. Apparently, she saw something she wasn't supposed to, which keeps her quiet about having revealed it to us."

"Or she's a double agent," Jax mused. "How secure is your operation?"

She replied with a thin grin. "Completely. We surveil our contacts' comms at all times. A clever little piece of software that someone at the Academy designed at our request. We hear and see everything that occurs in proximity to the devices."

Kimmel said, "That must be a big job."

"It is. But our Artificial Intelligences don't complain."

Verrand inquired, "Another gift from the Academy?"

Their host chuckled. "As I'm sure you're well aware, Maarsen isn't really in the habit of giving gifts without strings attached. Let's call it an exchange of services."

Jax asked, "So where does it lead?"

"That's the fun part. We don't know. But I'd wager my whole business on a bet that what you're looking for is going to be wherever that thing goes."

Once she'd given them all the intelligence she could think to offer and answered all the questions they could think to ask, Lady Elle bid them goodbye with a parting, "Don't forget, companionship on the house when your task is complete."

When they were in the elevator heading back down toward the casino floor, Cia muttered, "Yeah, and it comes with free surveillance video, no doubt, to be used at a time of her choosing."

The female guard who'd ridden up with them was their escort again. She gave a small snort at the comment but didn't reply. That was confirmation enough for Jax, but he couldn't resist the opportunity to tease Cia. "You never know. They might have someone really interesting for you, and you'd want the recording."

She glared at him. "No thanks. I prefer to find my dates the old-fashioned way."

Verrand chuckled. "Hit them over the head with a club and drag them back to your cave?"

Cia grinned. "Exactly."

The elevator passed the casino level and continued down to a basement. Like the Administration building, the gaming hall had secrets. They included an underground garage with an anonymous delivery vehicle they'd use to get close to the building when it was time for them to make their move. The truck would be vanished afterward by Lady Elle's people.

With a soft whoosh, the doors parted to reveal the back-backstage portion of the casino. Noise aplenty filled the air as mechanical and human workers did laundry in a huge area to the left, and a substantial kitchen was sealed off from the rest of the space by a thick transparent material to their right. Ahead was a large garage with several kinds of conveyances, and to the side of it was a room-sized metal box that looked like it could double as a safety bunker in case of orbital bombardment. The guard's palm print opened a number pad, and she shielded it from their view as she typed in a string of fifteen digits, based on the sound of her nail tapping on the screen. The heavy entry portal swung out to permit access.

Inside, it was as spotless as the upstairs had been. Weapons adorned two of the four walls, and shelves laden with various other items took up the rest of the wall space. High tables filled in the middle portion, and benches at intervals were placed in the remaining area. He looked with longing at the tactical uniforms hanging in a corner, but that wouldn't work with their cover as pirates. The requirement to perform reconnaissance had been rendered moot by Lady Elle's resources, so now it was all about getting in, getting the stuff, and getting out clean. To accomplish that, they'd need to keep up the illusion of being freelance pirates, which meant wearing what they came in.

But that didn't mean they were equally limited in their choice of equipment. Even the most roughly outfitted crew would be expected to put their money into their gear, and they could scuff up or otherwise cosmetically damage whatever the room had to offer before taking it into the field. He said, "We're going for quiet. No grenades unless they're web grenades." Despite that command, he slotted a pair of flash-bangs into the belt he'd pulled from one of the shelves. It was worn enough to mostly fit the image they'd be trying to pull off, and if their foes managed to examine it closely and pierce the illusion, he'd likely be too dead to care.

He trusted each of them to make their selections and focused on his choices. He added a second holster and moved his pirate handgun to the left, replacing it with a better-looking model from the casino's inventory. Military rifles lined one section of the wall, and he pulled one from its clips and gave it a once-over. *UCCA military, a couple of generations old. Probably still too obvious, even if it's familiar.* He replaced the weapon and grabbed another, a Confederacy model that was similar in function but would be a little less natural to operate. He announced, "Stay away from Alliance weapons. Stick with neutral or Confederacy stuff. We don't want to give them any reason to think this was a sanctioned operation." *Which begs the question, is Stephenson approved to be pursuing this inquiry? Ultimately, since it's through the Academy, does it matter?* He gave a mental shrug. *Now's not the time to worry about it, in any case.*

When they finished, he performed one final check of his team. Nothing seemed glaringly out of place, and he was impressed at the variety of additions they'd chosen, each of them consciously or unconsciously supplementing the selections of their teammates. Since the situation was mostly unknown, options were essential. He nodded at the guard, who was standing beside the door. "I think we're ready to go."

She returned the nod and handed him a rectangular box. "Boss said to give you this. It's a magic key. Should be able to open most encrypted locks, unless they have the latest military-grade stuff. In that case, you're on your own."

He accepted it and slipped it into his inner jacket pocket. "Good deal. Convey our thanks."

She frowned. "Don't get too appreciative. Since we can't have anyone tracing that item to us, if it's not back here or in the truck in two hours, it'll explode rather impressively and ruin your whole day. So, don't get caught, and don't dilly-dally."

"Excellent advice." He raised his voice. "Let's go, people. Clock is ticking."

CHAPTER NINE

The truck was either autonomous or remotely piloted. In any case, Jax and his team didn't need to worry about it. They waited in the back as it rolled slowly along the service lanes that ran mostly unnoticed through the middle of each city block. The guard had told them it was shielded from detection and would provide a reading that showed only foodstuffs hidden within if it was scanned. He noticed a sense of discomfort at the thought and decided it was due to the confidence he'd been repeatedly called upon to place in others not in his chain of command. A lot relied on the Professor being a good judge of character. If not for the reassurance that Stephenson was involved, he might not have been able to deal with that level of trust in unproven people.

When the truck stopped and the rear door slid silently open, he was ready. He pulled down the black full-face mask to obscure his features, jumped out of the back, and crossed to the Administration building's rear entrance. He pointed at the palm lock, and Maria Verrand got to work on it with a multi-tool. Anton Sirenno leaned his shoulders against the wall with his hand hovering over his pistol on the far side of the entry, and Cia and Ethan Kimmel positioned themselves next to him. Their rifles were in sturdy duffel bags that served the double purpose of making the run look like a simple theft. The team would snag anything that looked valuable during the operation as misdirection.

He handed Verrand the magic key once she'd exposed the line that connected the palm reader to the security system, and it did its thing in less than five seconds. A click sounded as the door unlocked. Sirenno pulled it open and led the way forward. The rest of them followed and held inside until Verrand finished reattaching the plate and joined them. Instead of wasting time to relock the exit, she slipped two thin pieces of metal from her belt pouch into the frame and wedged the doors closed. "Won't hold for long," she muttered softly, "but it'll keep out any random passersby."

He nodded and reformed the line, using gestures to command his people. Sirenno and Kimmel freed their rifles and guarded forward. Cia and Verrand did the same and stood next to the doorway they'd come through. Their entrance had deposited them into the receiving area, as expected. To the left was a locked storage cage filled with boxes and crates. Ahead was the door that led to a small kitchen, according to the blueprints, and to the right was the reason that coming in the back had made perfect sense: a freight elevator. He pointed Kimmel toward it, and the computer expert grabbed his bag.

During their planning session, they'd agreed that while the magic key would probably be enough to get the lift moving, it might not be adequate to keep that activity secret from the building's security systems or personnel. So, accessing and compromising the network was their first priority. Kimmel attached a line from his tablet to a maintenance port inside the elevator. While the primary means of communication was almost universally wireless, many individual pieces of equipment still had local accesses for repair purposes. To the right person with the correct gear, they provided a potential way in.

Kimmel stood and waved them into the lift. He whispered into Jax's ear, "As they thought, it doesn't go down. But it'll be invisible to the system for the next ninety-seven minutes. The other security systems will also think everything is fine until then." All of their actions were now tied to the timeframe of the two-hour time bomb he'd handed off to Verrand.

They rode to the top without incident and exited the lift, leaving it locked down at that level. He checked his wrist comm, a poor replacement for either his military version or the Academy's, but one that would be appropriate for a pirate crew, and pointed at the wall to their left. "Kimmel, see if you can find a wireless access for the thing. Everyone else spread out." The floor was what you'd expect from an administrative building. Their entry area had a doorway connecting it with an office section that closely resembled every other example he'd ever seen, multiple corridors with reasonably large chambers along them. The nicest ones were at the front, with broad windows looking out over the street. He grabbed several items that looked expensive but not sentimentally valuable, stashed them in his bag, and returned to the rear.

Sirenno and Cia were already there, and Verrand stepped through moments after he did. Kimmel emitted a soft "Yes," of triumph, and a wall panel slipped away to reveal the elevator behind it. The computer wizard pointed up at tiny indentations in the ceiling. "Focused holographic projectors to hide the seams. Clever stuff. Never seen it used that way." Another moment and he had the doors open. Jax held up a hand to still his team until Kimmel announced, "We're good. Security systems in the lift are ours too. I can't say what we'll find at the other end, though. There's nothing on this system that suggests anything below surface level."

Verrand's scowl was audible in her words. "They've thought of everything. Bastards."

Jax chuckled. "If it weren't for competent enemies, we'd all be out of a job. Let's see what they're hiding."

The ride down was silent. It wasn't only a lack of conversation; the oval-shaped car transmitted no sound at all from beyond it. The experience was eerie and surreal, reminding Jax of the quiet moments during a space jump before you hit atmosphere and things got wild. His fingers twitched on his rifle. *Here's hoping this thing isn't delivering us to something too hot to handle.*

He pointed at the selector on his weapon, prompting the others that theirs should also be set to stun. There was no value in leaving bodies behind them if it could be avoided. The people in this building were their political enemies, but not personal ones. If they could eliminate the obstacles in their way without actually *eliminating* the obstacles in their way, that would be a total win. Cia whispered, "Yeah, yeah, who would have thought that the big, bad, Special Forces captain would be such a mewling pacifist?"

Grins accompanied the reply, along with a snort from someone behind him. Jax shook his head and forced his game face on to cover his smile. When the doors opened, he was ready, right foot back, rifle extended, sighting down the barrel. But he was completely unprepared for the shock that greeted him.

He squeezed the trigger in reflex at the sight of the monstrosity that stood ten feet away down the corridor. The stun blast hit its metal skin and flowed over the surface with a familiar pattern of dissipation circuitry, accomplishing nothing. He'd faced other combat robots, but they'd tended to be based at least loosely on the human form. This one would probably be featured in future nightmares, if he survived.

It had four legs, each with a joint in the middle and ending in a small tripod that flexed as its weight shifted slightly. The torso section, if you could call it that, was a thick cylinder that reached from about a foot off the floor to about five feet high. Even now, it was in motion, spinning to bring one of the many wicked-looking melee weapons attached to it to face them. Where a head would have been, had this thing had any sliver of normalcy to it, was a turret. Or, more accurately, four double turrets, one pointing in each cardinal direction. The two barrels facing him belched out an attack.

Jax yelled, "Down," and dove forward into the corridor. Staying in the elevator would be nothing short of suicide, and he needed to clear enough space for his team to get out as well. On his way down, he automatically analyzed his surroundings. *Flat walls, floor, and ceiling. No doors. It all appears to be plastic or white metal.* A dark chuckle echoed through his mind. *Probably for easy cleaning.* Projectiles flew over his head, and he recognized them as a steady stream of small caliber rounds. He hit and rolled on his shoulder, then came up with his rifle raised and the selector already flicked to the energy setting. He pulled the trigger hopefully, then cursed as the dissipation circuitry drained the power away. The impact made the thing wobble a little, but no more.

Jax ducked and scuttled to his right as the line of bullets slashed at him. A pair of grenades appeared from behind, sailing over his head toward the robot. Its center portion swiveled and something that looked like a cricket bat smacked one of them out of the way, but the other detonated, coating the enemy in sticky strands. It seemed to struggle against them, the middle section and top part moving in different directions to try to pull it apart. Then it simply sprayed flame out of the turret facing to the right. The attack rebounded from the wall to splash over it, burning away the white tendrils that had momentarily held it captive.

"Damn it," Jax breathed, then fired with his rifle on its third setting. Bullets hammered into the robot, and it deployed a metal shield from its torso to absorb them. The barrier covered it from top to bottom and protected it at the cost of limiting its ability to attack. *For at least the next five seconds, until my magazine runs dry.* His mind raced, seeking options and finding nothing more promising than charging it and trying to shove his flashbang grenade into a vulnerable spot, maybe one of the places where its weapons emerged from the central cylinder.

Fortunately, his team members had better ideas. Cia and Sirenno stepped up next to him, and as his rifle ran dry, the pilot's took over. He swapped magazines and waited for a turn. Verrand yelled, "Nobody move," and slid into view through Sirenno's parted legs, holding a brick of brown clay with a small chip in the center. She stayed to the right, out of their line of sight, and sprinted up beside the shield. Her throw left her hand at the same moment that a blade scraped along her side, slicing through the leather of her coat and splashing red blood onto the white wall. She backpedaled with a shout of pain accompanied by a curse. "Stupid mother-scratching toaster, blow it!"

An explosion emanated from behind the shield, and pieces of metal made tinkling noises as they flew away from the robot and slammed into the walls and ceiling. Its defenses dropped, and Jax opened up on its turret head. The thing fired back, but Verrand's move had apparently damaged something important because the bullets went up into the ceiling and traversed down to the wall rather than hitting them. Sirenno stopped firing and yanked Verrand out of the way an instant before the line intersected her position.

After another tense second, the combat robot suddenly shut down, going from active to immobile without any transitional moment. Kimmel, sounding shaken, said, "Okay. We're good. I have it in a loop, and can keep it there."

Jax lowered his weapon slowly, fearful that the thing would prove the other man wrong, but it stayed passive.

He crossed to where Verrand sat on the floor, her back against the wall and her hands pressed to her side. She managed a weak grin. "I probably didn't think that all the way through."

He returned the smile and shook his head. "Maybe not, but you gave us enough time for Kimmel to shut it down. Good work." He grabbed the medical pouch strapped to his thigh and withdrew a compression bandage covered in clotting powder. Sirenno was already helping her out of her jacket to expose the wound.

Kimmel said, "She did more than that. Without her blasting it, I wouldn't have been able to get past its defenses. The shell was hardened against signal intrusion. If it hadn't been cracked or broken, we'd be toast."

Jax laughed. "Toast. Toaster. I sense a theme." He met Verrand's eyes. "This is going to hurt. Ready?"

She gritted her teeth and nodded, and he slapped the bandage onto her bare torso below her ribs. It was a great tool, made for the military, but the designers had cared far more about healing than comfort. The edges gripped the skin like a bunch of tiny claws and pulled, latching the outer portion solidly into the wounded person's flesh. Then they squeezed, making sure the bandage was taut. The actual contact with the clotting agent was no fun either, but compared to the rest, that sting was almost laughable. Verrand screamed and went pale, then panted as she mastered herself. Jax patted her leg. "You'll have a cool scar and an awesome story to go with it. I'm going to leave you here since we needed a rearguard in any case. Think you can handle it?"

Verrand looked like she'd argue for a moment before

sagging in agreement. "Okay. That's probably for the best. I'm not moving very fast, but I can surely shoot. And scream. Try not to get yourselves killed."

He nodded. "That's the plan."

Cia snorted. "And everything's gone perfectly to plan so far, right?"

"Shut it, flygirl."

"Bite me, jerkwad."

Jax shook his head, rose, and led the way forward. "Okay, let's finish this and get the hell off this planet."

CHAPTER TEN

Jax had expected a wide array of challenges, given how powerful the greeter at the elevator had been, but apparently, the building's defense planners had figured that the monstrosity would be sufficient. They encountered no other active defenses—electronic, mechanical, or human—as they explored the basement. Kimmel pointed out alarm triggers and cameras as they moved through them, but he had his teeth into the security system and was blocking anything from getting out. The masks that covered their faces except for eyes and mouth would prevent any visual identification after the fact, but Jax was confident that the tech wizard would find a way to erase those before they left as well.

The lower level was filled with unfamiliar equipment of every size and shape. Among the recognizable items was a set of 3D printers in sizes ranging from tiny to almost twelve feet high. Anton Sirenno shook his head at the last one. "Wonder if they built the robot thing's body out of that. Would explain how they managed the seamlessness."

His occupation when not at the Academy was as a robotics expert for Sondfora, one of the biggest names in that field. "Seems like it would have some disadvantages for repair and such. I can't imagine they're disposable." He lapsed into thought, and Jax led them on to the next room.

Finally, they found a lock that Kimmel couldn't access, preventing passage to an area that he couldn't see through the security system's eyes. Jax said, "Well, that certainly seems promising," and opened up the wall panel to expose the connections for the magic key. It flashed to indicate it was working, and almost a full minute passed without any additional information. The door slid open seconds before he was ready to give up and try something else. He put the panel back in order as a matter of habit while the others explored the room.

Kimmel swore loudly, and Jax hustled into the room to see what had prompted the outburst. The seamless walls, ceiling, and floor resembled those he'd seen in biological research clean rooms, where the entire cube that comprised the chamber was formed as a single unit, rather than joined pieces. It didn't hold any of the furniture or workspaces he'd expected to find. The only notable object in the room was what appeared to be a medical pod. "What's the matter?"

Kimmel gestured at the creche. "It's inductive. Requires the user to be wired. None of us are."

Jax frowned. "Are you telling me that the only way to get the data out of this room is to lay in that thing and what, absorb it through the skin?"

The other man nodded. "Maria, er, Verrand would probably know better since she works with AI and internal wiring is sometimes a part of that. But, yeah. My layperson's understanding is that the wires are close enough to the surface that a very short-range field can access them. It allows for much greater transfer speeds since the whole body is essentially a conduit. Of course, other augmentations are necessary." He shrugged. "It's out of my expertise. All I can say is that we don't have what we need to get the data. And if they're guarding it this carefully, this portable might not have the computing power to crack the encryption, even if we could access it."

He turned to Cia. "Ever encountered anything similar to this?"

Like him, she appeared to have lost any measure of humor with the situation. "Not personally. But I've heard of it. Sometimes people who are super paranoid about security will use wired couriers to move data. We've never had a reason to need one, and I'm not aware of any government using it. More like a criminal, black market, kind of thing."

He wished he had a way to talk the situation over privately with her, but he couldn't without offending the others, and he had no real operational purpose for it, anyway. "Could this be the Professor's doing? One of the 'learning moments' he so enjoys?"

Cia shook her head. "No chance." Kimmel and Sirenno echoed her. He sighed and said, "Okay, let's open up the comms. Give Verrand a look at it." While their computer wizard conferred with their missing team member, he circled the object, looking for any way in, any other option to access whatever it held. Like the room itself, it appeared to be made as one solid piece, with no ports, holes, or joins to exploit.

Kimmel's next words were the ones Jax had expected. "She's got nothing. We're screwed."

He'd been involved in failed operations before, and there came a moment where you had no option but to bag it and move on to the next phase of the mission. *And clearly, that instant has arrived.* "Okay, double-time back to Verrand. Kimmel, keep an eye on the security stuff. My instincts tell me that this is a hidden room for a reason, but who knows, maybe it's a third system that's talking to the other two."

Their exit from the building was the reverse of their entrance, minus the killer robot, and they made it out to the street with no further issues. Jax summoned their escape vehicle, and another of the food delivery trucks, or perhaps the same one, stopped in front of them a moment later. They climbed inside, carefully helping Verrand move without exacerbating her injury, and pulled the door closed behind them.

As the truck started to move, lights came on in the cargo area. Two rectangular crates about four feet long were secured to the sidewalls near the cab, and above each floated two words. The one on the left said, "Empty me," and the one on the right, "Fill me." Jax opened the first and found energy bars, electrolyte drinks, and a med-pack. He took them and passed them out. Everyone waited while Verrand scanned them for poisons, then tore into the refreshments as soon as she pronounced them clean. He pulled off his rifle and borrowed pistol and dropped them in the second box, along with the other items they'd taken but not used. He kept back only the medical pack and placed the exploding magical key carefully on top of the rest of the equipment he'd deposited.

The others did the same, and by the time they arrived at their destination, they looked no different than they had coming in, other than the duffel bags carrying their stolen goods. Cia and Sirenno had argued that leaving them behind would be the safer play, and he'd offered the counterargument that their role as pilfering thieves required them to pilfer. Plus, he didn't want anything to blow back on Lady Elle if the truck was somehow captured.

He watched their autonomously departing escape vehicle as it drove away before turning to the others. "Okay. Verrand, this is going to feel great, then it's going to suck. Everyone, we need to be back at the ship by the time it wears off, or we'll be carrying her." He positioned the injector at the side of her neck and pressed the button, discharging a mix of drugs that would kill her pain and give her energy, at the cost of eliminating the warning system that would keep her from hurting herself further. "Let's take it slow and steady."

They entered the terminal and walked casually toward where the *Jigsaw* awaited them. The transit hub was busy even at this time of night, and more security forces and soldiers were in evidence than he'd hoped to see. They didn't appear to be searching for anyone specific, and in general, the place seemed to be operating as it had when they'd passed through it earlier.

That lasted until the moment they reached the doors to the spoke leading to their ship. At the far end of the terminal, the tube opened and a squad of local security personnel stepped out, six in all. Unlike the others, they were looking for someone, as evidenced by how they kept glancing down at their wrist comms and out at the people moving through the building.

"Go, go," Jax muttered just loudly enough for those around him to hear. They pushed open the doors and increased their speed as soon as they'd closed behind them. He ordered, "Kimmel, keep a hand on Cia while she spins up the ship."

Cia shook her head. "It's not the *Grace*. This one doesn't have that capability."

"Damn it. I assumed the Professor would have given us something at least nearly equivalent."

The pilot chuckled, and he heard the nervousness behind it. "Did you *look* at that ship? The thing is flying on bonding tape and a prayer."

"Okay. New plan." He'd spotted the fuel line that led to their ship from the central hub near the terminal. "Did we set up refueling?"

"No. Didn't need it."

Jax replied, "Perfect. Now run." He drew his unimpressive pirate pistol, set it on overload, and threw it at the long metal cylinder that ran about six feet away along the walkway, pitching it as far toward the terminal as he was able. He'd been involved in spaceport sabotages before, and assuming this system was set up in standard fashion, the explosion would be contained to the compromised section since no fuel was flowing to the ship. Internal valves closed in the absence of pressure to keep them open and stayed locked until a signal from the control station reactivated them.

Security personnel charged through the doors behind them and screamed in panic as the fuel line went up in a giant fireball. The brutal heat that had lessened with the setting sun returned with the ignition of his artificial one made of rocket fuel, and the concussive blast sent their pursuers and Verrand stumbling. Sirenno and Kimmel grabbed an arm each and kept the wounded woman moving, and the ladder slid down from the hatch at their approach. Cia climbed up first, then Kimmel, who assisted him in keeping Verrand steady as she ascended. By the time Sirenno was inside, and the door closed, the security forces were halfway toward them.

He followed the sound of muttered curses to the cockpit and strapped in as the *Jigsaw* lurched upward from its pad. The ship negotiated with his comm, and he joined the conversation between the control tower and Cia already in progress. An angry male voice demanded, "Put that ship down, now."

She replied sweetly, "Under whose authority?" She killed her mic and muttered, "You festering scumbag." Jax chuckled despite the anxiety building in him as the questionable vessel around them creaked and groaned as the pilot rotated it and pointed it toward the sky. She activated the intercom and shouted, "Ten seconds, strap in or find a handhold."

He started counting down in his head while she engaged in another testy exchange with the tower. The man said, "The damn Confederacy government, that's who. Do it now, or we'll shoot you down."

She snorted into her open mic. "Please. You don't have the personal authority for that, and by the time you get it,

I'll be back home on planet Pouturn. You be sure to tell all your friends how you tried and failed to persecute an innocent person on the entirely mistaken assumption that she's somehow a lawbreaker and a pirate." She flicked off the connection as her counterpart sputtered an indignant reply, and told Jax, "That's a planet deep in Confederacy space. They won't believe it, but someone will have to waste time checking it out."

At ten seconds on the dot, the ship lurched as she threw it into the maximum acceleration they could tolerate without blacking out. He knew this because of the telltale sparkles creeping in at the edges of his eyes before the speed stopped increasing. Conversation was an impossibility, so he focused on holding on and promising the universe all sorts of wonderful future acts if only he were allowed to survive Cia's piloting.

CHAPTER ELEVEN

The universe ruled in Jax's favor, and they made it to the jump point, then to the *Grace*, and finally to the Academy without further challenges. Maria Verrand spent most of the trip in the medical pod, which proved to be as advanced and effective as Cia had promised. Her scar was barely noticeable by the time they reached their destination, and she was mostly back to full functionality.

They arrived at the castle during the night, allowing them all to rest up some before needing to face the results of their misadventure. They'd sent word ahead, but gotten no response other than curt instructions to return. Thus, the opportunity to sleep and reset his brain and body before dealing with whatever the day would bring was welcome.

He was the first of the group to arrive in the dining hall for breakfast, but by the time he'd finished his initial cup of coffee, the rest of the team had joined him. They all seemed a little more somber than usual, something he chalked up to the uncertainty around coming back having failed to achieve their objective. It wasn't a situation that any of them would be accustomed to. The Academy didn't generally admit students overly comfortable with failure. Quite the opposite: everyone he'd met was a high-flier who only needed a push to fly higher still.

Cia chomped noisily on a piece of bacon, a gesture doubtless directed at him. He scowled and demanded, "What? What do you want, woman?"

It drew laughs from the rest, and she finished chewing and swallowed with deliberate slowness. Finally, she said, "So, I'm thinking that when they ask why things didn't go well, I'm going to blame you. I wanted to suggest to everyone else that they do the same." She ended with a wide grin and received nods and promises to act accordingly from the others.

Jax shook his head in false dismay. "Honestly. Ever since I met you, everything is, like, ninety times more difficult than it should be. You're not a pilot. You're an albatross."

She put her hand over her heart and sniffed. "You wound me. Deeply. I'm wounded. Ow. The pain. Ow. I just...can't...go on." She fluttered her eyelids and slid sideways out of the chair onto the floor, uttering a loud gasp before falling limp. Jax led the team in a round of light applause for her acting skills, and she bounced back up happily.

Ethan Kimmel asked, "Seriously though, what's going to happen?"

Jax shrugged. "I'm guessing we'll all get to chat with the Professor at some point, either alone or together. He tends to do that with everyone after missions, as near as I can tell." They nodded, confirming his opinion. "So, we give them the truth. There's nothing to hide. Hell, the op was going well until we came up against a challenge we were in no way prepared to deal with. Technical inadequacy is kind of a binary, not something that can be massaged or improvised around."

Cia observed, "*You're* inadequate," and Jax flipped her off to renewed laughter.

He met Kimmel's eyes. "Ultimately, the responsibility rests on me. So, I guess Cia's right. Any blame is appropriately placed there. When the Professor asks, tell him what you did and why you did it, and why you thought maybe we as a team should have done something different, if you're of that opinion. After-action stuff is all about identifying things we can learn from, rather than finding reasons to punish people." He paused, frowned, and added, "Unless politicians are involved. Then, your favorite phrase is, 'I'm sorry, you'll have to ask my commanding officer.' Works every time."

Verrand gave a thin smile. "So is that what you are? Our commanding officer?" The way she said it wasn't a challenge, but it was more than a throwaway inquiry.

He considered it for a moment and replied, "I think the right phrase here is team leader. Every effective group needs someone to wear the mantle of responsibility. Since that particular mission was associated with some stuff I'm involved in outside the Academy, I'm probably the logical choice in this instance. However, that doesn't mean we won't have a different arrangement in the future."

Anton Sirenno sipped his coffee, then peered through the steam at him. "So, you wouldn't have a problem following one of us if the situation demanded it? Isn't that a little at odds with your military background?"

The question sparked understanding. *They think military equates to regimented and hierarchical and such. True in some cases, less so in the Special Forces, and likely even less than that under Major Stephenson.* He nodded. "Well, any of you except Cia. I try not to put myself under the authority of insane people." In truth, he'd probably trust her more than the others, since he knew her better and had witnessed some of the impressive things she was capable of.

An edge of relief colored their laughter, and the conversation turned to other matters. He stood to refill his mug, only to feel the familiar buzz of the Academy comm on his right wrist. He checked it and saw that the location was Maarsen's office and the time was only five minutes away. None of the others were reacting to their devices, so apparently, he rated a one-on-one meeting. He lifted his wrist and said, "Guess I need to take my coffee to go. The Professor is calling."

Maarsen's office was the same as always. He'd half expected to see Stephenson sitting there waiting for him, but it was only the two of them. This time, the older man handed over a tumbler of whiskey despite the early hour and Jax happily sipped it, savoring the deep, smokey taste. He sighed. "Thanks. I needed that."

The Professor chuckled. "Some mornings are like that. So, to business." He leaned forward and rested his arms on the desk, which was empty of anything other than his notebook, pen, and the tray with the decanter and glasses. "Did all the members of your team make it through okay? Any problems we need to deal with?"

Jax shook his head. "Everyone did great. It was almost textbook. Well, after the encounter with Lady Elle, anyway."

This time it was a laugh. "Ah, Elle. I'm so glad the occasion worked out for you to meet her. She is truly one of a kind. A treasure."

"You can say that again." He paused, then shrugged mentally. *He has to be aware of it already, right?* "You know what she does on that planet, I assume?"

The other man nodded. "Oh, yes. She's an excellent spy. Her means are widely varied, but always contain an element of vice. She was born to it. In another time, she'd be an empress."

"Well, she kind of is one. Stepping into that casino is like entering a whole different world."

"Indeed. She has done a wonderful job with it."

Jax took another slow sip. "What's the Academy's interest?"

Maarsen shifted from conversational mode back to lecture mode, a switch only detectable in his eyes, which seemed to focus intensely on a vision only he could see. "We provided seed money for the enterprise. In return, we take a portion of the profits. But more importantly, Elle was a student, and she has unquestionably made the most of her learning. She leads a life she enjoys, and we are often the beneficiary of it." Jax sensed the story included many more details than that, but the other man shifted topics abruptly. "So, clearly something of value was present. We were correct about that."

"Definitely. Kimmel, Verrand, and Sirenno all agreed that the setup was for high-density data transfer into a wired courier and that such a thing would only be useful for the most sensitive information. Or criminals, but I imagine we're crossing the possibility of the Confederacy engaging in black market activities off the list of likely occurrences."

"The odds do seem to lend themselves to the first interpretation. So, with that in mind, we'll need to come at this from another angle. It's not likely that we'd be able to break into that facility again even if we had the proper equipment, correct?"

Jax nodded. "You never get two shots at something like that. There are probably four times as many murder bots by now, and a whole host of other added security measures. Might even be the case that they've upgraded the security in all the buildings that are part of whatever trouble they're up to in that one."

The Professor sighed. "It's certainly not your team's fault the effort failed. I have to say that I didn't imagine the fallout would be quite so dramatic. I watched the security video. That was an impressive explosion." He paused for a moment, then shrugged. "But all we can do is keep moving forward, correct?" He nodded as if answering his question. "Okay, Jackson, thanks for coming. Your time is your own for a bit while I work some things out. Stay ready, though. I'll have something more for you to do before too long."

He finished the whiskey in a gulp, surprised at the sudden dismissal. It burned warmly as he rose and shook

Maarsen's hand. "Good deal. See you soon." *An empty calendar? I have just the thing to fill it.*

Jax casually strolled into the medical lab as if he followed a momentary whim, rather than something he'd been looking forward to for weeks. The place was busier than he'd seen it, with doctors and patients interacting in several locations, most of them involving some sort of equipment he wasn't familiar with. He failed to detect his quarry, so he continued his stroll. Maintaining the illusion of random chance got more difficult as he moved farther into the space. Finally, he gave up on it and tapped a young woman staring at a display showing cellular activity on the shoulder. "Excuse me, where can I find Doctor Cray?"

She turned her head away from the screen and glared at him. "What do I look like, the peppy cruise director? The concierge? You were fooled by the blonde hair, right?"

He lifted his hands in defense. "Whoa, none of that, I'm sorry. You were the last person I saw in the room after walking through the rest. No offense intended. And the hair didn't enter into it."

She kept him pinned with her glare until a familiar voice sounded from behind him. "Try not to be upset, Hannah. He's not much on social skills but does have some redeeming qualities. Not being drawn in by stereotypes is one of them, based on what I've seen so far."

The younger woman grunted and returned her attention to her display, and he whispered, "Sorry again," as he swiveled to take in the sight of Dr. Juno Cray. The grin leapt to his lips before he could stop it, and he was encouraged, even buoyed, to see a matching expression grace her face. "Hi, Doc."

"Hi yourself, Captain. Is this a medical call?"

Jax shook his head. "Nope, purely social."

Cray tilted her head toward the entrance. "Then let's get out of the way so these people can work. Fancy a coffee?"

He laughed. "You're speaking my native tongue, Doc."

She led him through a door at the side of the lab that had blended so perfectly with the wall that he hadn't noticed. *Or maybe every time I've been in here, I've been distracted. It's certainly possible.* On the opposite side of the portal was a long hallway with doors on either side. It had the same modern, high-tech look as the lab itself, clearly not part of the original castle's interior design. He imagined that rough stone walls hid behind the white surfaces. *The past trapped by the future. Poetic.* He laughed at himself, at the realization that his pleasure at seeing Juno bordered on giddiness. *Yeah, I might be a little infatuated.*

Her name was etched into a small piece of silver metal attached to one of the doors, but she ignored it and kept walking. The hallway turned at the end, opening into a medium-sized space. One wall was dedicated to refreshments, with snack bars in a woven basket on the counter next to a refrigerator. Another smaller cooler with a glass front displayed beverages, from soda to energy drinks. She headed directly for the complicated looking espresso machine, an authentic old-school model, the kind that had long since been generally replaced by synthetic versions.

He followed more slowly, taking in the rest of the

room. Where the lab was sterile and functional, living things filled this chamber. Plants hung from the ceiling, were arranged on shelves in medium-sized pots, and stood in larger planters on the floor. Several small cubicle-like areas jutted from the wall opposite the entry, with displays mounted in each. A pair of green couches sat at right angles to one another in the center of the space, looking entirely comfortable. Between them rested a wooden coffee table, and a quartet of stuffed chairs completed the rectangle they'd started. The room was intended for comfort and relaxation or maybe given the cubicles, working in a different setting.

She asked over her shoulder, "Espresso straight?"

"Perfect."

"Good deal. Have a seat. I'll get these arranged; then you can ask me out properly."

CHAPTER TWELVE

Jax looked up as Juno turned toward him, a small white cup held in each hand. She'd selected a less noticeable lipstick than the first time he'd seen her, a deep scarlet that went well with her white skin and the straight dark hair that occasionally swayed across her chin when she moved. Her dark eyes sparkled with amusement, probably at his expense, and her face was perfectly proportioned, at least in his opinion.

He'd chosen one of the stuffed chairs, not wanting to appear too bold, and she sat on the couch nearest it. She passed a cup to him and leaned back against the cushion, crossing her legs. Neither of them spoke for a moment, savoring the bitter brew's taste, then she broke the ice. "So, you're here for your second visit."

Jax nodded. "I am. Second one. Back again. I seem to recall something important tied to that number." He pretended to search his memory. "I can't quite put my finger on it, but I think it had to do with some rule of yours."

Juno laughed softly and shook her head. "Smooth, Jackson, really smooth. Yes, well, that particular prohibition is no longer in place, since it's not your first time at the Academy."

"So, I guess the question now is whether I meet your standards for someone you might go out on a date with. I'm guessing they're pretty high." He stared woefully up at the ceiling to illustrate his view.

She nodded solemnly. "They are indeed. Tell me, why should I spend my precious few moments of free time with you, Captain Reese?" The grin that stretched her lips as his gaze was drawn back to them belied the formality of her words.

He pretended to consider it, with his elbow on the arm of the chair and his chin in his palm. Finally, he said, "I've got nothing. Guess I'll go." He made as if to rise, and she laughed. "Okay, seriously though, I think that's the reason. You seem to laugh a lot when I'm around."

She lifted an eyebrow. "Perhaps I'm laughing *at*, instead of laughing *with*."

He shrugged and sipped the espresso. *Damn, there's something to be said for the old ways of doing things now and again.* "Either way, as long as it's making you happy, I'm good with it. Plus, you know, I am devilishly handsome. Any woman would be the envy of all her friends to be seen with me."

Juno snorted. "First, I'm impressive enough on my own, thanks. Second, I don't really have friends."

He gestured with an open palm. "Well, there you go. I'm a great friend. Ask anyone. Wait, don't ask Cia. Ask anyone else."

She laughed again. "Okay, I'm sold. What's your plan, Captain?"

"I'm pretty sure Maarsen will be sending me out again in short order, and I don't want to have to stand you up for our first date. How about we agree that when I get back, that night we'll go out? Until then, maybe we could meet for coffee now and again."

"Smart thinking. I'll need to add the caveat that I might have to be the one to stand you up if work calls."

He nodded. "So it's a deal?"

She grinned, leaned across, and touched his arm, sending a thrill of anticipation washing through him. Her eyes sparkled as she said, "It's most definitely a deal."

Jax kicked around for a few hours without a particular direction, wandering the exterior grounds and the interior corridors in search of some distraction. He didn't find any, but enjoyed the time anyway, right up until the moment his wrist comm summoned him again. This time, though, it was to a location in the classroom wing of the building. He frowned at the sight and muttered, "This better not be more juggling," then followed the map to the appointed destination.

It did indeed turn out to be an instructional space, but not the kind he was expecting. It held no chairs, no lab tables, no displays, or computers. Instead, it was a wide rectangle with sunlight filtering through the tall windows on the long stone wall opposite the door. On the right end were four identical armoires, each about eight feet high and carved meticulously enough that they were undoubtedly original furnishings of the castle. Target dummies for swords and martial arts held station at the other end.

Also notable were the two men standing off to the side, neither of whom he recognized. One was in the Academy's standard staff uniform, a well-tailored suit in black with orange and yellow accents. He radiated health from his compact form, likely developed from decades of martial arts. The other was dressed as if he'd just arrived at the castle, in comfortable business-casual appropriate for traveling. His button-down shirt was dark blue with a hint of a white t-shirt at the collar, his trousers khaki, and his shoes a shade of brown that perfectly complemented the other two. Coordinating footwear was something Jax did only in service of an undercover assignment, and the man's effort to do so spoke to serious attention to detail. The same quality was present in his precisely styled short brown hair, maintained eyebrows, and blemish-free face.

The uniformed man nodded. "Jackson, thank you for coming. I'm Harrington, weapons master here at the Academy. I'd like to introduce you to Kenton." Jax shook hands with each in turn. "This is Kenton's first day with us, and I thought you'd be a good match for a proficiency test."

Jax frowned. "Okay. What did you have in mind?"

Harrington gestured at the armoires. "You have some experience with knives, I believe?" He nodded. "Excellent. Then knives it is." He opened the doors wide, pulled out a drawer set in the bottom, and withdrew four blades. He handed two to each of them. Jax examined his, holding the edge up to the sunlight. While they were weighted as if they were authentic, they were dull, probably plastic, and clearly meant for training. He noted that the other man was doing the same thing, demonstrating that he had some experience with blades.

The weapons master withdrew a pair of padded jackets from the upper part of the wardrobe and handed them over. Jax shrugged into his, finding it comfortably tight and not too heavy. He'd trained in worse on any number of occasions. His opponent set his knives down on the floor and donned his with deliberate care, as if it were a dinner jacket. He retrieved his weapons as their instructor announced, "Torso only. Slashing and stabbing are both in bounds. No punches and no grappling, as the stone floor under your feet is rather unyielding. When it meets bone, bone loses. Begin when you're ready."

Jax and Kenton both chuckled at his words and began to circle slowly. Jax rolled his wrists, loosening them up for the contest to come. The other man stretched his neck, which cracked with a loud *snap* that bounced around the room before fading away. Jax positioned his left knife with the point forward and the cutting edge down, and his right reversed along his forearm with the sharp side facing out. He kept his gaze locked on his foe's eyes, watching for something that would give him a clue to the man.

When his opponent copied his positioning with familiar ease, Jax knew he'd been trained by the military. When he shuttled forward, slightly off-balance, Jax decided Kenton's lessons had stopped after basic. His experience was rather more extensive, both in the classroom and in the field. *Careful, Jackson. He could be hiding something, or he could have tricks you've never seen. Don't get cocky.* His foe led with a slash from his right blade. Jax stepped back out of range, then pivoted to stab at the triceps of the attacking arm with his left knife.

His rival spun out of the way. It wasn't a move Jax would have chosen, but in this particular case, when exposing the back of the head was safe, it proved effective. He circled with rapid sidesteps, forcing his opponent to keep turning with him, and saw several moments where a quick kick or a bull rush could have ended the contest. Then his foe rallied and darted in with a flurry of stabs and slashes that Jax was hard-pressed to defend against, given the limitations the instructor had set. He had put himself into position to counter when the weapons master yelled, "Hold."

Jax and his opponent dropped their arms and retreated out of range. Harrington stepped between them, nodding. "Well done, both of you. I'll take your weapons back. Our session is finished, but you're both expected in the Professor's office in," he checked his comm, "exactly thirty-nine minutes. I'm sure you'll get your notifications shortly. And, just a suggestion, you might want to shower beforehand."

He hadn't realized how much he'd been sweating and laughed as he unzipped the padded jacket. "No question about that." He traded grips with the other man. "Good to meet you, Kenton. Guess I'll see you in about thirty-eight minutes."

"Until then." He offered an easy grin, then headed for the door, peering at his wrist comm, probably for directions. Jax turned to the weapons master.

"Want to give me a clue as to what that was about?"

The other man grinned. "Nope. Maarsen's prerogative to share or not."

Jax sighed. "Naturally." He nodded respectfully before departing, already anticipating the pleasure of the hot water in his quarters' shower.

———

At least this time there was no pre-meeting, Jax thought as he walked through the Professor's office door on Kenton's heels. He headed for the left-hand chair, only for the other man to do the same. Jax solved the conflict by surrendering the field, such as it was, and chose the one on the right instead. *Closer to the whiskey.*

Behind his uncluttered desk, Maarsen smiled at them. "Welcome, gentlemen. Harrington told me you performed quite well at your initial meeting."

Kenton asked the question that was also at the top of Jax's mind. "What was that all about, anyway?"

The Professor grinned. "As with most of what we do here at the Azophi Academy, it has different purposes for different people. For you, Kenton, it was about assessing whether your statement about one of your abilities was accurate, or whether you were over or understating the situation. Obviously, it is in our best interests as educators to know if a given student is too humble, or a braggart, or has adequate self-knowledge."

He frowned. "And what was the result?"

For a second, Jax thought Maarsen would let him twist, but then he answered. "You did indeed accurately assess your abilities in that form of combat." Kenton nodded, looking satisfied.

The Professor turned to face him. "And for you, Jackson, it was a chance for you to meet someone you're going to need to rely on in the near future."

Jax kept his scowl hidden and managed to maintain a neutral tone. "Oh really? How so?"

Maarsen said, "Kenton, tell Jackson a little about what you do."

The other man shrugged. "I started out in the UCCA military, medical division. Took a liking to it, but didn't want to go the whole doctor route, so now I'm a bioengineer for," he paused, then continued, "a big company. I do all sorts of things for them, but my main area right now is in human cybertech."

Jax asked, "Like prosthetics and such?" That would make sense. *Maybe he's here to help me tune up my arm.*

Kenton raised his hand and wiggled it from side to side. "Sometimes, but not really. My division is working on implantable technologies."

That clicked immediately, and Jax turned to face Maarsen. "I see. Well, it's true, I have a lot to learn where that field is concerned." He hoped that the older man would fill in what he was supposed to be teaching the new student since that was an explicit part of the deal, but that desire went unfulfilled.

Instead, Maarsen said, "You'll have your chance, I'm sure. For now, you need to pull your team together and get ready to depart. We're sending you all out to secure an item that will be of great use to the both of you."

Jax asked, "My arm and leg, you mean?"

The older man nodded. "And it should be useful in the big picture effort you're a part of here at the Academy. For

Kenton, it'll be a chance to see what some of his competitors have been up to."

His new teammate replied, "Sounds good to me." His confidence struck Jax as more ego than earned. "When are we leaving?"

"The plans won't be finalized until tomorrow. In the meantime, I'm certain that Jackson can introduce you to the rest of the team and get you squared away."

Jax grinned. "Sure will." *Being the new guy in the training room ought to smack that attitude down a bit.*

CHAPTER THIRTEEN

The first couple of hours after the meeting were spent preparing for a training session. He'd debated stopping by to see Juno, but as his inner voices fought to a standstill on the idea, had abandoned it. *Don't want to seem desperate. Plus, work before play.* Maarsen had provided the name of a tech, and after a short discussion, Jax had seized on an option he thought would be valuable both as preparation for the mission ahead, whatever it might be, and increasing the bonds among his teammates.

Long experience had taught him that shared hardship was the best way to strengthen those connections, and he'd put that philosophy to work in his planning. Now, as he stood in the yellow-lined ready area on the far end of the empty training room, he focused on suppressing his grin at the chaos about to ensue so he didn't give away the surprise. The introductions had been taken care of. Gentle insults had flown back and forth as Kenton Marshall proved he could hold his own, and they'd donned their gear with a sense of positive anticipation.

Such a shame I'm going to have to wreck that for them. Or not a shame in the least, he chuckled inwardly. He activated his comm and ordered, "Button up the helmets, people." They complied, and he continued, "All right, let's start the show." Floor and ceiling panels moved aside, and objects ascended and descended to create a blocky street scene, if that street had been the location of a pitched battle between a pair of giants. Randomly placed cubes simulated rubble, light posts tilted at an angle instead of displaying proper verticality, and line of sight was limited to the few clear feet in between obstructions. The biggest obstacle rose to about ten feet high, the smallest only half a foot.

Cia growled what Jax knew his whole team was thinking. "What the hell is this, Reese?"

"We're less informed than usual about our next mission, which given our normal cluelessness is saying something. It seemed like a good time to practice our ability to sneak around. The field in front of us is undoubtedly a security nightmare. I told the tech to make it as detection-heavy as possible, and by the way she laughed, I'm guessing she fully embraced the idea. Our goal is to get to the far end without getting spotted. As always, nothing in here is powerful enough to cause actual damage, but it's entirely likely that setting off the defenses will put one or more of us into some moderate-to-severe pain."

The pilot countered, "You suck."

Jax laughed. "Perhaps so. Doesn't change anything. Are you volunteering to take point?" He paused, but she didn't reply. "Oh, that's the other thing. I'm not leading this operation. No one is. We'll come to decisions as a team and see what we can achieve. Every time we fail, the scenario resets and we start over with whatever knowledge we've gained." That wasn't a particularly real-world scenario. Effective target reconnaissance would accomplish the same objective without the pain and repetition cycles.

The tech's voice joined the comm conversation. "Training active in ten seconds. Good luck." He heard the unspoken "You're going to need it" in her tone.

Ethan Kimmel's helmet bobbed in a nod. "Okay, the first step will be to run a full sensor scan. I've got the strongest equipment for that, so I'll do it as soon as we're live."

Anton Sirenno replied, "And when you find a security device, what do we do with it? I mean, I'm happy to blast it, but I'm not sure if that's the best plan."

Marshall's voice sounded part confident and part hesitant, although the latter was fairly well concealed. Jax heard it because he'd been trained to search for people's tells; he imagined Cia had undergone similar instruction during her lessons on trading and negotiation. "I've got military experience that includes deactivating explosives and stealth techniques. I can probably sneak up on things to take them out if they're not too high up."

The timer expired, and Kimmel announced, "Scanning." Jax activated his suit's scanners, as he did at the start of any combat situation. He was confident his team would be doing the same. Only breathing sounded over the comms for almost twenty seconds before images began to appear in his helmet display, overlaid on the exterior view. The light posts all had cameras on them, now faintly glowing in red. Based on their computers' calculations, the units operated in a 200-degree line of sight, and triangular shapes in the same color appeared to demarcate their detection zone.

Audio detectors were highlighted in blue and seemed to be scattered mainly around the periphery. Again, the computer offered its best guess as to the devices' area of influence. Simply avoiding the systems would be impossible, since they overlapped and covered all or most of the available territory. *There goes Plan A.*

Purple spots appeared, and orange ones, and finally yellow. The computers didn't fill in any additional details about those, meaning the sensor system could detect they existed but not figure out any other data about them. They could be anything from motion-sensing rocket launchers to tiny robots that would laugh at them if they made the ground vibrate near them. He muttered, "Well, that's ugly, Kimmel. Way to go."

Nervous laughter followed the comment, and the technical wizard of the group replied, "Hey, I've only got the souped-up detectors. Not my fault that some jerk put together a wicked scenario."

Cia clarified, "Jerkwad. It's jerkwad. Jerk isn't quite descriptive enough."

The smile was audible in Kimmel's voice. "I stand corrected."

Marshall said, "How about this? We can get in range to take a shot at the nearest camera, as long as we stay on the far side. If I blast it with a low power stun burst, maybe it'll look like it broke if a human was tasked with watching it?" He started to move in that direction.

"Hold up," Verrand ordered, curt enough to make him stop as a reflex. "We need to think this through a little more before we go shooting things. Kimmel, any way to hack into their network?"

"I've been trying. No dice. Whoever designed this thing didn't want us taking the easy route."

Five helmets swiveled to face Jax, who held up his hands. "Wasn't me. I said make it hard. Anything after that you can blame on the technician. Or the Professor. Whichever you prefer."

Marshall insisted, "I think we need to shoot the cameras. That will give us a path around the audio sensors, at least."

Jax replied, "Anyone have a better idea?"

No one answered, so he gestured at the newest member of the team. "Have at it."

With a decisive nod of his helmet, Marshall hefted his rifle and exited the safe zone, moving over to the right wall. His route would keep him out of the cameras and away from any of the other sensors, that much was true. What would happen when he shot it was an unknown. Unfortunately, Jax had to agree that without the benefit of being able to compromise the security system's network, they needed to take out at least some of the actual devices. Whether the plan to disable it with a stun blast would be less noticeable than destroying it outright was another unknown. *In my other gig, I'd have the* Cronus *raze the approach from orbit, then sprint for it.*

"Here we go." Marshall pulled the trigger. Sparks shot from the camera above, and the field it had projected vanished from their displays. He pumped his rifle in the air in celebration of his success. "I'll go after the next one." The reappearance of the field two seconds later surprised all of them, indicated by gasps over the comm, but the biggest shock was reserved for the shooter who had advanced into the detection zone. An aerial combat robot swooped down from the ceiling and blasted him with a bolt of energy, locking up his suit and lighting up his nerves. The scream as he fell sounded exactly like the ones Jax always gave in those situations, a combination of frustration, surprise, and pain.

The tech's laughing voice came over their comms. "Scenario deactivated for one minute. You'll have to drag him back to the safe zone before his suit will unlock."

Jax said, "Verrand, Sirenno, go get him. Kimmel, did we learn anything from that experiment?" He was hoping that like the robot they'd faced in the basement of the Confederacy building, blasting the thing would offer access to the network controlling them.

"Nothing other than the fact that stun blasts are only a temporary reprieve. I can't see a way forward other than taking out the camera with a full power burst, then moving on to the next. If we were doing this in the field, I'd say we'd be best off to blast it all and opt for speed, but somehow I don't imagine that's what you're going for with this training session."

He nodded. "It's not, and more than that, I bet our friend in the booth up there has enough security drones to make that a seriously unhappy experience for all of us. No, we'll need to use finesse more than force."

They reset and tried it again. And again, several times more. Each of them made it a little farther before getting blasted and dragged back to the start. After forty-five minutes of experimentation, every one of them was tired and annoyed. But, for the first time, Jax thought they had a handle on what they needed to do. He discussed the plan with the group, then they put it into operation.

In the end, the team had determined that a combination of speed and craftiness was required to win the day. Rather than destroying the cameras, which had resulted in the immediate dispatch of multiple drones, they'd come up with a new solution. Marshall got into position and nodded to indicate his readiness. Jax said, "Ready, set, go." While the rest of them took off at a run, their designated camera gunner stepped out and stunned the camera. Repeated experiments revealed that it ran on a three-second cycle, so he would shoot it in two-second intervals until they were all through. Another was positioned further along their planned advance, and whoever reached it first would repeat the process.

After those obstacles was a sonic sensor. They'd discovered that if all the sound detectors got a signal at once, the computer discounted it as a mistake. In the real world that would be entirely unlikely, but it made for effective training in problem-solving. Kimmel, now in the lead, and Sirenno, behind him, each threw a flash-bang grenade to a location where it would trigger multiple units. The purple devices had turned out to be thermal scanners, which their suits defeated by lowering their temperatures a couple of degrees. It wasn't comfortable, but it was better than being blasted by the drones yet again.

The motion detectors, in orange, they were able to weave through without activating. It involved a lot of parkour—vaulting over obstacles, crawling under others, and one particular spot where the lead person had to kneel so the rest of the team could use them as a jumping platform. Jax had chosen that role for himself, figuring that if someone was going to hurt from this, it might as well be him. His first inclination had been to assign it to the new guy, but that was too cruel, even for him. *At the Academy, at least. If it were my Special Forces people, I'd do this enough times that they all had to be the step stool.*

The ones pulsing in yellow were the most annoying of the bunch. Several could be avoided, but a straight-line array of them entirely blocking their progress was the final barrier to their objective. They'd tried running through and going over, and neither had worked. Blasting them resulted in the shrill whine of another combat drone, followed by a scream and the thump of a locked-up suit hitting the floor. The only tactic they hadn't yet investigated was to shut down the electronics in their suits, because only on the last run had they finally eliminated every option save one: the devices had to be reading electromagnetic emissions, given all their other failures to defeat them.

Verrand had volunteered to test the theory, and she panted, "Shutting down now," before her comm channel went down. She raced through the line of detectors and slid into the finish box marked on the floor in front of the far wall. He held his breath as he waited for another drone to emerge, but it didn't. He broke into a grin and said, "All right. Everybody into the pool. We've beat this thing."

CHAPTER FOURTEEN

Jax had secured permission to postpone their departure to the following morning so he could take them all out for a drink. At least, that was the announced reason. The actual purpose of the delay was so he could recover from the damage that being a launching platform had inflicted on him. A trip to the medical lab had been both good and bad. Good, because he'd gotten a shot of quick heal meds that would have him ready to go the next day. Bad, because Dr. Juno Cray hadn't been present.

Not that he'd gone there mainly to see her, with the injury as an excuse. *Surely not.*

They'd all gathered at the castle entrance, their number requiring a large van for the ride to the airfield. Kenton Marshall held up his end of the conversation but didn't quite seem to be gelling with the others the way that Jax would have liked. *Maybe that's what he needs to learn. How to trust. That would be ironic. And just like the Professor.*

Sighting the *Grace* was as spirit-lifting as always. Her logo at the bow of the ship, a musical note with a line through it, seemed freshly polished, as did the rest of Cia's pride and joy. The pilot was the first out of the van and up the cargo ramp, her enthusiasm inspiring the others to increase their pace, probably without even realizing they'd done it. The familiar crates that usually accompanied them were secured inside the cargo section, filled with various pieces of equipment that might come in handy during the mission ahead.

The mission that's still mostly a bloody mystery. Since the Grace *is wearing her normal identity, we're either taking on a task that doesn't need deniability or heading to a waypoint to change rides.* When they'd left the *Jigsaw* behind, he'd hoped he would never have to see that ship again. He'd been half-convinced it would break apart during landing and would lay odds that something had at least bent during the process. Trianna had flown it off the rock where it had previously been stored, presumably for repairs. He couldn't be sure, because the woman still hadn't said a word to him. *Apparently, I failed to prove myself a non-chucklehead.*

He tapped Marshall on the arm and pointed forward. "Quarters are toward the bow. Galley and rec area are above us. You'll want to be strapped in somewhere when we're ready to take off. The others can show you where." He strode ahead, leaving the team's most recent addition to find his way with the rest of the team. *Gotta happen some-time.* He slid into the right-hand seat in the pilot compartment next to Cia, and she laughed.

"What, you assume that you're always going to be my second? What if I preferred the new dude, who I might add is far cuter than you, up here to fly with me?" Her hands never stopped moving, performing the ship's preflight routine with practiced confidence.

He shrugged. "I figured you'd tell me to go away when you wanted me to. It's not like you're particularly reticent about sharing your opinions."

She frowned at him. "That's a big word for you. Did you, like, get a dictionary as a gift or something?"

Jax sighed. "You're not as clever as you think you are, shorty."

Cia laughed. "Ooh, resorting to the short jokes. Definitely a sign of defeat. And at least I'm capable of it. Thinking, that is." She lifted a hand to cut off his reply. "Yes, Tower, this is the *Grace*. Ready for a tow." To him, she added, "Check to be sure the hatches are closed, please."

He peered down at his display screen and poked through the menu until he found the right information. "Confirmed. Sealed tight."

She nodded. "Good." The next couple minutes were filled with her faux-flirtatious banter with the driver of the tow vehicle, which left her laughing and shaking her head. She toggled the ship-wide intercom. "All right, people, we're taxiing to the runway. You have about a minute before the engines will do their best to smash you into jelly on the hull, and I do not want anyone getting my girl messy. Be sure you're strapped in before then."

Jax tapped on his controls until the navigational images appeared again. He saw that they ended at the jump point out of the system. "You don't know where we're going either?"

Cia shook her head. "No word yet. I mean, worst case

we can loiter around until our supplies run out, but it's not really something I'm jazzed about doing."

"Professor's being unusually *reticent* about sharing information, don't you think?"

She scowled. "I think if you don't quit saying reticent, I'm going to kick you out of the compartment. And yes, I agree. Not sure why. Maybe he doesn't have it all yet?" She deftly steered the ship onto the end of a long runway and spoke to the passengers again. "You have ten seconds before we go. Shout now if you're not ready."

He asked, "What do you think of the new guy?"

The pilot shrugged. "Meh. Military people are always annoying. Now stop talking, I'm trying to work."

She pushed the throttle, and the ship roared forward, headed for the stars.

By the time they'd reached the jump point, the data package containing the details of their mission had arrived. The jump itself went off without issue, and Jax reviewed their orders on his wrist comm as he walked toward the galley where the rest had gathered, Cia pushing him in the back as he slowed while reading. "Move it. Stop being reticent."

He let out a long, exasperated sigh. "Do you ever quit?"

She slipped past him with a grin lighting up her face. "Nope. Never. Better learn to deal with it.

He took the stairs one at a time, which was doubtless unimpressive to the rest of the team gathered around the dining table since she'd vaulted all of them in a single leap.

He shook his head. "Enthusiasm abounds. That's because she hasn't seen our mission yet."

Verrand nodded. "Lay it on us, Reese."

"I don't wish to alarm you, but the success of this operation seems to rest on Cia's shoulders."

The pilot straightened in surprise from where she'd been whispering in Kimmel's ear. "Say what now?"

Jax nodded. "Yep. Apparently, you are the key to us getting access to what we need. You know someone by the name of Muip Vardebron?"

She scowled. "That guy is a total dirtbag. My family quit working with him years ago."

Marshall asked, "Your family?"

Cia rolled her eyes. "Rearden. Based on Mars. Trading house, a pretty big one."

He nodded. "I've heard of it. I think my company has employed them on occasion."

The standard shrug she used when discussing her family appeared. "Most companies have, really. We have our claws into everything."

Jax said, "So, is he going to be happy to see you?"

"Uh, no. Not likely. We'll need to find someone to act as a go-between."

Sirenno, who'd been sitting quietly with his arms crossed during the discussion, said, "And will your family's contacts be able to help with that?"

Cia sighed. "Maybe. But my knowledge of them is out of date. So I'm going to have to make the ultimate sacrifice."

Kimmel twisted to look up at her with a smile. "I'm sure that talking to your family isn't that horrendous."

The pilot shook her head. "You haven't met my family."

Cia departed to send some messages, and Jax tapped Marshall on the shoulder. "I'd like to show you something." The man rose obediently and followed him back into the exercise area at the rear of the recreation section.

Marshall emitted a low whistle. "This ship really makes the best of what its small size allows." A note of condescension was present in the statement, which was part of why Jax had decided he needed some one-on-one training. Or, as a former instructor had referred to it, "A verbal smack upside the head to hit the reset button buried deep within the dense mulch that lives where the brain ought to be."

"The *Grace* is a marvel. I've never been on anything other than a naval vessel that can outshine her, and some of those would find it a close competition." He shook his head and handed over one of the collapsible batons he'd grabbed from the rack of training weapons as they'd entered. The other man flicked it out with a casual twist of his wrist. "Let's do some basic strikes and blocks while we talk. Take it through the numbers. Quarter speed, no damaging one another, please."

Marshall nodded and stretched his arms across his chest, then swept them wide to limber his muscles. Jax did the same with his baton. Each attack vector was assigned a number for practice purposes, and the other man would have learned them in basic just as Jax had. The cycle began with inward strikes at the head from each side, then the torso, then the legs, followed by an upward strike at the groin and a downward one at the skull. They slowly worked through the sequence, learning one another's movements, then naturally increased the tempo on the second round.

Jax asked, "How do you think you fit in so far?" He angled a block to throw the other man off pace, but his partner quickly recovered.

"Well enough. I think my prior military experience makes it pretty easy to slide into a team operation, you know?"

Jax blocked high, then took the offensive for the next sequence, arcing his left stick in at about a third speed toward Marshall's head. The man deflected it cleanly. "About that. You have to remember that these folks don't have the same fundamental experience we do. They won't necessarily react to things the way you anticipate."

Marshall frowned. "Are you saying they're not up to the task?"

He suppressed a sigh. "Not at all. I'm saying that they can reach the same destination, but the path they take to get there could be a little different than the one you or I might see most clearly. I've found that I have to adapt more than expected, but that their ideas are often as good as or better than mine."

The other man took over the role of attacker, and the speed increased again. Their heavy plastic batons cracked as they intersected, the beat pushing them both to increase their velocity. His breath was coming a little faster with the exertion, and as he spoke, it was clear that his opponent's was, as well. "I'm sure they'll be great to work with. Don't worry. I can find a way to be part of any situation."

Not quite the introspective acknowledgment I was looking for, to be honest. The vibration of his wrist comm forestalled his reply. He stepped back out of range and lifted his hands in a gesture of surrender. "Cia wants me up front. We'll have to finish this another time."

Marshall grinned. "Maybe we can take it to full speed."

Jax nodded. "Maybe." He returned his batons to the rack and headed for the pilot compartment, thinking that his new team member might wind up being as much a problem as an asset. He laughed inwardly. *And it's fair to say that maybe, just maybe, the same has been said about me in the past.*

CHAPTER FIFTEEN

The capital of planet Nacopra wasn't nearly as grand as the last city his team had visited. That one had been solidly under Confederacy control, in a system they'd held for decades. This one was on the fringes of Confederacy territory, on the boundary of that occupied by the Alien Coalition, and had changed hands a few times in the previous decade. The UCCA hadn't made a play for it, figuring they'd leave the precarious system alone and let the others argue about it.

The *Grace* plunged through the clouds into the lower atmosphere, and Cia cursed as a bolt of lightning cracked near the ship. "Damn it to hell." She swerved but was careful to keep them in the yellow rectangular tunnel overlaid on the exterior view. His navigation controls presented the same information, but as a wireframe diagram, for reasons he didn't really understand.

They were buffeted by gusts of air and torrential sheets of falling water as they made their way to the spaceport.

The pilot muttered, "Place like this, you'd think they'd have indoor landing spots."

Jax laughed. "Umbrellas are a thing, you know."

She gestured at the display. "In this wind? Probably even a portable shield wouldn't hold up against that nonsense." A shake of her head sent her short hair swiveling. "No, we're going to get wet. The best we can hope for is that the *Grace* is assigned a berth near the walkway."

Naturally, the ship wound up parked about as far from the walkway as it could be. However, the large vehicle that pulled up beside the ship once her engines were shut down alleviated all concerns. Cia put the systems into standby, ready to be activated remotely at need, and gathered them all in the galley. "Okay, I've arranged for an invitation. Our host has sent a bus to pick us up, looks like a luxury model. Probably trying to look good in the hopes I'll say something positive about them to my family."

Ethan Kimmel interrupted, "I take it that this person doesn't know that you all don't get along?"

"No, we keep that information close. If asked, my parents and siblings simply claim I'm out 'experiencing life' before joining the business formally. It's far from unheard of in their circles. And I don't contradict that story, except among those I like. Well, and Jax, since I'm stuck with him."

The fact that only a couple low chuckles sounded in response was a good gauge of his team's nervousness. He said, "So, if I hear you right, what you're saying is that we can't trust the contact you've, uh, contacted, or the person they're taking us to meet."

She nodded. "Your hearing seems perfect. Exactly so. We should assume that the bus is wired for audio and video, at least, and probably a full-body scan isn't out of the question. Also, I wouldn't recommend partaking of anything that might be inside."

Sirenno frowned. "Like what?"

Cia's shoulders lifted and fell in a shrug. "In the past, I've been greeted with alcohol, drugs both legal and not, and men, women, and pleasure robots for the taking."

Marshall made a shocked noise. "Seriously?"

"Seriously. Where there's money in hand and money to be made, there's no limit to what people will do. Again, not my family, and not my people, but morals are extremely flexible with this crowd. The same warnings apply when we see Vardebron."

Umbrellas were sufficient to protect them as they relocated to the bus, and sure enough, refreshments awaited them. Fortunately, the vehicle was empty except presumably for a driver in the closed cab and Cia's contact waiting in the back. He didn't rise at their appearance, simply nodded and gestured toward the seats on either side. When she arrived, however, he stood and in a display of obsequiousness more impressive than Jax had ever seen, welcomed her to the planet and thanked her for contacting him. He was thin and jittery, his limbs seeming to shake even in those moments when not deliberately in motion. His nose was sharp and a little too small for his face, offsetting his eyes, which were a bit too big. His hair was wispy and turning to grey. For all of that, his clothes were elegant and his manners flawless. *Strange combination. And Cia's warning wasn't necessary—I would never trust this guy.*

Her shift into what he'd come to think of as "trader mode" was seamless. Although she hadn't dressed to impress, came with her hand out for help, and was maybe a third of his age, she clearly held the position of senior partner in their relationship. She deflected his flattery without fully acknowledging it and took a seat a few away from him, denying him the status that a closer choice would potentially have conveyed. Once the initial greetings were done, she asked, "So what can we expect?"

The man's hands were gripped tightly together, but that was his only sign of nervousness or displeasure. He sounded like he might have been discussing a fine evening at the theater when he replied, "Oh, the usual. Lots of guards, lots of guns, lots of effort to make visitors feel threatened. He hardly ever goes through with it, though. And certainly, he'd be a fool to try such a thing with someone like you, Master Rearden."

She returned a dismissive wave. "Which is not the same as saying he would never threaten me. Intentional?"

His eyes crinkled a little, signaling concern. "I wouldn't wish to speak badly of another, but there has been some question of late as to the, shall we say, mental acuity of our friend Vardebron. His actions have tended toward the impulsive."

Cia nodded, her face neutral. "Examples? Explanations?"

He shrugged. "Capriciousness, Master Rearden, in matters personal and business both. It would be inappropriate for me to say more than that." *More like, you're afraid of losing your value as a go-between if she decides to give this up as a bad idea, which is more and more what it appears to be.* "People I trust have ventured that perhaps he has found himself in some sort of straits that are distracting him from focusing on issues of import."

That drew a frown from his pilot. "It would need to be something significant to draw that one away from operating his business."

"Exactly what I've said, Master Rearden. But I have not been able to ascertain what it might be, despite considerable investment in attempting to do so on your behalf." Jax highly doubted the man had done much of anything on anyone's "behalf" but his own for some time, but it was a nice play. Cia's hint of a smile suggested she'd noticed the wordplay and felt the same.

"All right. Anything else we should know before we brace the dragon in his den?"

Her contact held up a data chip. "Only this, which is the latest information I was able to procure on the layout of the interior, the nature of the security systems, and the current complement of guards."

She bestowed a genuine smile on him. "Oh, very well done, Uzur. Thank you for anticipating my needs so expertly." He beamed under her praise as she accepted the chip and handed it off to Kimmel, who carried a small palm computer with no wireless connectivity specifically for moments like this. He slotted the item into it to test it for viruses, malware, or other hidden surprises. A moment later he nodded, withdrew it, and inserted it into his wrist comm, which then sent it to all of theirs.

Cia shifted a couple of seats closer, tapping Marshall to get him to move and receiving a small scowl in return. Then, she put her hand on Uzur's arm. "So, tell me what your company is up to these days."

The darkened windows of their ride kept them from seeing the city areas they passed through, although Jax watched their progress on his wrist comm's map. *Need to get some autonomous drones for these situations. Maybe make them standard equipment on the* Grace. He filed it away as a suggestion for afterward, since wishing for things he didn't have was not a productive way to spend pre-mission time.

When the vehicle stopped and he hopped out of it, he was greeted by the sight of a lavish and decidedly gaudy domicile. The mansion stretched for a distance to the right and left, and had two separate ornate front entrances, each with a circular lane so cars could drop guests off under the canopies that extended to more than ten feet away from the house. The doors before them were two stories high and the same white mixed with grey color as the polished stone that was the house's primary construction material. Gold filigree rendered symbols he didn't recognize on them. *Probably a family crest or some such thing.* They opened as Cia stepped from the bus. *Clearly, she has a status that the rest of us lack in the eyes of the person we're meeting.*

She swept forward and stopped in front of a man in a tuxedo. "Cia Rearden and company. Please convey our thanks to Mister Vardebron for receiving us."

Jax had originally thought the man might be their host. He downgraded him to butler after Cia's comment. The servant was tall, stately, somewhere between thin and muscular. The way his black coat moved over his starched white shirt suggested the presence of a pistol underneath his arm. That hadn't been part of the briefing they'd received, although it was certainly in keeping with the owner's overwhelming concern with the security of his home. He'd installed systems and backup systems, plus at least half again as many personnel as Jax would have detailed to protect the place. Cia's discomfort with him was coming into focus since only someone who didn't always stay on the legitimate side of the business line would need such a substantial number of guardians.

He led them to a spacious den with entry doors almost as large as the ones they'd already passed through. Inside was a portly man, probably in his fifties to judge from the thinning hair and skin that was starting to wrinkle. He sat on an uncomfortable-looking couch with thin cushions and metal arms and legs. Arrayed around him were equally unappealing chairs, to which the butler directed them. Cia took the one nearest their host. Her neutral expression, so different than those he was used to seeing on her face, told him she didn't see the man as an ally by any means.

She cleared her throat. "Thank you for meeting with us, Mister Vardebron. I respect you too much to waste your time, so I'll get right to the point. We've been sent to acquire a certain item that I believe you have the connections to secure. Money *is* an object, of course, as it always is, but not an insurmountable one as long as the terms are reasonable."

He nodded. "Do go on, Master Rearden." The way he said it raised the hairs on the back of Jax's neck. He was insulted on Cia's behalf and braced himself for her to respond in kind.

Instead, she shrugged and replied passively, "It's all

right here." She held up a data chip, and the butler inserted it into a tablet that he extended for his employer to view.

The man rubbed the short beard on his chin and made soft noises as he took in the data. Finally, he said, "What you ask for is possible, but I'm afraid it's going to take more than money to accomplish it."

"What do you mean?"

"There's another business deal I'm working on completing that requires something of a show of force. I notice you've brought a group that would serve that purpose adequately with you. So, for the payment of handling my needs on this other transaction, I will secure the item you desire and sell it to you at cost, plus ten percent."

If it had been him in the seat next to the man, he would have been bristling with outrage and trying to control his voice. Cia maintained an air of perfect calm as she replied, "We accept. Shall we get to the details?"

CHAPTER SIXTEEN

"The details are annoying, is what they are," Cia groused as she lifted the *Grace* from its pad and aimed it for the skies above. "The extra ten percent was a deliberate insult. Later, when I have time to think it through and do it right, he's going to pay for that."

Jax laughed. "You have more of a killer instinct than you let on."

"I haven't left the expectations behind just because I'm not currently part of the family business. You don't do something like that to a partner."

"Clearly, he doesn't see us as partners."

She stuck her tongue out at him. "You think? Anyway, how weird is it that we're heading out to visit the Dhelear? Right after you encountered them in your other life?" He'd shared the details with her, but not with the rest of the team, during the first part of their trip.

Jax frowned thoughtfully. "I'd say it's random chance, but relying on that would be stupid. I'll send a message to Major Stephenson before we jump, letting her know what's up." He'd been composing that letter in his head since discovering who was on the receiving end of their current mission. "Despite Vardebron's assurance that this is simply a show of force to ensure the handoff goes well, somehow I don't believe him."

"That's because you're not the biggest idiot in the universe. Third biggest, maybe." She grinned in his direction. "There's definitely more to it. Can't be a simple smash and grab, though, because a ton of better options are available in his sphere of contacts for that sort of thing. No, it's bound to be something stupid and annoying, like I said."

"You can always make a bad situation seem a bit worse, Cia. It's a gift. Treasure it."

She laughed. "Whatever, Mister Whiney Whinerson. Hey, speaking of whining, Marshall didn't like it when I took his seat, did he?"

Of course, she noticed. That's what she does. "No, he did not. I think he has some issues when it comes to teamwork."

"And the Professor sent him out with you. What's that about? Like two wrongs making a right?" She flicked on the ship-wide comm. "You're free to move about for the next fifty-seven minutes until we reach the jump point. Don't break anything on the *Grace* unless you fancy a stretch in the medical pod." Killing it, she continued, "Do you think that Maarsen wants you to make him understand that he needs to learn to control his desire for control, like you did?"

He sighed. "I will never stop regretting sharing that bit of deeply personal insight with you. Marshall's not quite the same as I was. Am. Whatever. It's something a little different. I wouldn't have been upset at you taking my seat, even back then."

"Makes sense. Well, I hope you figure it out before we're home. Returning to the Professor with a second failure won't do much for your standing at the Academy." She hit the autopilot button and stood, stretching with a groan. "I'm going to shower and change into something that hasn't been in the proximity of Vardebron, that slug. I'll be back for the jump."

Jax watched her leave and considered the question of Kenton Marshall. *Yeah, I do need to identify what's lacking, and it seems like it might be more a challenge of narrowing it down from the many possibilities than simply finding where it's hiding.*

The planet Accides wasn't the birthplace of the Dhelear, according to the records the *Grace* carried, but had been one of their first conquests. Looking down at it from space, approaching on the night side, the sheer enormity of the area of the world covered by cities was almost over-whelming. Jax shook his head. "Damn, that's a lot of civilization right there."

Cia gave a soft snort. "I'm not sure civilization is the appropriate word. They've developed a lot, but at their core, they still like to eat with their hands." She pantomimed flexing claws, and he nodded.

"One more reason to handle this by stealth, as much as we can."

The pilot's grin held an edge to it as if she'd tasted

something bitter. "Although Vardebron said he wanted a 'show of force,' I'm sure he'll be satisfied with whatever approach gets him the item he needs." The additional details he'd provided had revealed that the man had no compelling reason for his belief that strong-arming the other parties in the transaction was the right tactic to use.

Once they'd learned that the Dhelear were involved, Jax had discarded that idea entirely. He had no desire to go up against them on their turf if it could be avoided. *Or anywhere, really. Those claws are downright scary.* "How close will the landing pad be to the target?"

A frown illustrated her answer. "Not close enough. We're going to have to cover a decent distance to get there. Figure an hour walking, if no one bothers with us."

"And the likelihood of us being left alone on an alien world with few humans, at night, is probably pretty small."

Cia nodded. "That sort of insight is no doubt why they pay you the big bucks." Her tone lacked her normal mirth, signaling her concern.

He stared down at the planet as they grew closer. "What about a touch and go?"

"You can't be thinking of what I think you're thinking of, because that would be insane. Better explain." He paused while she exchanged words with the spaceport and steered the *Grace* onto a new descent path.

"You bring the ship in as low as you can somewhere close to the target, set down for a moment, then take off again."

She snorted as if he'd said the most ludicrous words she'd ever heard. "First, there's nowhere to land. The area is covered with buildings, and they're probably not rated to have a bloody spaceship on top of them. Second, their control people would have a massive hissy fit that would almost certainly get us shot down. Third, you should really think about showering more and washing your brain while you're in there. It's clearly not working properly."

He ran frustrated hands through his short hair. "Okay. Can you fly over a nearby area slowly?"

Cia sighed. "Yes. And for the record, I hate this idea."

Jax grinned as he slapped the release for his safety harness. "Not as much as Marshall is going to hate it."

The choice to bring the team's new addition was a natural one since he was the only other person with official military training. All of them had some sort of basic combat in their backgrounds, either as a hobby or competitively, but none had actually enlisted like he and Marshall had. Jax summoned him to the *Grace's* small armory and arrived at the same moment he did. "We're going to have a little fun."

The other man tilted his head to the side quizzically. "I'm not sure I love the sound of that." His tone belied his words, and Jax realized that Marshall might have interpreted his selection as confidence in his overall abilities rather than the specific difference of his training. *I'll have to be more careful with what I say and do in the future if I'm going to help him truly become part of the team.*

"You need a suit, armor plates, pistol, rifle, and some web grenades. *Only* web grenades. We're going for stealth here." Jax pulled his civilian clothes off and climbed into his battle gear. "This stuff isn't military-grade, but it's pretty good."

Marshall nodded and started gearing up. "I would think that with the contacts they have at the Academy, you could improve on it." His tone held a slight hint of disapproval, and Jax chose to assume it was directed at the equipment itself and not the Professor and his people. *Or me.*

"That's a good point. I've been working with the docs on my prosthetics, but I'm sure that they must have some staff or students that can do some adjustments. The rifles are top-notch, anyway." The crates below held heavier gear, but it wouldn't serve their need for quiet well. And it, too, probably wasn't as innovative as it could be. He finished with his suit and armor plates, then secured his boots in place, stomping to be sure they were set. "All right. You finish getting ready and meet me in the cargo bay. I have a couple of things to pull together."

Marshall nodded, and Jax left him to wrap up, moving with haste through the corridor leading to the back of the ship. He activated his direct comm to Cia. "What's our timeframe?"

"A minute and a half until the course change. You'll need to be out fifteen seconds after that. You know, I can't guarantee that they won't see you. Or detect you on one of a thousand other kinds of sensors."

Jax shrugged and climbed down the stairs into the cargo bay. "It's the highest building around for blocks, so they might not have considered an aerial assault. Sometimes those blind spots are baked into the design. Anyway, I sure don't have a better idea at the moment. If this doesn't succeed, you and the rest can go in and run with the original plan, with the added challenge of getting us set free if we're captured."

He heard her scowl. "And if you get killed? You know, I've put a lot of time and effort into accepting you as you are, flaws and all. I'd hate to see that work go for nothing. Plus, the Professor will probably blame me, or something."

He responded with a laugh. "I love you too, Cia."

"Shut it. One minute. Get your ass in gear."

Marshall arrived a moment later to assist, and together they pulled out heavy black cables and harnesses from one of the Academy crates. The pair worked quickly to prepare for the action to come. When the ship heeled sharply to the side, they donned their helmets and Jax hit the button to open the cargo door. A countdown glowed in the corner of his display, now at seven seconds. He walked forward to the edge of the ramp, seeing the city moving below, faster than he would have liked. "You ready for this?"

The other man's headgear bobbed. "Totally." Jax heard the pre-battle jitters that randomly afflicted everyone, in his experience.

"All righty then. We jump at zero. The cables are the correct length to keep us from slamming into the side of the building, but we might have to cut loose and drop. Cia's an amazing pilot, but this is asking a lot." The timer hit zero, and they jumped together. His stomach stayed in the ship as his body fell. After what felt like at least an hour of hurtling toward the ground but was probably only a few seconds, the line snapped taut and yanked him forward. The overlay on his display showed him his target; without it, he would have been too disoriented to pull off the maneuver. *Would be interesting to explain at the spaceport why the* Grace *has two people dangling from her.* He yanked the release at the right moment and dropped only a couple of feet, then collapsed and rolled to absorb his momentum.

When he stopped moving, he bounced up and looked for Marshall. His partner was a short distance away, pulling himself up on some sort of piece of equipment with a groan. "Did you hit that?"

"Yeah. Bad aim. Ow."

"Injured?" Jax moved toward him.

"Nah. Just a little dinged. I'm good. If it gets problematic, I'll take a shot of painkiller. I'm ready to roll."

"Perfect. Let's get what we came here to get."

CHAPTER SEVENTEEN

Every building he'd ever seen, aside from the most secure ones, had at least one roof access to permit maintenance personnel to do their jobs. It was too inconvenient to do otherwise. This proved to be no exception. Two eight-foot-high protrusions were present, each with a heavy door blocking entry. The *Grace's* gear had included an electronic lockpick, and he held it over the palm pad, hoping it would be sufficient. He was confident the device would handle a normal level of security, but feared that this structure, home to a criminal organization masquerading as a company according to the materials they'd been given, might prove resistant to its demands.

After a full minute of waiting, he sighed and packed it away. Marshall noted, "Too bad we didn't keep the ropes. We could have gone down the side and through a window."

"That would pose problems without Kimmel here to compromise their systems. No, we're going to have to do this the harder way." He retrieved a second device from a belt compartment and pulled off a backing to free the adhesive. He placed it over the palm pad and activated it. A moment later the green light on the front glowed, indicating it had found and spoofed the local alarm signal. Again, the gadget wasn't anything like military-grade, but neither should the security be, especially up here on the roof. He stepped aside to make room for Marshall, who quickly and efficiently pried off the pad to expose its connections.

The other man said, "Old style. We haven't used stuff like this in years." He made some adjustments, the latch clicked, and the door moved slightly outward.

"Nice work." Jax gripped his rifle in both hands, checked by touch to ensure the stun setting was active, and pushed the door wide with the gun's barrel. It revealed a staircase leading down. He advanced, noting how the steps seemed a little bigger than what he was used to. *Probably one of a ton of differences, given that aliens built this world.* His experience hadn't often involved non-human-designed cities, and he had to keep reminding himself not to assume anything at all. *Even the size of the stairs.*

His helmet rendered the sight in greys and greens, due to the lack of illumination. He'd spent enough time using night vision that it was almost as clear as daylight to him, but wasn't sure about Marshall's experience. "Keep it slow and steady. Careful on the steps, they're oddly sized." He continued down and found the expected door at the bottom. A hand dipped into a belt pouch and came out with a thin strip of metal with adhesive on it, as well as another of the security-confusing bricks. He opened the door and applied the latter above the palm pad on the other side of the wall, then used the former to prevent the door latch from closing again. It would have read momentarily open to a security system, but he hoped the signal would be dismissed as a potential glitch that had resolved itself.

He led the way into the hallway beyond. It was industrial-looking, similar to the service corridors he'd seen in countless buildings and on an equal number of blueprints during his military unit's downtime review of construction schematics. His display adjusted, adding color now that sufficient lighting was present. The walls and floors looked to be plastic, but somehow not. They had an opalescent sheen to them that unsettled him, as if the whole thing was constantly in motion.

Marshall apparently felt the same way. "That's bloody eerie." The line-of-sight comm connection would keep their conversation secure, but more importantly, wouldn't set off sensors looking for wireless emanations.

"Yeah, it is." A door stood before them, and their hallway stretched down to the left and right to end in more doors. "There's no way to know how the aliens think, but if they're anything like us, the powerful folks hang out on the top. We might get lucky and find the item the first place we look. Let's go left." He walked slowly in that direction, keeping his footsteps light and his rifle pointed forward. Marshall stayed a consistent three feet back and enough to his side that the fisheye view in his display allowed him to see the other man. When they reached the door, he pulled out the third rectangle of the four he'd brought, and another metal strip.

He repeated the process of securing the door and stepped out into a far more lavish room. It had comfortable-looking couches on the left and front walls, and a high round table in the middle sized for three, to judge by the number of tall chairs. A counter held something that looked like a beverage dispenser, and a large cabinet that could be a refrigerator. *Or, for all I know, a meat locker full of smoked human flesh for snacks.* He snorted inwardly. Their research hadn't suggested the aliens ate other sentient species, but that had been a pivotal component in many movies he'd seen, and it was difficult to leave all that informal training behind.

Marshall quipped, "Stop for a coffee, boss?"

Jax smiled and shook his head. The other man was equal parts charming and grating. In a military unit, any competent commander would make him run until exhaustion eliminated the negative part, but that wasn't an option at the moment. "Get in, get the stuff, get out." It seemed like Maarsen's constant mandate for him. The right side of the room opened onto a central meeting area of some kind. An oval of curved displays hung from the ceiling with an opening on each end to allow access to the arrangement's interior. Inside, he found blank screens and emptiness. He mused, "Might be a control area? But for what, I don't know."

His partner said, "Maybe running ops. People with cameras feed the displays, and the bosses are here giving commands in real-time. I've never seen this kind of design, but it does remind me of those kinds of rooms." Jax had to agree. He'd never worked out of one himself but had been on the opposite end, in the field feeding back visuals.

"Sounds legit. I see three doors, symmetrical in the center of the walls to our left, right, and forward."

"Confirmed."

"Let's try the one ahead first." He gave a verbal command to summon the image of their objective, roughly fist-sized metal cube, silver, with no seams or markings. "It's probably too much to ask that it's being used as an ornament or something." The door was a standard interior model, and the electronic lockpick took care of it easily. *Not quite paranoid enough, friends.* The space inside held no work furniture, only more hanging displays. Shelves hung on the walls, filled with an interesting array of objects that in no way resembled what they were looking for. He and Marshall wandered around the room scanning for hidden safes or other secrets but found none. "Okay, right or left?"

His partner replied, "Right. I feel good about right."

Jax muttered, "I don't feel good about any of this," and headed for the door the other man had mentioned. He unlocked the door and swung it open, then spun at a sound behind him. A stun blast from Marshall's weapon barely missed a fleeing figure racing out of sight in the far corner. Jax raised his rifle and traversed it across the room, and realized a moment too late that his partner was in motion. He'd already made it halfway to where they'd last seen the alien by the time Jax ordered, "No, wait."

Marshall's tone betrayed the fact that the excitement and adrenaline of the moment had blown away his restraint. "I can get him, no problem, boss." Then he, too, vanished out of sight around the corner.

Jax yelled, "Marshall, stop," but instead of a confirmation he heard another stun blast go off. He charged down the corridor shouting mental curses at the man and banged through a doorway that led into a service stairwell. It had the same look and feel as the hallway they'd entered through, and even the railings along the stairs were made of that same strange plastic. He peered over the side as he ran and spotted the alien two levels below and Marshall a floor behind him. He shouted again, "Kenton, stop right there," and the other man unexpectedly complied.

A moment later, an unfamiliar sound emerged from below, and his partner was wreathed in energy. He fell like the surrounding gravity had tripled, his rifle clattering on the floor as he collapsed. Jax growled and charged ahead, reaching the half-level above him to find two aliens in the familiar scarlet armor pointing large guns at him. He scrambled backward and flicked the selector to projectiles, then leaned around the corner and fired blindly at an angle that would ensure he wouldn't hit his ally.

The translated voice came unexpectedly from above. "Put down your weapons, human, or we will kill the other." He turned his head slowly to see that two aimed large rifles at him from the landing ten feet above, with another pair peering down over the railing from higher up. With a sigh, he released his rifle to dangle from its strap and lifted his hands. *Dammit, Marshall. Just when I thought we were on the right path.*

Jax hadn't enjoyed having his helmet removed and replaced with a fabric hood that prevented him from seeing. He also put being handcuffed and marched along with powerful grips on each of his biceps on the list of things he wouldn't be doing on his next vacation. But being thrown into a chair as if he was no more than a child by someone strong enough to do it was the least appealing of his recent experiences.

He blinked at the bright lights of the room as his captors ripped the hood from his face. Before him stood an alien in a forest green version of the armor suit that the others had worn. Four more in the scarlet variety, two on each side, had the attentive posture of guards. A non-human who was a few inches taller and significantly brawnier than the rest strode into position beside the one in front of him, then turned to glare. His blue suit didn't quite go with the green one his boss wore. Jax twisted from side to side, but Marshall wasn't anywhere in the room. "Where's the person who was with me?" he demanded.

A moment passed, probably as translation occurred, then the alien spoke words he couldn't understand. An accented voice emanated from all around him. "His life is forfeit."

He shook his head. "That's a little steep for a little breaking and entering, don't you think?"

The being in front of him scowled. "He has disrespected me by injuring one in my service. Your offense is lesser since you proved incapable of doing damage."

Jax was doubly offended. First, because of the danger to Marshall. Second, because the bastard alien judged him less "capable" than the other man. "You would have done it already unless you had something else in mind. Care to share?" *Whatever it is, I bet it's going to suck.*

CHAPTER EIGHTEEN

I knew this would suck. I seriously underestimated the degree. Jax was being marched in cuffs again, this time at least without a hood covering his head. He felt like they'd moved far enough in one direction that they weren't in the same building anymore, but couldn't be sure. The walls and floors were the same opalescent white plastic-ish stuff and had no joins that he could see. *Maybe everything on the planet is extruded from some mammoth construction vehicle. That wouldn't be the most bizarre thing I've heard today.*

That honor had to go to the proposal he'd accepted, given that the alternative was Kenton Marshall's death, and probably his own shortly after. Even the translation of the being's words had sounded smug as he offered Jax the same deal that Captain Jensen had offered the Dhelear ship they'd encountered. One-on-one. Hand-to-hand. Or, more specifically, hand-to-claw. *There's something more going on here than simple punishment, but I have no idea what it might be.*

Fortunately, a lifetime of experience had prepared him

for the times where he had to put the big thoughts away and focus on more pressing issues, like how not to get killed by an enemy with better weapons. As soon as he'd realized what was going on, he'd listened with only half attention, focusing his mind and senses on the aliens that had surrounded him. Unfortunately, no obvious weaknesses presented themselves, and the analysis did nothing to diminish his fear of their retractable claws. *Speed will be the key. If my opponent gets an opportunity for a clean hit, I'm toast.*

The realization that he'd been hearing a distant rumble from ahead for several seconds penetrated his thoughts. The corridor ended at a blank wall, and the low roar sounded as if it was coming from behind it. When they reached it, the aliens pushed his face against it and held it there while they removed the cuffs. Through the wall, he heard an enthusiastic voice speaking, or shouting, words he couldn't understand. The cadence seemed familiar, as did the call and response pattern with the other voices. *It sounds like a sports fight.* Combat was still a prime form of entertainment in the universe, both to engage in and to enjoy as a viewer, and was one of the most popular contests for wagering, legal and illegal alike. *Great. I'm going to be a sideshow attraction, on top of the actual maybe dying part of the equation.*

He straightened and rubbed his wrists as the pressure let up. A muffled cheer came from behind the wall, followed by a pause and some more words. Without warning, the surface in front of him slid upward out of sight, revealing a large dark area around a brightly lit center. Hands struck his upper back, sending him forward in a stumble, and the crowd made a strange sibilant sound as a spotlight caught him. He realized the space wasn't as big as he'd thought at first, about twice the size of a regular gymnasium for basketball. As his eyes adjusted and he could keep them open for more than a second at a time, he spotted an audience on all sides standing in neat lines, each row a little higher up than the one before it.

In the wash of lights in the middle, which was clearly intended to be a combat ring, stood the burly alien he'd last seen in the office, dressed in a dark blue version of the bodysuit they all seemed to wear. The being had displayed his teeth as his boss described what Jax had to do to save his partner's life. It was simple, really. Weaponless combat, his hands against his opponent's claws and teeth. If he won, he and Marshall would go free. If he didn't, he'd die at the hands of the lurking goon and the newest member of his team would likely be tortured for fun, then killed. *So, you know, lose-lose.* He wasn't sure he believed that winning would result in freedom, but at this point, he had little left to lose and had to cling to whatever opportunity fate chose to offer him. The aliens had sweetened the pot when he'd shown initial reluctance, promising to hand over the item he'd been attempting to steal. How they knew what he was there for was a question that he devoutly hoped to find the answer to one day.

He caught sight of Kenton Marshall, standing between two impassive guards with his arms bound behind his back. His expression was glazed and defocused. *They must have slapped him around some on the way here and concussed him. Or could be drugs. Either way, the option of grabbing him and running is off the table.* It wasn't viable in any case, given the sheer number of aliens surrounding them.

Guess I'll have to do it the hard way. Correction, the really, really, really hard way. His escorts gave him one more push, but he was ready for it this time and maintained his dignity as he walked into the rectangular combat field. He noted the metal line that ran along the boundary and figured it would be a nasty surprise for anyone unlucky enough to intersect it during the fight. His opponent stared at him, had been staring at him during his approach. He seemed calm and confident, and Jax sensed eagerness in his expression, despite the differences in their physiology.

The alien voice spoke again over the room's speakers, and the crowd responded with cheers. No provision had been made for translation, and although he would have liked to understand, it wasn't important. The minimal rules and regulations had been shared up in the office. A fight to the death, however it could be achieved. He'd managed some vague plans, mainly hinging upon the ability to get some sort of makeshift weapon once the battle began. The marked perimeter argued against that likelihood.

The voice stopped, and his opponent advanced. With an electrical sizzle, a shield sprang up at the edges of their fighting space. *Good, maybe I can knock him into one of them and fry him.* Jax shifted into a back stance and circled to his right, then reversed direction after his foe changed his line of approach. He had plenty of room to use, which was a bonus. He'd fought in smaller spaces any number of times and was glad to be without those limitations.

The alien lunged, his fist snapping out at Jax's face. The

creature had covered an unexpected amount of territory with the move, and the back of Jax's mind added that speed burst into the list of things he had to worry about, immediately under the thing's claws, which held the top position. He skipped to the side to avoid it and flicked his human arm up to knock it out of line. It passed to the left of his head, and he bolted to his right so it couldn't come back in a swipe.

His opponent didn't offer a follow-up attack, only continued to stalk him slowly. *Playing for the crowd or cautious enough to see what I'm capable of. Either way, I'm not a fan.* The part of Jax that respected an intelligent and competent enemy was absent at the moment, given the odds against him and the life-and-death stakes. If it were possible to cheat to win, he'd do it in a second and figure out a way to atone for it later.

He feinted to his left, then leapt forward and slashed a roundhouse kick at the alien's thigh, aiming for where the nerve bundle that would numb out the leg on a human was located. He connected with a glancing blow and was almost certain the sound his opponent made in response was laughter. *Sure, be smug because you're like the jolly blue giant.* He dove to the side and shoulder-rolled to his feet to avoid a kick from his foe that absolutely would have removed his head from his shoulders and launched it into the back row of the audience had it hit him. *Bloody hell, he's fast. Okay, time to make something happen.*

Jax pretended to go on the defensive, circling and adopting an alarmed expression, which was easy given the attack of a moment before. When the alien punched again, Jax snapped his left arm up in a rising block with the power of his whole body behind it. His artificial limb smashed into the alien's forearm, fortunately on the underside rather than on the bony plate that covered the top of it. His opponent's face twisted and he snatched the arm back, abandoning the follow-up punch he'd been halfway through throwing. He shook it out and gave Jax a nod. He sensed no respect in it, merely a cataloging of his abilities. *Damn and double damn.*

The next flurry of exchanges put Jax on the defensive, the alien's speed as impressive as anyone he'd ever fought. It wasn't lost on him that his opponent was playing with him, as the claws had yet to make an appearance. That was the only reason he was willing to bide his time and conserve his energy while trying to get more information on his rival's fighting style. The moment they showed up, every move would be potentially fatal. His foe tried low, middle, and high attacks, and he offered the same in return. The crowd cheered and hissed at different moments that seemed unconnected to any particular action, and the announcer's voice was a drone behind the sound of his breath and the blood pumping through his body.

The attack-and-counter routine led Jax to a conclusion he didn't like a single bit. *I'm going to have to take a blow to deliver mine.* They could play cat-and-mouse all day until one of them tired, but he wasn't the predator in that scenario with this particular adversary. *Triple damn.* He steeled himself for the move and waited for the right opportunity.

It came about half a minute later, after another flurry of punches thrown and blocked by each. The alien drew back its off hand for a blow, and Jax hurled himself forward. He landed a foot away from his opponent with his arms raised to guard his head and chambered his leg almost all the way to his heart. He pivoted and thrust it out, channeling all the momentum of his leap into the blow. The alien's fist connected with the back of his right shoulder, causing it to go instantly numb, then blossom with pain.

But it was worth it because his heel slammed into his foe's chest hard enough to drive it stumbling backward, directly into the shimmering electrical field behind it. Jax retracted the kick automatically, grinning at the success of his move and his unexpected victory.

Right up until the alien bounced off the shield, which turned out to be a physical barrier that didn't fry, electrocute, cook, or otherwise damage him. This time, the grin on the thing's face was unmistakable as it found its balance and held up its hands to show off its claws. *Uh-oh. That's really not good.*

CHAPTER NINETEEN

The claws extended from the tip of each finger like nails, each about an inch long, and resembled dark, jagged stone. They were sharp everywhere, and he'd need to watch out for both slashing and stabbing attacks from them. He backpedaled in a rush to get out of range, but his opponent displayed no matching haste. Instead, he seemed to be playing to the crowd, strutting around the perimeter of the combat area as if claiming it as its own.

That's fine, buddy, you do your thing. Gives me more time to figure out how the hell to deal with your new toys. His mind raced, but with a purpose, sorting through all the fights he'd been in before and searching for something he could use. In a situation where an enemy had a knife and he didn't, the best tactic was to take the weapon away. That wasn't a possibility here. Any kick or punch that lingered an instant too long would be an opening for the alien to cut him. *And once I start to bleed, it'll be the beginning of the end.*

His instructors had always advised that if he was

157

fighting a blade, he should assume getting stabbed or slashed was guaranteed, and be ready to follow through when it happened. That way, when the cold metal parted flesh, it wouldn't be a shocking moment, but an anticipated one. He'd found it useful on many occasions, but it offered no comfort in this particular circumstance. His opponent finished his prancing and turned back to him, a change in his demeanor signaling that they'd passed playtime and were now into the endgame, as far as he was concerned.

Jax switched his stance, putting his dominant arm forward. It would lessen his ability to deliver full-power blows with it, but the prosthetic wouldn't bleed when stabbed. He would need all the enhanced speed the limb offered, and momentarily wished he'd pushed the training faster. He set that worry aside, along with every other thought except his advancing enemy.

The alien's pattern of attack changed. Rapid blows replaced his previously powerful ones. He was no longer trying to smash Jax, but going for slices and punctures with his wickedly sharp fingertips. It took only a couple of passes before the creature figured out his strategy, which consisted of blocking with only his front arm and dodging the rest of the attacks. His foe added in quick kicks, which Jax intercepted with the sole of his foot before they could rise high enough to threaten any vulnerable parts.

He muttered inwardly about how much he hated this battle, hated the spectators, hated the enemy trying to kill him. A fair fight was acceptable if undesirable, but this was the next best thing to a bloodletting, with him as the sacrificial lamb. He focused his will until his teeth ached from clenching them and continued his blocks and evasions, waiting for an opening, any opening at all, that might give him a chance.

When it came, no conscious effort guided his actions. He'd become all reflex, the change a necessity to continue picking off the nasty attacks coming at him. A small voice cautioned that he was going to get hurt, but the opportunity was too good to pass up. The alien had extended himself a little too far, and his front foot slid as his weight shifted momentarily, locking out his knee. Jax's left arm, which had been on its way up in a block, reversed course as he let himself fall forward, channeling his whole body into a downward elbow strike. It hit the thing's knee, which was protected by one of the bony plates, and smashed through it.

The alien screeched when its joint bent the wrong way. It didn't stop him from slashing claws down Jax's unprotected chest, and a feeling of sharp cold was immediately followed by the warmth of his blood rising through the five parallel slices. He ignored the pain and pushed himself to his feet, circling the alien's recumbent form at a safe distance, heading for its skull. His foe screamed in rage and suffering as he rotated to try to keep up with his motion, and made the attempt to rise only to fall in agony. *Sorry, pal. It could have easily gone the other way, with me being the one to slip. One day it probably will, but today is not that day.* He lined up the thing's head and kicked it as hard as he could, then continued his assault past the point where his opponent had ceased moving. There had been no question that simple unconsciousness would be insufficient to claim victory.

When the alien was wrecked beyond saving, he turned

and walked with as much dignity as he could toward his bound teammate. The guards freed him, and Marshall immediately peeled off his shirt and pressed it against Jax's wounds. The once-military-medical man said, "Keep pressure on it. The slices are shallow, but they're bleeding a lot."

Jax nodded and turned to the men who'd been holding his partner. "All right. Tell the boss it's time to make good on his commitments."

With no power to compel the aliens to adhere to their promises, Jax had set the odds at one in three at best that he'd survive the day. It was with no small surprise that he found himself patched up, in possession of the item they'd come to get, and out on the street an hour later. Kenton Marshall looked rough, his eyes haunted, and Jax imagined they must have worked him over a little, but not enough to do any permanent damage. His movements were stiff but sure, so any issues were probably mental or emotional. *Which is totally legit, but shouldn't prove an impediment to us getting back to the ship.* New shirts had been provided for both of them, and he'd received bandages and tape to bind his wounds.

The city was confusing, the languages unknown. It wasn't meant to be a place where humans belonged. His wrist comm had been taken away before the fight, and his hope that they'd left Marshall his had been dashed. He'd done enough map memorizing that he felt like he knew the proper direction, but figured it would be hours of walking even if they could manage a straight line, given his exhaustion and his partner's weakened state. He pointed and asked, "That way, correct?"

The other man choked out a laugh. "Yeah. A nice stroll to end the day, right?"

Jax turned to face him and put a little command in his voice. "Kenton, look at me." His partner lifted his eyes from the ground. "What happened back there sucked, and at some point, you'll have the time to process it properly. At the moment it's playing with your head, which is totally natural. You need to pack it all away and focus on one thing: getting the hell off this planet. After that, anything is possible. Until then, nothing is."

Marshall drew a deep breath, squared his shoulders, and nodded. "Right. You're right. I'm good."

Not quite, but if not good, at least good enough. "We'd best get started then." They walked for a dozen blocks, avoiding eye contact with the aliens walking on their side of the street. Vehicles drove to their left, pod-like things that were taller than the cars he was familiar with and also about three-quarters as long. The uniform spacing between them suggested they were controlled by some central system or used the same internal programming. It was kind of a surprise to see personal transports. Somehow, he'd figured it would all be shared. *Sneaky assumptions are sneaky.*

He turned to comment on it to his companion when one of the vehicles pulled over to the side and the doors to the passenger compartment folded toward the back. Maria Verrand lifted an eyebrow at them. "Hey soldiers, need a lift?"

"And that's why we decided we'd drive around at a distance at the top of every hour, in case you showed up." Verrand was all smiles at having been the one to find them. Apparently, there'd been a wager involved.

Jax shook his head and addressed the third person in the medical bay. "Cia, I figured you'd be out of here, good riddance to bad rubbish, off to the stars."

Her laugh was chiming and happy. *Dare I believe she might have been worried? Surely not.* "I made the argument, but the others wouldn't let me leave you behind. It seems that whatever brainwashing you did, or mind-altering drugs you injected them with to think that you're worthwhile, was a success."

He snorted and scratched the healing wounds on his chest. The medical pod had accelerated the process, and he'd be back to normal in a few hours. Or, as the pilot had put it when she'd shared the pod's readout, "As normal as you ever are."

Jax changed the subject. "So, we got what your friend wanted. Will he hold up his end of the bargain?"

She shook her head. "Remember, he's not my friend. The opposite. And no, I wouldn't trust him as far as I could throw him."

That resonated. "Do you think he deliberately set us up?"

Cia scowled in silence for a few seconds before shaking her head again. "No. He wanted the thing, and he's getting the thing. Unless he had some backdoor deal to deliver us to the aliens, there'd be no profit in it for him. And if such an arrangement did exist, I don't imagine they'd have given you any chance to walk out alive."

He nodded, having come to the same conclusions. *Always good to perception-check, though.* "Unless their spirit of competition is that honorable or something. All right. Next question, do you think he's going to try to screw with us when we drop this off?"

She grinned, but it was more feral than happy. "Count on it."

He rose with a groan. "Okay, then." To Verrand he said, "How about you go have a chat with Kimmel? See what he was able to pull about the defenses at the scumbag's mansion. We tried to be polite and play this straight, but this time we're going in ready for whatever trouble he tries to bring."

She nodded and departed on the task, and Cia asked, "You okay?"

Jax shrugged. "I'm pissed off, to be honest. But more than that, I'm worried about Marshall. They gave him a beating, at least. Might have done something more to him. We need to keep an eye on him, in case he's been compromised." The odds were slim. Even a master at breaking and reprogramming would have found it challenging to accomplish in the time they'd had, and they had no evidence the aliens understood how humans functioned enough to manage it regardless of duration. Still, paranoia was a survival trait in his business, and he'd learned to listen to the crazy ideas from the little voice in his head. *I probably shouldn't describe it to Cia that way, though. I'll never hear the end of it.*

Cia asked, "Should I let the others know? I can cycle

them through the pilot compartment for training as a plausible excuse."

"No, let's keep this between us. I don't think it's a real concern, and biasing them against him because of it would be bad. Right now, he's going to need every bit of support he can find, so if you hear anyone giving him trouble or thinking about doing so, make sure they don't."

"Is he okay?"

Jax chuckled. "I'm not convinced he was ever *okay*. He has some garbage to deal with. We've all gone through it, and now it's his turn. I'll help him as best I can, and if there are still issues when we get back, maybe Juno will have some suggestions."

He knew it was a mistake the instant the words left his tongue. Cia's mouth formed a perfect O for a moment, then she grinned and her eyebrows shot up. "Juno, is it? Not Doctor Cray?" She exited into the hallway singing, "Jackson and Juno, sitting in a tree...." He rolled his eyes, sighed, and went to look for Kenton Marshall, currently the second most annoying person in his life.

CHAPTER TWENTY

Cia had hit up her contact for another ride, which he was more than happy to provide. When they climbed aboard the same luxury bus, he was unexpectedly absent. In his place was an equipment crate, strapped to the seat he'd used on the previous trip. The pilot pressed her palm against the reader and the box unlocked. Jax undid the straps and opened the container, then let out a low whistle. "Dang, he doesn't like that other dude, does he?"

She laughed. "No, he does not." Ethan Kimmel had managed to pull all sorts of interesting data during their prior visit to the mansion; so much, in fact, that Jax was shocked he'd avoided detection. That observation had earned a shrug from the young computer wizard, who still thought he was immortal despite all the challenges they'd faced so far.

Among the discoveries was that while they'd been scanned for metal and explosives, they hadn't endured a full-body analysis. It seemed like an odd gap in the security of the place until Cia explained that some old-school criminals were willing to consent to the first, but not to the second. They didn't appreciate the idea of some person or AI peering under their clothes without their permission. He thought that view was rather archaic, and definitely wouldn't fly in any governmental or military installation. But it gave them an opening he fully intended to exploit.

The ship's workbench had provided each of them with a pair of plastic knives. The first was almost flat and had a sharp cutting edge. Jax's was currently hidden up his right sleeve. The other had a triangular blade with a point, designed to puncture a foe and prevent the wound from being easily closed. That one was in his left sleeve. None of their other weapons would pass muster, however, and they'd been prepared to go in with only the blades.

But Cia's contact had improved their situation significantly. The pistols were small and used compressed air to shoot flechettes. No explosives or metal to detect, which would get them past the sensors, and their size, no bigger than his palm, made them easy to conceal. He tucked his inside his boot and pulled his trouser leg down to hide it. The box held one for each of them. He observed, "Now we owe this guy, don't we?"

Cia nodded. "Yes, but it'll be simple enough to discharge. I'll have the family route some low-level work his way. Nothing that will make him a big fish, but something to get him out of the food tank and into a better one. Who knows, it might even lead to more work for him from folks at my family's level." She shrugged. "My obligation will be fulfilled after I make the connection for him."

Jax frowned. "Is there any exposure for us if he decides he's upset with that?"

"Depends on how the meeting goes, I guess. As long as things end without major injuries or deaths, I don't see a problem. Sure, he can say I was here, but only at the risk of earning my family's displeasure, which is something he should know not to do."

Anton Sirenno interjected, "What, because they'd whack him?" His fake gangster accent made them all laugh.

"Exactly." Cia rolled her eyes expressively. "No, because they have enough influence to ensure his business was driven into the ground. They've done it before. I should say *we've* done it before. There are some real bastards out there who don't deserve to continue their scumbag ways."

Jax blinked but didn't push. She was drawing an interesting ethical line. While he was deeply interested in knowing the details of its boundaries, their impending arrival, plus the others listening in, made it the wrong time for that conversation. "All right. So, we'll assume everything is going to go well. Everyone displays excessive respect and deference, right up until the moment Cia or I decide otherwise." He stared into Kenton Marshall's eyes to ensure he knew he was included in the warning. "Got it?"

They confirmed they did with words and nods. Jax grinned. "Then there's no way we're walking out of there with anything other than everything we came for." Once again, he belatedly realized that setting himself up like that for the universe to slap him down was always a bad idea. *But it got me last time, at the resort. Surely it won't happen twice.*

The bus lurched to a halt, and they repeated their entrance to the mansion, were greeted by the same butler, and escorted to the same den. He spotted a couple more guards standing around along the way, appearing to be in conversation but watching them with hard eyes as they passed. Cia's face went into its neutral mode, which told him she was either irritated or worried. He blanked his expression and stretched out his fingers, warming up his hands for the possibility of action.

Their host awaited them on the same couch, this time with a glass of wine in his hand. He swirled the dark liquid lazily as they took their seats, then tilted his head at the butler. The uniformed servant asked, "Have you brought the item?"

Cia nodded, and Ethan Kimmel handed the cube over. Marshall said, "We worked hard for that." Jax glared at him, but the pilot covered the statement.

"Not that you care what we had to go through to get it," she affirmed. "Nor should you. The point is that we have fulfilled our side of the agreement."

Vardebron nodded. "We must wait but a moment while my people ensure that you've gotten what I asked for. Not that I doubt your integrity, Master Rearden, but these are suspicious times. There's no telling what those alien bastards got up to while it was in their possession."

So it's not something of theirs. Interesting. Jax had subjected the cube to all the light scanning he could manage on the *Grace*, including running the thing through the medical pod, but hadn't managed to get a look inside. He'd resisted anything more aggressive for fear of damaging whatever it contained. The butler returned without the box, but with a meticulously carved stone cylinder. The container extended just a little to each side of the palm he used to present the object to his patron.

Vardebron took it and ran his hand across its surface. "This is from Coth, one of the first planets the Confederacy claimed after it had set down new roots. I thought it would be appropriate to offer you this along with my apology. When we came to our agreement, it was with the understanding that I would be able to supply the entire package he desired. Unfortunately, only half was available."

Jax couldn't suppress his scowl. He did manage not to speak, which he took as a small victory. Cia's tone hadn't changed. "Unfortunate. I would say that you've incurred a debt by failing to provide what was agreed upon."

Their host nodded. "I have. And in partial payment of that obligation, I will share with you all the information you need to find the portion I was unable to secure. Unfortunately, the agents I sent to accomplish that task were far less skilled than you all, it appears."

Jax watched Cia carefully, looking for a sign that the time had arrived to cause some trouble. He was sure that the guards had repositioned to a spot near the doors so they could react to such a move, but at the moment he found it hard to care. *I would never make it in the world of a trader. Too many people trying to screw their partners out of a fair deal rather than working together.* She gave no such signal, only accepted the container, rose, and offered her thanks and farewells.

His last sight of Vardebron was the man's smirking face, and his palm itched to put a needle into it on general principles. Instead, he maintained his cool all the way to the bus, then he and Cia talked about unimportant things until they were back at the ship and out of the vehicle. As they climbed up the ladder to the hatch, he asked, "Do you think that bastard bugged the bus?"

She nodded. "I'm sure. Standard practice. The fancy container, too. We'll get that into an emissions cage as soon as Kimmel gets his butt up here." Jax played co-pilot as they got the appropriate clearances and headed back to space for the return trip to the Academy.

He laughed suddenly. "Well, we didn't get everything we wanted, but at least we managed a half-success. Who knows, we keep at it, we might manage to complete a mission one of these days."

Cia gave a soft snort. "I think the real question is, was there ever a possibility of getting the whole thing? And if not, was the Professor already aware of that when he sent us out? Was Vardebron?" She shrugged. "There's no way to know for sure. It might be that we accomplished everything we were supposed to."

"Do you ever get tired of the mystery?"

She laughed. "You'd think I would, wouldn't you? But no, I really don't. I love being part of the Academy, and I'm learning a lot of useful stuff along the way. So we didn't get to the destination we thought we were headed for. That only means we need to find a new path, and that maybe where we're meant to go is someplace different."

Jax nodded slowly. "There's definitely more to you than there seems to be at first glance, Master Rearden. You've given me something to think about."

"Does it hurt? Thinking? Because of how unfamiliar you are with it? I bet the medical pod has a solution for that. Lobotomy, maybe."

He rose with a sigh. "On that note, I should go have a

chat with Marshall, make sure he's not going to explode before we get back. Then I need some sleep. Those quick-heal drugs are rough."

"Good plan. Send Kimmel up here. He's a way better conversationalist, anyway."

Jax lifted an eyebrow. "Conversation. That's what you kids are calling it these days, huh? Well, you know, try not to wreck the ship while you're *conversing*." She sputtered, and he bolted before she could take away the thrill of his momentary verbal victory.

CHAPTER TWENTY-ONE

The *Grace* landed in the early morning hours at the airfield northwest of the castle. Her crew had managed fitful rest, except for Cia, who claimed she slept better on the ship than anywhere else in the universe. A van awaited them, and they filed out to it and climbed in. Overall, he thought the team seemed depressed. It was a normal response, the post-action blues they were sometimes called in the Special Forces. Likely exacerbated for them all by their failure to come away with a clear victory.

One of the staff members met them as they arrived at the Academy. He addressed them as a group. "The Professor wanted me to congratulate you on your success and inform you that you're invited to share a meal with him at noon. Until then, your time is yours to rest and recover."

Kenton Marshall gave a low snort. "It appears lunch is mandatory."

Anton Sirenno replied, "Everything here is mandatory in one way or another. We have only the illusion of choice."

Maria Verrand shook her head. "Sounds like you boys need a nap. See you at chow time." She strode off around the corner of the building, headed for the side door.

Jax nodded. "Sounds right. Later, y'all." He waved as he started down the etched sidewalk, the crest of a long-departed family continuing to provide a reminder of them in each concrete block. Although he'd planned to change clothes and head for the exercise room to burn off some of the tension he still carried, his bed looked exceptionally inviting. He fell into it without regret until the alarm he'd wisely set woke him to prepare for a meal with the Professor.

He dressed in the black quasi-uniform that was the standard garb for the Academy and followed the path his comm displayed. It took him toward the rear exit that had led to the social event during his first visit to the castle, where he'd learned about Juno's position on dating students. *Heh. It's still bizarre to think of myself as a student. But I guess they need to call us something, to distinguish us from those who are here primarily to work rather than learn.* He'd come around to the notion that everyone in the place was learning in one way or another, and he found he liked the idea.

An opening lay beyond the midpoint of that hallway, and he crossed the threshold to discover Cia and Ethan Kimmel had beat him to the location. He wasn't sure if they were an actual couple, despite the teasing he'd been sending the pilot's way, but he had an inkling they'd be pretty good for each other. The chamber itself was a formal dining room that had probably served the same purpose during the castle's entire history. Windows filled the long wall of the rectangular space opposite the door. To the right, behind the head of the table, a massive fireplace with an equally impressive mantle above it occupied most of the wall. On the left was a stone surface covered in paintings, asymmetrically arranged with thin bands of grey block showing between them. The remaining area on the periphery was devoted to serving tables and cabinets.

The table itself could have seated sixteen in comfort but was currently set for eight, three on one side and four on the other, plus the end chair nearest the fireplace. He nodded to the others. "You got here early. Hoping to snag the best snacks before the rest of us arrived? I mean, I can totally see that sort of behavior from you, Cia, but honestly, I thought Ethan was made of better stuff."

She flipped him off, and they laughed together. Nikolai Maarsen entered at that moment and asked, "What's so funny?"

Cia replied, "Jackson. Really, everything about him, but you can start with that ridiculous chin and work your way from there."

The Professor raised an eyebrow at him, and Jax shrugged. "You admitted her to the Academy. You deal with her."

A few minutes later the rest of the group arrived, including Anika Stephenson. Jax shook hands with his superior officer, who he was always sincerely happy to see. They sat around the table, with the Professor at the head, Jax and his boss in the chairs closest to him, and the others fitting in where they liked. Maarsen said, "Food will be along momentarily. In the meantime, I'd like to welcome Major Stephenson, who was a student here for a time and continues to work with us on a wide variety of things. Please introduce yourselves and let her know a little about you."

They went around the table very much like students on the first day of class. The expressions his colleagues wore suggested they also found the requirement amusing, but everyone complied without complaint, to a greater or lesser degree. Verrand proved the most reticent—*heh*—and Kenton Marshall the most verbose. *Kind of figures, given his abundant self-confidence.* When they finished, Stephenson nodded and said, "I'm a major in UCCA Special Forces. Jackson is one of my captains. It's my fault he's here, so I apologize for that."

A momentary pause hung before the table burst out in laughter. Jax sighed and shook his head with a smile. Maarsen took over the conversation again as uniformed servers bustled into the room with bowls of soup and set them in front of each person. "So, rather than having individual conversations with you all, since we're suddenly in the middle of an operation instead of at the end of one, I figured it would be more productive to have this discussion as a group. Plus, you deserve a good meal for what you've been through." He was looking at Marshall as he said it but smoothly swept his gaze across the rest of them as he continued to speak. "So, go ahead, try the soup."

Jax breathed in the steam coming off the dish and smelled onion, and the sight of tofu chunks in the broth confirmed that it was one of his favorite Academy offerings, miso soup. He was suddenly famished, and wanted to lift the whole bowl to his mouth and drink it down in a gulp, but restrained himself to proper etiquette. The

Professor sampled his, then set his spoon down. "All the information we had, speaking for the major here as well, showed the data we needed was all in one specific location. However, those in possession of it apparently decided to split it up so neither of the partners could use it without the other."

Verrand nodded. "A smart move. We've done similar things at my company when it comes to intellectual property agreements with others. Sure, the courts could decide any issues, but having the pieces only work when both parties are involved is a much more dependable solution."

Stephenson added, "And since we're talking about governments here, they're even less likely to trust one another than corporations."

Sirenno shook his head. "You haven't worked with the right corporations, Major. Mine is far more suspicious than any government I've ever seen." Kimmel, Verrand, Marshall, and Cia all nodded their agreement.

His superior laughed. "I stand corrected. Anyway, I spoke out of turn. Sorry, Professor."

Maarsen smiled. "No problem at all." He paused while the soup bowls were exchanged for salads heavy on beets and bleu cheese. "This leaves us in a bit of a pickle. Now that we have one half of the equation, those in control of the other half will expect us to make a play for it. Unfortunately, time is of the essence, or we could simply wait for it all to die down."

Jax frowned. "Does this have anything to do with the whole fight thing on Accides?"

Stephenson shook her head. "Only indirectly. Vardebron knew that the Dhelear had the item we were after."

Cia growled a curse, and the Major nodded with a low chuckle. "Yes, he had you retrieve the very thing you were after and returned it to you in a different form. But somehow, he also tweaked to the fact that Jackson was part of the group that gave the aliens a bloody nose a while back. So he made a side deal to give the captain up to them. You messed with the plan by not following the path he'd set out for you. Might have inadvertently protected the rest of the crew by doing it, too."

Cia's fingers were turning white around the knife she held. "That worm is going to get his, count on it."

Jax nodded. "I want in on that action."

She offered a thin smile, probably all she could force through her anger. "Done and done."

Maarsen spread his arms and put his palms flat on the table. "All of that is a side issue. What matters now is how to obtain the rest of the code that we need. The Artificial Intelligence that one of the alien species is building with the Confederacy must not remain a secret from us."

Marshall asked, "Us the Academy, or us the UCCA?"

The Professor shrugged. "Both, really. That's why the major is here. Our interests are very much aligned on this project."

Conversation stopped as the main course arrived, a thick hunk of steak accompanied by mashed potatoes and asparagus. Jax's mouth watered at the sight of it, and he had to hold back a moan of pleasure as he cut into the meat and saw that it was cooked perfectly, right in the middle of rare and medium. The table was silent except for the sound of chewing for a few minutes. Then small talk broke out until the dinner plates were taken away and large mugs of coffee and bowls of berries with whipped cream were placed in front of them.

Maarsen sampled the dessert and the strong coffee before leaning back in his chair. "Now it's time to figure out the best path forward. Since you will likely be the ones to travel it, Major Stephenson and I wanted you to be part of the planning."

Jax asked, "Where's the other half?"

His boss sighed. "According to Vardebron, it's on the Confederacy homeworld."

Cia's response wasn't quite a snarl, but it was most of the way there. "And do we really think that scumbag is telling us the truth this time?"

Stephenson nodded. "We'll check it out, of course. But our quiet SF investigation has provided corroborating information. So it's likely you'll need to go there to get it."

Then there's only one approach. Jax said, "It'll have to be an undercover op. Like at the resort. New identities, disguised ship, advance team, backup in place."

The Professor replied, "Agreed. It's the only option I can see, as well."

It was strange to hear Kenton Marshall being the voice of reason. "Wait a minute. You're talking about sneaking into the actual seat of the Confederacy, stealing something incredibly valuable to them, and tiptoeing out again with no one the wiser?"

Jax exchanged looks with Stephenson, then they both nodded at the same time. He said, "Yeah, that's about right."

"That's insane."

Cia laughed. "Welcome to the club, Kenton. We're all crazy here."

CHAPTER TWENTY-TWO

Nikolai Maarsen waved Major Anika Stephenson into a chair on the visitor's side of his desk. The call he was about to make was an integral part of what he thought of as the "AI Situation," and since she was already on site, he didn't see a reason to resist including her in real-time, rather than providing a report afterward. He busied himself with ice and whiskey, preparing a tumbler for each of them and sliding hers across the wooden surface.

She sipped it and smiled as he took his seat. "You always have the best stuff. Refreshing after that amazing meal."

"And sufficiently bracing for what lies ahead, I hope." He unlocked the secure drawer in his desk and retrieved a smooth silver cylinder, about three inches in diameter and a third of that high.

Stephenson nodded. "Yeah, me too. Am I far enough away?"

"Yes. The device has a very specific pickup pattern, and

it's one direction. Stay quiet, and there's no way the recipient of the call will detect you."

"You're sure? He provided this, right?"

Maarsen laughed. "He provided something, yes. I had some students crack it and replicate it from scratch, keeping only the data that allows the connection to work. He's probably realized that by now. Hell, he likely planned for it from the beginning." In many ways, Zavian Arlox was his dark twin. The man's intellect was off the scales. Unfortunately, so was his obsession with drawing power and authority to himself, ostensibly in service of the UCCA. *And, to be fair, much of what he accomplishes does benefit the Alliance, often significantly. But they're fools if they believe that's all he's interested in.*

Major Anika Stephenson was far from a fool. She'd detected the spider at the center of the web without knowing who it was, as had he. They'd worked together to put a name to the strand-puller, and had agreed to clandestinely oppose him whenever possible. He held no doubt in his mind, not even a hint of one, that Arlox had designs on whatever the Confederacy and the alien species, either alone or on behalf of the Coalition, were creating. *Zavian probably isn't behind it directly, but there's no way he's unaware. And that means he'll want it, too.*

Which was another reason the project was so important. Not only did they need to get it to maintain balance with the factions opposing their government, it would put the Academy in danger if Arlox got his hands on it before they did. *Choosing sides has consequences, always, but I'd prefer they were a little further in the future, thanks.*

He pulled himself out of his thoughts. "Any other questions?" Stephenson shook her head and gestured with her glass for him to go ahead. He straightened his spine, faced the machine, and announced, "Activate." The holographic display sprang into being above the disc. "Connect to Zavian."

The device negotiated connections with its counterpart, somewhere in the UCCA-held systems of the universe. The intelligence arm of the Alliance had many installations, and Arlox spent a goodly amount of time on site or on one of his division's ships traveling from one to the next. A countdown popped up in the corner to indicate that the other man would be with him in two-and-a-half minutes. Maarsen used the delay to rehearse the points he wanted to address.

When the other man's face appeared, it wore a scowl. *Although it's fair to say that even when he's not unhappy he looks like that.* It exacerbated the wrinkles that age had brought to his otherwise flawless skin. Dark hair was slicked back from his widow's peak, exposing a high forehead with perfect eyebrows and piercing eyes beneath. Maarsen always figured it was the fever that shone in them that caused the man to remain as thin as he was, burning away his flesh like a ship's runaway engines devoured fuel. His deep voice sounded in an annoyed, "What?"

He'd learned to take the other man's rudeness in stride. He assumed it was probably the way he was with everyone, the typical conceit of those with extreme power. He smiled. "Zavian, lovely to speak with you, too."

Arlox shook his head. "Get to the point, Nikolai. I'm rather busy at the moment."

"As if there's a moment in which you are not." He raised

his palms to forestall a response. "I will do as you ask. It has recently become apparent to me that there is a plot unfolding that connects the Confederacy and the Coalition. Are you aware of any such thing? Do you have information that you can share?" Maarsen worked with the military and government often enough to have a mid-level security clearance from them. Of course, most of what that allowed him access to he could already count on one or more of his students to share or acquire on his behalf, depending on their positions and proclivities.

The other man closed his eyes and gave a slight head shake as if the question pained him. "That's rather broad, old friend. Perhaps you'd like to be more specific? Or are you simply fishing? As you well know, there are always plots between all the players, including you, I'm sure."

Maarsen chuckled. "Fair enough. This has to do with the development of an Artificial Intelligence."

The eyelids raised and his eyes narrowed. "Do you have evidence of such a thing?" The Professor nodded. Arlox growled, "I'm going to need whatever information you've collected, immediately."

He'd anticipated the demand, and a heavily sanitized report of things the other man doubtlessly already knew was dispatched to him with a gesture. "On its way. I'm afraid we don't have much yet. This is rather new to us, which is why I'm calling you." He was never sure what percentage of what he said his rival believed, only that they were involved in a game with rules that changed from moment to moment. Sparring with Zavian was one of the true pleasures in his existence.

"Standby." The other man's image froze for almost a

minute. When it came back to life, Arlox said, "You're not kidding, that's seriously thin. What I can add to it is this: Yes, they're doing something, and you and your school would be well served to keep your noses out of it. It's a priority for my department, and getting in our way would be a bad choice for you and your people both."

The Professor wasn't about to be dismissed so casually. "Now, now, Zavian, you know me better than that. My burning quest for knowledge can never be so easily quenched." He thought the other man's mouth quirked toward a smile for an instant. "I've provided you with what we have. Surely you're able to point me in a useful direction at least." He'd built up a great deal of capital with the other man during the years they'd interacted, and the unspoken inviolable rule of their relationship was that everything was a transaction. Maarsen had given, and now something of value was expected in return.

His rival sighed as if he hadn't already planned to hand over his own sanitized report. He gestured, and an icon appeared on Maarsen's display. Arlox said, "That's what I can give you. Is there anything else? I'm late for my next meeting."

Sure you are. He chuckled inwardly. "No, that's all. Good to see you, as always, Zavian."

The other man nodded. "Nikolai." The image vanished, and Maarsen returned the disc to the secure drawer, then took a deep drink of his whiskey before speaking.

"So, what do you think?"

Stephenson shook her head. "I've seen videos of him, of course, but they don't convey the sheer gravity of talking to him."

"It's true. He *is* a force, and one should never forget that when dealing with him or his people. He probably has as much power as anyone in government, and yet your average person thinks he's a run-of-the-mill administrative figurehead. Which, I might add, is an illusion he's quite happy to propagate. It's always misdirection and lies, but now and again we can discover a grain of truth."

The file had been automatically transferred to his tablet, and Maarsen reviewed it quickly, then nodded. "Most of this we know, but it does serve to confirm the probability that the thing we need is on Chesyira."

Stephenson shook her head. "You realize what a challenge that's going to be, right? I'm sure Jackson is up to the job if anyone is, but this might be bigger than the Academy's people can handle."

He shrugged. "Do you feel comfortable turning it over to the Alliance spies, knowing that Arlox has them all in his sphere of influence?" Even the ones that didn't work for him directly took payments, or were being blackmailed, or shared information because they considered it their patriotic duty.

She sighed and drank the rest of her whiskey. "No, I really don't. But you need to play this one big. Make sure he has access to every resource you can provide. Because it's entirely possible even that won't be enough to allow him to succeed. I'd like to have him back when this is over, rather than knowing he's rotting in some Confederacy prison awaiting trial for espionage."

Maarsen nodded. "He'll have it. They all will."

That night, Jax summoned his team to the bar in the basement of the castle. The tables in the middle were packed, as were most of the booths that ran around the periphery. Some sport he didn't recognize was being shown on the wall-mounted displays. The place was busier than he'd ever seen it, even on trivia night. His date with Juno had sadly been postponed to the next evening, as her warning that she might have work to attend to proved prophetic. *Although, to be honest, meeting her after a full night's sleep will be much nicer, even though it means waiting another twenty-four hours.*

He'd half expected to hear from Stephenson or the Professor after their lunch, but no new information had been forthcoming. He was reluctantly forced to admit that he might not be the most important thing on either of their agendas. The lack of knowledge irked him. That wasn't a feature of his other profession; most often, he was in the group of people who needed to know the things that were restricted to need-to-know.

He stopped at the bar and exchanged greetings with Coach, the part-time bartender, part-time sparring instructor, and the Academy's go-to for any odd job that popped up, as the other man described it. Sweat stood out on the dark skin of his bald head as he moved quickly to keep up with the additional press of customers. His impressive mustache, though, was as perfect as always.

Coach's voice was deep and gravelly. "What'll you have tonight? Irish whiskey?"

Jax shook his head. "Keeping it light. Cider. Strongbow if you have it."

"I'll let you off the hook for ordering an English drink

in a Scottish bar this once, Jackson. But you're going to need to make up for it with a proper scotch tasting one of these days."

He grinned. "Only if you'll join me."

Coach matched his expression and dipped his head in a nod. "Done. Tomorrow?"

"Can't. Have a date."

The other man turned away to yank the tap handle and discharge his drink into a pint glass. He set it on a coaster in front of Jax and lifted an eyebrow. "Doctor Cray, huh? I don't know that I've ever seen her willing to go out with a student."

Jax coughed as surprise caused him to try to breathe the cider. "What the hell? Is this place a hotbed of gossip or something?"

Coach snorted. "No, but your pilot is. Speaking of which, she just came through the door."

Jax turned to scold her, but she was accompanied by the rest of the team, and calling her out in front of others would require additional planning. *Okay, revenge will have to wait, Cia. But when it comes, it's going to be brutally delicious.*

CHAPTER TWENTY-THREE

They met at a booth, the only option that would fit them all in the crowded space. He slipped in first, Cia did the same across from him, and the others filtered in after. Anton Sirenno, on one end, headed to the bar for drinks. They made small talk until he returned, then Jax asked the question at the top of his mind. "So, how crazy is this idea, really?"

His team responded with laughter, eye rolls, and several shaking heads. Cia replied, "I've heard things that were more insane, but it's a lot more like a spy novel than something I expected to face in real life. Probably the first requirement is knowing whether you're capable of it, because you have to be more qualified than the rest of us."

Jax nodded. "I've been asking myself that, too. It comes down to the cover identities. They need to be plausible, so no one takes too hard a look at us, but also comfortable for each of us to play the appropriate role. That was pretty easy at the resort, since we were mainly vacationers. But this may require gaining legitimate access to whatever installation it's in, either for recon or for the operation itself. Any other way, we have no deniability at all. And I, for one, am not interested in spending the rest of my days as a guest of the Confederacy penal system."

"Seconded," Maria Verrand offered. The others nodded their heads in approval of the sentiment.

Cia took a long pull on her drink, which was a reddish cider he'd definitely have to try at some point. "So, what roles give us the greatest chance of success?"

Kenton Marshall answered, "Corporation of some kind, surely. Most of us are comfortable in that environment, and Jax can certainly fake it."

"Okay," Ethan Kimmel, predictably seated next to Cia, said. "What kind of corporation?"

Sirenno replied, "Robotics. It's close, but not too close, and we all have some sort of skills that apply."

Verrand snapped her fingers. "What if we went in as a team working on the technology in Jax's arm? The prosthetic is cutting edge enough that it should hold up to inspection, and we can work together to come up with some improvements that look good on paper. Maybe we're a small company, trying to make a breakthrough?"

Jax nodded slowly. "That one has some potential. But the company would need to have a presence on the planet, too, right?"

Kimmel shrugged. "Simple enough to hack the public databases and put in records of one being there. The advance team can go in ahead to secure a base of operations-slash-business address. It seems pretty likely the Academy already has some people either on that planet or deep in the Confederacy, don't you think?"

Jax blinked and tilted his head to the side. "You know, that never occurred to me, but you're probably right. I spend too much time thinking of Maarsen as a teacher and too little viewing him as an intelligence-gathering puppet master." He wiggled his fingers in the air like he was manipulating a marionette and got a laugh from the others. "I'm glad we're not working against him, that's for sure." He noticed Cia frowning and asked, "What's up?"

"The sky, the clouds, planets. Maybe read a book," she said absently as her frown deepened. "I'm less than comfortable with this plan. Feels like we're under-prepared and under-resourced. It would be great if people are on the ground ready to assist, and I really hope there are, but we're still talking about a world deep in Confederacy territory. That's about as 'operating without a net' as you can get. Even then, I'd probably be okay with the situation if it weren't coming on the heels of Vardebron and his games. A lot of potential leaks are hiding in this particular tub of secrets."

Jax nodded. "You're not wrong. Anyone else feel the same?" The others appeared to agree with her, even Marshall, which came as a surprise. "We'll have to either trust the Professor, I suppose, or refuse the mission."

Kimmel asked, "You'd do that?"

"Of course I would if I thought the risk was too great. We're not military intelligence, and the Academy doesn't own us. Well, except maybe Cia, although why they didn't return her right off the bat is anyone's guess." The pilot stuck her tongue out at him, and he bared his teeth at her. "I said this before, and I'll keep saying it—we operate as a team, including the decision of whether we take on a given assignment or not."

Sirenno snorted. "Maybe that's why the Professor always holds back some details until the last minute. So it's harder to refuse to do what he wants, since we're already halfway there."

Verrand drummed her fingers on the table. "That won't fly with this one. If we're going to make a decision, we need all the information up front. Do you all agree?"

The others nodded, and Jax replied, "Me too, with one reservation. It may be a situation where some of what we'd really like to know isn't available. So we'll want to have an option where we make an initial decision with a specific designated point in the future where we either affirm or change our choice. Right before we jump into Confederacy space, say."

General agreement followed, and he asked, "Anything else at the moment?"

Cia grinned. "Yeah, why are you hanging out here with us instead of with Juno?" She stretched out the woman's name in a singsong. "Did she dump you already? Thought better of the whole thing? It's understandable. Really, you have so many flaws." She went on to list each of them, much to the amusement of those around her, while Jax shook his head in helpless surrender.

They'd passed the rest of the evening in light conversation, learning more about each other's pasts and putting together a vision for what their fake corporation on

Chesyira might look like. By the end of the night, they'd created an array of logos and names, each more ridiculous than the last. Finally, his team had drifted away one by one until it was only him and Marshall left.

The other man returned from the bar with drinks for them both and slid into the booth opposite him. The tavern had emptied out when the clock hit midnight, and now only a few stragglers shared the place with them.

Jax asked, "So, doing okay after our little adventure?"

Marshall waved a hand. "Yeah, that's not what I stayed to talk about." *Which means you're not doing okay, but aren't ready to deal with it yet. Been there.* "I have a thought on this mission I wanted to run by you before I shared it with the others."

He took a sip of his cider, noting absently that he was feeling the effects of the several he'd had so far. "Okay, hit me."

"I don't think it's possible for this to be entirely a government operation unless they're a lot different than we are."

Jax frowned. "Say more."

"All right. Look. The biggest brains don't go into public service, or at least they don't spend much time there. So the likelihood of a private company involved on the Confederacy side for brainpower purposes is pretty high. Add in the possibilty of someone in government, or even the royal family, having a personal stake in some business that will make a handsome profit from working on this, and the chances increase that much more."

A sense of excitement began to build in Jax, the same feeling he got when a military operation was coming into focus. "And a private company, no matter how security-conscious or where it's located, will be safer and probably more susceptible to our efforts."

"Exactly." He leaned back and took a drink of his stout. "And it just so happens that we have a lot of people on the team who are part of big corporations. And you know how connected those all are. The chance that one of our businesses has a way in with companies in the Confederacy is pretty high."

"How would we go about finding out?"

The other man shrugged. "With your okay, I'll talk to the others and see what they think. We can work on it tomorrow morning, before the afternoon training session you're going to announce."

Jax laughed. "And what gives you the impression I'm planning to do that?"

"None of us have much experience with spycraft, so that's a clear area of instruction. But you can't really do more than the very basics here. So, I figure you'll let everyone sleep it off, and we'll be off to Inverness or something to see how sneaky we can be. But you won't want to take it into the evening because of Juno." He stretched the word the way Cia had earlier, and they both chuckled.

"Well, you've got it mostly right. We're going to Edinburgh. Inverness is too close and too small. They'll have a natural suspicion that won't be present in a larger city. And yes, we do need to brush up our skills, and can't do it here or aboard ship."

Marshall frowned. "I almost hate to mention this, but Cia's family might have something to offer here, too. Their company, I mean."

Jax closed his eyes and rolled his neck as a sudden wash of tiredness swept over him. "Let's keep that one in our back pocket. Emergency use only."

"Affirmative. So, it's okay to talk to the others?"

"Absolutely. You've come up with a great idea, and you should definitely run with it."

Marshall grinned. "You got it, boss."

CHAPTER TWENTY-FOUR

Jax had offered the others no hint of what was to come at breakfast and studiously ignored the inquisitive looks that Kenton Marshall directed at him. Afterward, he borrowed a car and headed for the maglev station in Inverness. Right before he boarded the train, he dispatched a message to all of them. "Edinburgh, within three hours. Incognito. Arrive singly. Meet at the Brew Lab."

His research identified two potential targets, and he'd chosen the largest—Alfawerks, a long-standing robotics company that had grown up in partnership with the University of Edinburgh. It owned a twelve-story building a few blocks from their rally point that would make an excellent stage to test his team's acting abilities. If they failed and managed to break away cleanly, he'd also profiled the other one so they could try again, time permitting. *Sure, the job is important and all, but there's no way I'm going to be late for my date with Juno.*

He spent the ride staring out the window, enjoying the

momentary interval of peace in his otherwise rather exciting life. Even the knowledge that it would end with probably the most challenging mission he'd ever faced didn't dampen his appreciation of the countryside. He wondered idly about the distant future, considering whether being a part of the Academy in retirement might be an interesting way to pass the time.

The university coffee shop that was his destination lay at the end of a ten-minute ride or a thirty-minute walk. He decided on the latter, since the others wouldn't arrive for a while, and took stock of his surroundings as he traveled. His team would need costumes, and several options appeared along the way, including a second-hand consignment store. In his opinion, that was the grand prize since new clothes sometimes looked too new. A piece or two without that fresh-out-of-the-package feel would make the rest seem right, if a whole outfit couldn't be pieced together from others' castoffs.

The small coffeehouse was excessively cozy. A dark marble-topped bar ran down the entire left side, stretching about twenty feet before ending at the back wall. Baristas stood behind it operating complicated-looking coffee machines, some of them as old as the one Juno had used for their espresso-fueled flirting. On top was an array of snacks wrapped in bright bags, doubtless packaged to appeal to whatever nutritional fad was currently in ascendance. The walls and ceiling were an aged yellow, with coppery lights hanging on short chains, and the same colors had been incorporated in the wooden planks that made up the flooring.

Leather couches and low benches shared the rest of the

space with an eclectic mix of tables and chairs, as if the coffeehouse itself was a consignment shop for furniture. It had just opened, and the people behind the bar looked bleary as he ordered a flat white with a bonus shot of espresso, figuring he could use the energy from the extra kick of caffeine. When it appeared, he took it to a couch in the back that faced the door and called up a newsfeed to kill time until the others arrived.

Tensions in the universe continued on the upward trajectory they'd been on, or at least it seemed so based on the headlines. His Academy comm was unable to access the secure UCCA internal information feed that would give him a more definitive picture. But it was enough. *Given how much territory there is out there, you'd think we'd have learned to share it by now. But apparently neither humans nor the aliens we've met so far are wired that way.*

He wound up watching old movies until the others walked through the doors. To their credit, they entered singly, with enough space between them that it could be random, although Cia and Ethan Kimmel arrived only a few beats apart. *Which isn't unrealistic, either.* He pointed each to the counter, then waved them over once they'd gotten their drinks. Maria Verrand was the first to join him. She remarked, "So, this is an interesting diversion. What's going on?"

He substituted small talk for an answer until the rest of the group had gathered, then he leaned forward. "Today's task is a practice run at what we'll eventually have to do, assuming the current plan holds. You've all been put into an unfamiliar place and have to compromise the security of a private corporation." He tapped his comm to send the details to their devices. "We have ninety minutes to prepare, and that includes getting appropriate disguises." He reclined with a smile. "And here's the best part. I'm just along for the ride. Today you all get to tell me what to do."

Cia scowled. Her tone suggested he'd finally lost his remaining marble. "Are you serious?"

He nodded contentedly. "Eighty-nine minutes and counting."

The others pulled together a reasonably workable plan in two-thirds of that time, then they all set out to snag their disguises. It required one of them to play a teacher and the other the students, and he'd been selected for the leading role. *It's not that I look old, it's that I appear older than the rest of them. Because of my experience and wisdom. Yeah, that's it.* So, while his team hit the consignment stores with handfuls of cash, he was headed for a more upscale shop. Fortunately, he'd brought along a few untraceable debit cards secured from the Academy's quartermaster. The woman had glared at him suspiciously throughout the exchange of information for cash equivalents, and he planned to con Cia into returning whatever he didn't use so he could avoid another encounter.

The store was trendier than any he'd ever shopped in, although as a military officer who more or less lived his job, he hadn't had much opportunity to purchase civilian clothes anywhere other than on ship or on base in quite some time. A couple of other customers browsed the outfits, each with a worker assisting them, and another employee strode up to him with a wide smile. He was average height and weight, with sandy blonde hair and small round glasses. "Welcome to *Maison*. What can we put you into today?"

Jax slipped into his chosen role. "I'm looking for something comfortable yet formal. Something that will look right in front of a classroom."

The other man nodded and lightly touched his arm. "Right this way. I'm sure we have an outfit that will suit you. So, you teach at the university, I take it?"

He spun a tale of how he'd started his academic career across the ocean. After falling in love with Scotland on vacation, a chance meeting at a conference turned into an unexpected stroke of luck that allowed him to get a visiting position at the University of Edinburgh. He hoped for a permanent gig and needed to be sure he fit in properly. It was plausible enough to convince his salesperson, who likely didn't care, anyway.

He walked out in his new outfit, carrying the old one in a bag. They'd agreed to rally at the maglev station, where they could stash unneeded items in lockers until the trip back to the Academy. Cia and Kimmel were already there when he arrived, in business casual clothes that definitely made them look like graduate students reaching for a sense of formality. He pocketed the key to the rental locker and crossed over to them. "Students. May I join you?"

Cia replied, "Of course, Professor Hyde." The quartermaster had also provided new identities for all of them and promised that the computer experts at the castle would fill in the appropriate backgrounds for all of them at his request. He'd sent back the details before they'd left the coffee shop. He had become Jonathan Hyde, an expert in matters of Confederacy technology. Their trip to the company was ostensibly so his graduate assistants could get a look at the UCCA versions of early robotics on display at the company to inform their own work on the ways Confederacy innovations had changed the field. *Or something like that. I'm not going to hold up under too much pressure, but I can make a few things up.* If this had been a real op instead of a training exercise, he'd have been rehearsing that information for days, at least, maybe weeks, probably in close consultation with an actual expert.

He sat on the bench next to the pilot, on the side not already occupied by Kimmel, and talked across her. "And how are your studies coming?"

The computer wizard grinned. "Very well, Professor. I believe that the Confederacy technologies deviated from ours right off the bat, due to a difference in perspective about the ultimate uses of robots in that culture. Would you like me to explain?"

Jax lifted a hand. "No, I'm good, really. Thanks. Seems as if you've got it down, though."

The others arrived over the next ten minutes, all of them making it back in advance of the deadline. When they'd gathered, he asked, "Any last-minute issues? Everyone clear on their role?"

Hearing none, they departed for the Alfawerks building for their first test in coordinated espionage.

On the late afternoon train back to Inverness, Jax sprang for a private car so they could go over the results of the operation. They'd secured drinks before boarding, cans of beer and cider, which helped lessen the stress of the moment. Once again, they were headed home in something other than total success.

He asked, "So what went well?"

Sirenno replied, "The first part was perfect. You managed to convince the person at the desk that we'd scheduled a tour, although she had absolutely no record of it. Offering to call the departmental administrator at the university was a great move. Really sealed the deal."

He nodded. "Agreed. Unfortunately, I think we can expect that whatever target we wind up with for the real op won't be so easily fooled. We'll need to be sure to have people ready to play some remote roles in our game. What else?"

Verrand gave a soft chuckle. "The costumes. Those were good."

Jax laughed. "Come on now. It wasn't all bad. Kenton did a great job of asking questions while they showed us around the robotics display. Hell, I almost believed he was a graduate student."

The others nodded, and a couple clapped. Marshall grinned. "Well, I do have a pretty clear connection to technology in my job. After that, it was just exaggerating."

Jax turned to Cia, who seemed the most annoyed. "And what can we improve on?"

"We definitely need more information going in. I kind of thought we had the fundamental pieces, the essentials, but as soon as things started moving, realized we didn't."

He nodded. "Agreed."

Kimmel added, "And better technology. I was able to crack their most basic network level with my tablet, but that only gave us an appointment calendar and building layout. Anything more would have required more programs and more power."

"I think it's safe to assume we'll have higher quality gear all around when we do this for real. But what about taking on the roles? What would have made that easier?"

Verrand snorted. "More time to practice, for sure. This was kind of a jerk setup, Reese."

"Jerkwad," Cia corrected.

The other woman grinned. "Noted."

Jax shook his head. "The point wasn't to make us feel good but to see where we were lacking. Honestly, you all proved to be better actors than I expected, and whatever nervousness you felt should be less the next time around. I'm pretty sure we've got what it takes to pull this off."

"Assuming the right support is there," Marshall clarified, then changed the subject. "So far, I haven't gotten anything back from my corporate contacts about the target. Anyone else?"

Head shakes from Verrand, Kimmel, and Sirenno confirmed the lack of progress. Jax said, "Well, we've got time. No indications have arrived suggesting we'll be on our way tomorrow, so that's one more day to pull things together."

Cia laughed. "Yeah, but you'll be too busy for that, desperately scrambling to try to get Juno to go on a second date with you after you screw up tonight. 'Gets slapped before dinner is over' in the betting pool is mine, so don't let me down, okay? You know, just be yourself."

He closed his eyes and lifted a single finger in response, then settled in to relax, thinking about the evening ahead. *Pretty sure you're going to lose that bet, Cia. I've got a good feeling about this.*

CHAPTER TWENTY-FIVE

He split from the rest of the team in Inverness, opting to rent a vehicle for the trip to the castle. While his preference would have been a motorcycle again, it didn't seem like a good plan for a first date. Instead, he selected a car, a distant descendent of the Ford Mustang. It still maintained its muscle car looks although it was electric and highly computerized. The cherry red version almost swayed him, but he decided basic black was the right call for the evening.

The drive back was a pleasure, the car's responsive handling a joy to control. It caused him to take the curves faster than strictly necessary and put a grin on his face for the whole trip. Juno's last message had pushed their meeting for an hour, from seven to eight, which gave him more than enough time to ensure he was as polished as he could be beforehand.

He wasn't a suit and tie kind of guy, so he'd suggested they go to a relatively informal spot for the night's meal. His date had been amenable, and maybe even a little relieved, so he'd selected Rocpool for their outing. He'd noticed the restaurant on the corner several times in passing and had been intrigued by the comfortable elegance that showed through the windows.

Jax took another extended shower, one of his most basic pleasures at the Academy, then stared indecisively at his wardrobe. *Could be I should have bought a few more things at Maison today.* He turned to his old standby, a black button-down tucked into trousers of the same shade, with his single pair of decent dress shoes finishing the look. He rolled the long sleeves back once and strapped on his comms, then fussed with his hair for a couple of minutes. Finally, he shrugged at the person in the mirror. "Not much more we can do without extensive plastic surgery." *Or maybe transplanting my brain into a robot body, which seems like where my career trajectory will deliver me at some point.* He'd timed his preparation well enough that no extra was left for fretting, and he headed for the castle entrance to meet his date.

The sight of Juno in a long black dress gathered at the waist by a simple silver chain belt brought a wide smile to his face. It was a modest outfit, but the spaghetti straps showed off beautiful shoulders, and the fashionable boots had the right amount of heel to make the whole thing more formal than the individual parts seemed. She carried a small silver clutch in her left hand. With all the smoothness he could muster, he said, "Hi."

She gave a soft laugh from deep in her throat that thrilled him and an answering grin. "Hi yourself. I hear you had an adventure today."

He gestured at the door, and they walked toward it

together. "I did. Turns out we're not the most impressive criminal gang quite yet. But once we have time to practice properly, watch out."

"I look forward to hearing *that* story. I mean, the successful one."

He winced dramatically. "Okay, ouch." They reached the car, and he opened the passenger door and offered her his left hand to assist. She touched it as she climbed in, which he took as a message that while she didn't need the help, she appreciated the offer. "I'll drive there, and you can take the wheel on the way back if you want. It's a fun car."

He circled to his side and slid into his seat. She replied, "That sounds like a plan." Her dress had lifted enough that he could see bare shin above the top of her mid-calf boot, and he laughed inwardly at the memory of his teenage days, where any sight of flesh caused his heart to race. *Years and years later, and here we are again. Although I think it's got more to do with the person who owns it rather than the skin itself.* "So, where are we headed?"

"Inverness. Rocpool. The place has been there for a long time, almost an institution now, according to the travel guide."

Juno nodded. "I've always wanted to try it, but the occasion never seemed to be right. Besides, I don't get out of the castle all that much. Great pick."

He steered south onto the road that connected the Academy with the nearest reasonably large city. The conversation along the way was light and flirty, with his date giving as good as she got and frequently upping the sarcasm-ante. Cia had teased him about his infatuation with the doctor when they were alone in the pilot compartment during the last mission, suggesting he was engaging in classic transference. The theory went that she'd helped mend him, so he'd decided that he was in love with her. He'd shrugged it off by teasing her about Ethan Kimmel yet again, but the idea had stuck with him until he'd given himself a mental slap upside the head and declared, "It's just a bloody date. For fun. We're not getting engaged. There's time to worry about that garbage later, assuming I survive that long." It was enough that he enjoyed Juno's company, and hopefully, she found his equally inviting.

He surrendered the car to a valet and escorted her inside. The interior of the restaurant was comfortable, less posh than its menu would suggest while retaining an appealing elegance. Black booths and chairs surrounded dark wood tables and stood upon deep brown hardwood planks. Square lighting fixtures hung from above, their scarlet shades throwing tinted light around the room. Napkins and accent touches throughout the large dining area were white. Their outfits matched up well with what the other guests were wearing, and he gave himself a mental pat on the back for not overdoing it. Misjudgments in either direction, too formal or too informal, always left him uncomfortable.

His reservation had specified a desire for privacy, and they were led to what passed for it in such a crowded restaurant, a small table in the rear corner along the windows. He held out her chair, then took his. "What do you think?"

She smiled, drawing his attention for a moment to her dark red painted lips. He jerked his eyes back up to hers.

Focus, Jackson. "It's lovely. A little less stuck-up than I'd expected."

"Exactly my thought."

"There's no need to lie to flatter me, you know."

He tilted his head to the side. "Lying? Me? Never. Well, maybe in the service of a good joke. Or a benevolent surprise. Or to an enemy." He chuckled. "Okay, there are a lot of circumstances in which I might lie, granted. But I'm not lying to you, especially not to flatter you. I don't think you're the kind of person to appreciate such things."

She nodded. "You're correct. Nor do you seem like the type to bother with them."

"So, uh, why'd you say it in the first place?"

Juno laughed. "To make you uncomfortable, of course."

He lifted his water glass in a toast. "Well done, then." She clinked hers against his. Then their banter was interrupted by the arrival of a server. He outlined the specials, placed their napkins in their laps for them, and bustled off to get the bottle of wine Juno had selected from the list she called, "Impressive."

"So you know wine, then?" Jax had only enough knowledge not to embarrass himself.

"It was part of the required coursework at the boarding school I attended."

"Ooh la la," he quipped, "fancy. So, there's some money somewhere in your family line?"

She nodded. "Way back, and we've been coasting on it for generations. Fortunately, a solid history of service runs in my blood. In a given generation, we usually have at least one businessperson to keep the funds intact, at least one politician, and a scientist, or artist, or in my case, a doctor."

"So, the castle is pretty normal for you. And you'll be paying for dinner tonight."

Juno laughed. "Hardly. We're city folk. No estates, no grounds, only fancy apartments in fancier buildings. And you asked me out, so you get the bill. I'll do the asking next time, assuming there is one." The way she said it gave him hope that another date was likely.

Their conversation paused as the waiter took their orders and swiftly departed to fill them after performing the uncorking ritual. Jax tasted his wine and had to admit she'd chosen quite well. Merlot was a little thicker red than he usually enjoyed, but this one was probably the best he'd ever had. "So, what are the odds, do you think?"

She shrugged. "You're at a solid fifty-one percent likely right now. As long as you don't do anything stupid, I can see it getting up to maybe fifty-five, fifty-six." She held her neutral expression for a moment before breaking into laughter. "Okay, seventy-five percent and climbing, based mainly on the fact that you chose a good restaurant and were smart enough to agree that I should choose the wine. Plus, you know, you're not terribly hard on the eyes and have a decent personality."

Jax snorted and held out his glass to her for a refill. "Damn me with faint praise, isn't that what the play says?"

She poured and replied, "I try not to allow potential partners to get a big head too early. It's always a huge letdown later when my true insult-heavy persona comes out."

"Ah, kind of a Jekyll-and-Hyde thing. Sounds exciting. I'm in."

Juno shook her head with a broad grin. "You're something, Jackson." Their meals arrived, and they focused on eating and talking about food experiences. He accepted a bite from her plate, perfectly cooked beef cheeks with risotto. It had been dressed in red wine and shallots and tasted like a meal that might be served in heaven. She was equally affected when she tried his selection, a dish he couldn't possibly pass up, being in Scotland and all. It was a cut of local venison, with Parma ham and haggis accompanying it. He'd been shocked to find the Scottish historical staple wasn't on the Academy menu and impressed that his date was brave enough to try it now that he'd found some. He'd considered asking if they'd used a sheep's stomach to cook it in, then rejected the idea as perhaps impolite. When Juno requested that information from their server of her own volition, his infatuation climbed one more rung up the ladder.

They shared desserts as well, switching off halfway through. He started with fresh berries covered in strawberry sorbet and white chocolate sauce, and she began with a chocolate praline tart topped with honeycomb ice cream. Coffee arrived afterward, and he leaned back contentedly with the small cup in his hand, happy in the glow of a good meal and great companionship. "I have to say that this is perhaps the best first date I've ever been on."

Juno looked upward as if to beseech the gods to deliver her a less idiotic dining partner. "I'm sure you say that to all your first dates."

"Nah. So far, only to the ones where it's been true. Now, to be fair, they have gotten better as I've gotten older, but there's certainly no guarantee. I do have pretty high standards. It takes a lot to match up with this." He gestured at himself, the inappropriate level of self-congratulation in his words summoning a laugh from her.

"You're something special, that's for sure. So, toss me the keys. I have an early morning, and you do, too." She rose, and he followed. When they got outside, he handed the tag to the valet, and the teenage girl ran off to retrieve the car.

He said, "I don't have an early morning. There's nothing on my calendar."

She lifted an eyebrow. "I think you're incorrect. You might want to check your comm." He complied, and sure enough, he had instructions to head for the ship immediately after breakfast. He shook his head, and she laughed. "The Professor gave me a heads-up earlier because he wanted to be certain nothing got in the way of our evening."

Jax sighed. "The Professor knows we were planning to go out?"

Juno shook her head as she headed around the car to climb into the driver's side. "Maarsen knows everything. Haven't you realized that yet?"

He tried not to grumble as he got inside. It was a minor annoyance, given how well the evening had gone, and so was easy to set aside. "I guess I know now." He twisted in the seat and grinned at her as she pulled out into traffic. "So, what's the post-dinner likelihood of a second date?"

She gave a throaty laugh. "You're at eighty percent. Maybe a proper goodnight kiss will seal the deal."

He spent the rest of the drive trying to figure out what she might mean by "proper" and thinking that he'd met his match in Doctor Juno Cray.

CHAPTER TWENTY-SIX

They boarded the bus after breakfast, during which Cia was notably absent. The drive north to the airfield was filled with various theories about why she wasn't with them, from the ridiculous—she'd eloped with one of the other students, which was preposterous since Ethan Kimmel was with them—to the possible—the *Grace* needed extra preparation for wherever they were headed.

The moment they were on board, the cargo ramp closed behind them, and the pilot's curt tones came over the ship's intercom. "Moving in thirty seconds. Strap in now." He exchanged glances with Maria Verrand, who looked equally concerned over Cia's momentary—*hopefully* —personality shift, and they strode along the shortest path to the nearest safe spots.

The ship seemed angry, too, jostling and bucking more than usual during the takeoff and climb into space. A sense of foreboding grew in his gut, a familiar pre-mission feeling before entering into dangerous territory. *Well, I guess someone's got to do it.* When the ship's motion leveled off, he unclipped his harness and ran for the front, in case additional abrupt maneuvering lay in their near future. He had planned to jump into the right-side seat in the pilot compartment if needed but relaxed as he saw they were safely beyond immediate threats. He cleared his throat and said, "So, hi. How are you this morning?"

Cia growled an unintelligible response and hit several commands into her displays. Apparently, they were reluctant to work today, judging by the force of her actions.

Jax blew out a breath. "I'm going to climb out on a limb here and suggest that something has upset you. Is it Kimmel? Because, if so, I can throw him out the back right now. Say the word. I never trusted that little punk, anyway. With his staring and his computer wizardry and his ridiculous overconfidence."

His efforts were rewarded with a snort and a sigh. "No. It's not Ethan. He's fine. Everything's fine. I'm just tired."

He shook his head. "Nope. Not buying it. Try a different excuse. Or, you know, tell me the truth. Wasn't it you who had a problem with others holding back information that might affect them? Given that our lives are literally in your hands right now, I think that probably applies in this circumstance."

She smashed a fist down on the activator for the autopilot and twisted toward him. "I'm the one in the know today, and I really wish I wasn't."

He frowned. "Should I call the others together so you can brief us all at once?"

"No briefing is required right now. The Professor's instructions were quite clear. And he called ahead to ensure we'd do what he wanted."

Jax waited for several seconds, but she clenched her jaw and didn't continue. He held out for a couple more, then prompted, "And what is that, exactly?"

"Information gathering. He apparently agreed with Kenton-freaking-Marshall that approaching from the corporate side would better our odds. But when the others couldn't find anything on it, did he give up on the idea like a reasonable person? Oh, no, never. Instead, he locked onto that goal and set his smarty-pants brain to work on how to approach it differently. And you'll never guess what he came up with."

The pieces fell into place, and Jax's eyes widened. *That explains everything.* "No. He didn't."

Cia nodded with a look of sick satisfaction on her face at his flash of insight. "He did. He called my parents. We're headed to Mars to visit the Reardens."

The pilot refused to abandon her chair for the duration of the flight due to an expectation of increased traffic around the red planet. Jax wandered to the galley and found the rest of the team sitting at the table. He briefed them, resulting in looks of understanding on some faces, and something bordering on condescension on others. He shook his head and cautioned, "We have no idea what the background is here. Cia does. We're going to follow her lead, and nothing more. She may leave all or most of us on the ship. Whatever she chooses, this is *her* play, and we do what she says. Anyone decides to freelance, and we'll have words after."

Verrand frowned. "Are you team leader again?"

He shook his head. "No. Cia is since she knows the territory best. But I'm the enforcer if I need to be, just like if one of you currently held the key to our success. And if that's a problem for any member of this group, we can drop you back on Earth before we continue on to wherever this trail leads us." The steel in his tone caused the others to sit up straighter, stare at him harder. He softened it by adding, "Assuming there's another step. As usual, the Professor is keeping his cards entirely too close to his vest."

They all nodded, and Kimmel asked, "Is she okay?"

Jax shrugged. "She's stressed. Even at the best of times, it's hard for me to get a read on her, and right now I can't tell what she's feeling. If it were me, I'd be worried about seeing the family, upset that someone was making me do it, and probably frustrated that I couldn't do anything about it without letting my people down." He frowned down at them from his standing position leaning against the cabinets that held the cookware and dishes. "Don't underestimate this. Cia's taking one for the team here, and it's going to be painful for her. She left behind her pretty cushy family trader gig for a reason."

Their expressions revealed that the gravity of the situation had finally settled upon them. "She did tell me one thing. The crates have business wear in them, and we need to look like something other than 'scruffy pirate wannabes.' So, let's unpack and follow our leader's orders."

He rejoined Cia before their descent to the planet. He could have watched it on his comm from the bow camera, but he wanted to see it on a bigger screen and thought his partner might take solace from his presence. She was wound as tightly as he'd ever seen her, every move fast, sharp, and aflame with nervous energy. He asked, "Where are we headed?"

She tapped a panel, and the navigation information appeared on his control display. Mars was dotted with domed cities, and the marker for their landing was outside the largest on this side of the planet. He brushed his hand across the surface to zoom in the view, revealing a smaller dome a good distance away from the city. "Holy hell. Your family has a dome?"

She nodded. "Our own estate, own dome, own warehouses, own shipyard, and own landing pad with *its* very own retractable dome."

He whistled. "Hell. That's bigger than every military base I've been on. Why did you leave again? Got bored with having enough money to do literally anything you wanted to? Thought maybe you'd buy a moon instead?"

"Once you meet my family, you'll understand." She didn't speak again during the flight, except to coordinate with the AI in charge of the landing field. The trip down to the planet was the same as if they'd been landing on Earth, but instead of a runway in the distance, a bubble retracted as he watched. The final approach was vertical, the ship's nose tipping toward space as she slowly fell, Cia feathering the engines to control their descent. At the last moment, she gently brought the *Grace* back to horizontal and landed the ship without a bump on the pad. The dome began to reassemble itself overhead.

She rose from her chair and headed for her cabin. "I have to clean up a bit. Everyone should be ready to go. There shouldn't be any need for weapons, and anyway, you can expect full-body scans about three hundred times before we wind up near anyone worth killing."

He asked, "Lock picks? Other gadgets?"

She laughed darkly. "You've probably never seen security like ours. The people the government hires? They become available when we let them go because we've found something better." Cia shook her head. "There's no way to tell you what you're in for. You'll have to see it for yourself. But make sure no one tries anything clever. We also have a private defense force, and more or less our own laws. Tick off my parents and you all might vanish, never to be heard from again."

He almost laughed until he saw the look on her face. He nodded, swallowed, and replied, "Yeah. I'll tell them. Twice."

Cia studied the group for several moments and straightened Kimmel's collar before she hit the button to activate the cargo ramp. The Academy had sent along a present, because apparently that's how things were done among the wealthy, and Verrand held the brightly wrapped box in her hands. Each of them wore the same dark suits, well-tailored for their individual sizes and shapes. Different colored dark shirts and complementary ties completed the top part of the ensembles, and dark dress shoes the lower portion. Cia had selected her own clothes and wore a purple and black tunic with a long skirt in matching colors and pattern. It swished when she walked and showed knee-high black boots underneath that looked as if they cost more than anything he'd ever purchased.

She led the way out of the *Grace*, walking several feet ahead of the rest of them. At the bottom of the ramp waited a tall, thin man in a tuxedo featuring the same color scheme as her outfit. Jax murmured, "What the hell, do rich people all rent these guys from the same store?" Verrand snorted from beside him but wisely didn't reply.

When they got into earshot, the man was saying, "Lovely to see you again, Miss Cia. It will be my pleasure to escort you through to the house." He offered her a pin shaped in a stylized "R," and she sighed as she attached it to her shirt.

"My associates need credentials as well."

The man shook his head, and his slicked-back black hair didn't move an inch. "Mistress Rearden did not permit it, Miss Cia. She wished to ensure that they stayed in company with either you or me."

Cia sighed. "Of course, she did. At least it's perfectly in character." She turned to face them. "Okay, here's the deal. You need to be with me, or with Standring here. Otherwise, the security systems will react to your presence in ways that will be painful at a minimum, but probably more like fatal. There's a lot of intellectual property on-site, and we're very serious about keeping it secure." She looked down for a moment and drew a deep breath. When her face rose again, it was locked in a neutral mask. Her spine straightened, and her chin lifted a little more than usual. He'd done the same on any number of occasions, adopting a disguise before facing the enemy.

But the enemy had never been his family. He bowed his head in a nod of respect to her, raised his hand to block the butler's view of his face, and mouthed, "We've got your back."

Cia nodded, turned, and announced. "We're ready. Let's get a move on. Time is money, as father likes to say."

CHAPTER TWENTY-SEVEN

Standring and Cia walked ahead of them, engaged in a discussion Jax couldn't hear. The pilot had shifted into her role as Rearden scion with seeming ease, but he was sure it had cost her to do it, and she'd continue to pay that price for the duration of their time on the planet. *So quickly done is best done.* The rest of his team followed along and maintained their silence as they'd been instructed to do.

A luxurious tube car awaited them, constructed of white plastic and silver metal, decorated in the same colors as Cia and the butler wore. *This family is clearly serious about making sure you know you're on their home turf.* In the shoes of a potential business partner visiting to strike a deal, he'd feel firmly put in his place as "other" and "smaller" by the reception they'd received.

They sat, and it sped soundlessly toward the mansion. The tall windows that made up the upper half of the side walls showed the barren landscape of Mars' unforgiving surface. It was the only other planet in Earth's home system to have been colonized, as the jump drive had made it possible to explore widely for planets more easily conquered. Pragmatism overcame idealism once other options presented themselves, and the dreams of atmosphere and lush greenery covering Martian soil were abandoned as not worth the investment they would require.

They coasted to a stop with only a hint of motion, and the doors slid open to allow egress. He rose slowly as a reminder to his team, and they all waited for Cia and the butler to depart first. The luxury of their surroundings increased tenfold as they stepped from the car onto the platform. Metal and wood combined all around to create a sumptuous replica of an Earth train station from centuries past, but those facilities had never been as clean and perfect as this one. A high ceiling arched overhead, and light filtered through the copious windows set in it. Their footsteps echoed on the tile as they walked toward the exit, an array of eight doors arranged in pairs, translucent glass panes obscuring what lay beyond.

They opened automatically at their approach, and Jax finally got a good look at the Rearden home. He'd spent enough time in character to avoid visible reaction, but it was difficult to keep from gaping like a colonist who'd just visited their first real city. The huge reddish-brown stones stacked atop each other to create its facade had almost certainly been dug out of the Martian soil. He wasn't aware of a quarry on the planet, but evidence of one lay before him. A narrow patio ran along the front, the roof protecting it supported by seamless columns five stories high. As they approached, the enormity of the structure became clearer. *No wonder most of the family stays close. They could all live together and still not see each other for months if they wanted.* Oversized decorative double doors were set in the middle, and they parted at a gesture from the butler.

Inside stood two rows of security personnel, five members in the first rank, and four in the second. Eight of them stood stiffly at attention and wore the same garb. It was very similar to his Special Forces clothing, a black tunic and trousers with purple stripes and heavy black boots. Their belts held holsters on each hip with stun batons sheathed beside them. The ninth member of the group, a woman with short blonde hair severely chopped into a line on one side and shaved on the other, was clearly the leader. Her uniform had more purple accents and carried insignia on the collar. She stepped forward with a smile. "Miss Cia. Welcome home. You've been missed."

Jax heard genuine affection in the woman's voice, and in Cia's as she replied, "And I've missed you, Jaleni." She turned and called, "Jax, could you join us for a moment?" He approached and felt the security personnel's hard eyes track him as he moved. "This is Jaleni. She's the chief of security for the compound. What she says is law here." Cia swiveled her gaze to the other woman. "This is Captain Jackson Reese, UCCF Special Forces. He's part of an organization I belong to, and I trust him completely."

Jaleni nodded. "I am reassured, Miss Cia, but you understand I cannot allow him any additional liberties."

Cia laughed. "I never expected you would."

At that, a grin broke out on the Security Chief's face. "Well then, we'll have no problems. And do you both take responsibility for the rest of your crew?"

Jax nodded. "You don't have to worry about us. We'll

behave as much as you want us to." He tried a charming smile and got a deadpan stare in return. *Okay, no flirting with the security people. Check.* The woman turned to Cia and said, "You'll be staying the night, of course."

The pilot rolled her eyes, and sarcasm dripped onto the floor. "Why would I ever want to miss a family dinner?"

The chief nodded. "Indeed. I remember how much you enjoyed them." She gestured ahead. "Standring will show you all to your rooms. Please don't leave them without alerting us in advance. Guests found wandering will be judged a threat and acted upon accordingly by the security systems and personnel."

Jax asked, "Are we safe in our rooms without those pin things or whatever?" He knew the jewelry contained a transponder that would ID the wearer to the sensors that doubtless lay in each corner of every chamber.

She smiled, well aware of his game. "In the rooms, yes. Beyond them, very much no. And that includes the grounds, so no strolls through the landscape, please. The sentries out there are particularly violent." He had an image of the robot he'd recently fought and cringed inwardly.

"Gotcha, Chief. Thanks for the warning."

The security lead escorted Cia in one direction, and the guards accompanied Jax and the others as the butler led them to their rooms in what was likely a guest wing of the mansion. He spotted several places where he would have concealed doors, or cameras, or weapons, or maybe even traps if he were in charge of the place's defenses. The countermeasures would probably be fewer where Cia was headed. He wondered idly if she would be staying in her childhood bedroom, then got creeped out by the idea of growing up in a place like this. *A kid would need twenty-four-seven surveillance to ensure they didn't get lost trying to go from one wing to the next.*

His room was far nicer than the best hotel he'd ever stayed in, including the resort planet they'd visited during his last stint at the Academy. It shared elements of the family's color scheme but was mainly light fabrics and dark woods. The attached bathroom had a shower with a computer that controlled the spray, and he immediately put checking that out thoroughly on his to-do list for after their meeting with the family. A mammoth display filled one wall and cycled through artistic images of Mars accompanied by classical piano that followed him while he moved through the space, suggesting hidden speakers all around.

I'm sure they've got as many options for recording sound as for playing it back in this room. Before leaving the ship, they'd discussed the need to treat the house as an enemy location and assume no privacy whatsoever. Kimmel had naturally suggested that he could beat whatever systems they had in place, and Cia had explained to him that if he attempted it, she'd pull out his eyebrows a strand at a time and make him eat them. Jax hoped the computer wizard hadn't ignored the threats and promised punishments and tried to smuggle in technology anyway.

Jax lay back on the bed, which was about the size of his quarters aboard the *Cronus*, and closed his eyes as the comfort enveloped him. *When you have nothing better to do, get some rest for what comes next.*

Dinner was held in a room large enough for dancing. It probably could have hosted a formal dance and a meal simultaneously, as the long table down the center of the room only took up a third of it. This, despite being sufficient to seat twenty or more in comfort. Only one end had been set, with places for each of them plus five more. Etched metal tents with inscribed names sat atop small cloth pads on each plate to indicate their places. He was on the far end, away from the head of the table. Ethan Kimmel was already seated at the nearest position on the opposite side. *So, they took our measure somehow and put Cia's biggest supporters as distant from her chair as possible. Nice. Jerks.*

The rest of his team showed up shortly after, Verrand sliding into the seat to his right and Sirenno plopping down next to Kimmel. Before he could speak, the Reardens arrived *en masse*. The patriarch of the Rearden clan, Anders, was tall and well-built. His tanned skin glowed with health, and he had all the classical good looks money could buy. He lowered himself into the chair at the head of the table with a radiating confidence that it was *his* seat, and no one else could ever belong there.

Cia sat to his left, wearing a more formal version of the ensemble she'd had on earlier, featuring a more notable purple trim. Across from her was an older woman that could only be her mother. Michaela Rearden was so thin she was almost waif-like, and her pale skin and light hair made her seem almost to fade while you looked at her.

Beside her sat the youngest-looking of the family he hadn't yet met, which likely made him Grenthan. He was a carbon copy of his father, right down to the same swept-back dark hair and perfectly done eyebrows.

Across from him sat the other male scion, Travers. He must have drawn the recessive genes from each of his parents, because he was taller than both, had skin liberally dotted with freckles, and an unexpected shock of red hair that he seemed unconcerned with styling. Jax got the immediate impression that he was probably the second biggest troublemaker in the clan.

Finally, next to Maria Verrand, sat the last Rearden child that Cia had mentioned. Valenie was her older sister, and her mannerisms were much like her mother's, small and relentlessly proper. She had long dark hair that shone in the lights and fell in waves past her shoulders. Her features were perfectly proportioned; she could easily have been a model had that been her choice.

The meal was sumptuous, among the best he'd ever eaten. They'd enjoyed seven courses, with small bites in between as palate cleansers that would have been amazing on their own, and each better than the last. Exotic fruits from multiple planets contributed to their meal, and the main course was steak and fish from an alien world deep in Coalition territory. The meal held a message of power for those who were not part of the Rearden clan.

Those who were there spent the meal in barbed conversation, much of it directed at Cia. Her ability to hold her own in the face of it impressed him, and several of her comments cut deeply enough to draw visible reactions from her brothers and sister. Jax kept his eyes on the man at the head of the table and noticed that he seemed to enjoy watching his youngest daughter win rounds against her siblings. *Interesting, that.* At the end of the meal, Anders invited Cia into the den for discussion, and she in turn asked Jax to accompany them. For a moment he thought the elder Rearden would object, but he nodded neutrally instead and gestured toward one of the doors leading from the room.

The den was smaller than the dining room, but that was like saying that Mothra was smaller than Godzilla. Both were still pretty darn big. Dark wood with lighter wood as accents made up the main elements, and with the addition of thick fabrics in greens and browns, the space reminded him strongly of a forest. A uniformed servant awaited within, and as Anders took the leftmost chair near the fireplace, approached with a tray holding three tumblers of whiskey. Cia chose the middle seat, and Jax the one remaining, and when he accepted his glass and gave it a gentle sniff, he almost swooned from the delicious notes that hit his nostrils. He considered it an amazing feat of restraint that he managed to wait to sample it until his host had broken that seal.

It tasted as good as it smelled. A moan may have escaped him, but fortunately, Anders began speaking at that moment. "So, daughter, since you come in the company of a Special Forces captain and a number of other accomplished people, I presume you are on an assignment for your school."

Cia lifted the eyebrow that faced Jax before turning to face her father. "You know it's called the Academy. Why do you insist on the games? Especially since you know you'll never beat me?"

He laughed, sounding surprisingly genuine. "I've missed

you, Cia. I wish you'd come back to the business. If not now, then soon."

She shook her head. "Perhaps, but it's not time yet. I'm afraid you'll keep having to deny me for a while." The affection in her voice was unmistakable. He'd thought she disliked her family on a personal level, but this encounter suggested something else, at least where her father was concerned. *Expectations, maybe, and a desire to be free of them.*

He nodded. "Very well. So, tell me what I can do for you."

CHAPTER TWENTY-EIGHT

Cia said, "We think there's a company in the Confederacy working with the government on an AI project. Do you have a guess as to which one would be most likely?"

Anders Rearden's family resemblance to his daughter shone forth as he lifted his eyebrow. She had more of her mother's looks, but Jax was starting to think her personality and mannerisms had come from the other side of her parentage. "There are several. Do you have any more information to offer to narrow it down?"

She sighed and turned to face Jax. "He's impossible. You never get anything for free with this guy." She twisted back. "Okay, we think there's a third player. An alien species, either on behalf of the Coalition or working independently."

He nodded with a small frown. "That does make for a unique situation. How sure are you of this?"

Jax replied, "One hundred percent on the Confederacy and alien collaboration. Less so on the corporate connection, but several people we trust have made very compelling arguments as to why that's highly probable."

Rearden nodded. "Certainly. In fact, I doubt they could do it without private industry. Their government is even less adept than ours in most cutting-edge fields, which I don't have to tell you, is saying something significant." In the same tone, he said, "Tablet," and ten seconds later the servant handed him one. Their host tapped on it in silence, and Jax and Cia both used the time to sip their drinks. Jax stared around the room, adding to his earlier big picture several smaller notes: a framed certificate here, a family portrait there, and a cabinet filled with trophies gleaming in silver and gold.

Finally, Cia's father extended the tablet to his left, and the servant bustled forward to take it from him. Jax had the sense that if the other man hadn't been fast enough, Rearden would have dropped it to prove a point. *Thing probably costs more than I make in a month.* "There are two players who might have the brainpower and infrastructure to pull off what you've described. May I ask what you're planning?

Cia replied, "We're going to figure out a way to break through their security and steal their secrets." Jax groaned inwardly at the revelation, which he probably would have chosen to keep secret.

Rearden nodded. "Neither will be an easy task, but if your position is that it's likely to be easier than compromising a government building, and certainly far more deniable, that makes sense. After all, you can always claim it is corporate espionage at need, right Cia?"

She laughed. "You know me well, father."

"I'd like to think the reverse is true, so this question doubtless won't be a surprise. What's in it for the family?"

The back-and-forth conversation had left Jax's brain behind a while before, but Cia sounded as if she'd antici-pated the question. "Use of whatever we find, but only internal. Not as a product to be sold or shared. The Professor would never agree to that." Unspoken but easily understood was that Maarsen had agreed to what she'd offered, which meant she'd thought about it enough in advance to discuss it with him, even through the anger of being sent back to deal with her family. Again, Jax was impressed by his partner's ability and depth.

"Done. What do you need?"

She answered, "Credentials. Supplies as necessary. A couple of small upgrades to the *Grace*. Travers to be sent off to some backwater planet for survival training so I don't have to see him around."

Rearden laughed. "Yes on the first and second, within reason on the third, and a hard no on the fourth. Your mother would kill me."

"Coward."

"Admittedly. That woman hits hard." The conversation shifted to relaxed catching up on what had happened since her last visit, and Jax shook his head in bewilderment. *This is nothing like I expected. But, hey, the whiskey is amazing, and I'm safe and comfortable. Could be a lot worse.*

"I don't see how this could be any worse," Ethan Kimmel growled the next morning as he examined the credentials he'd been given. "Seriously, I'm an intern? I'm entirely too old to be an intern." They were gathered in one of the living rooms—the house had four of them, according to Cia—planning for their operation against the companies her father had identified. Once again, they'd find out *en route* which was their target. Fortunately, both had a presence on the Confederacy homeworld.

That had been a dismal revelation, definitely in the "couldn't be worse" category. Jax had held out hope that their targets wouldn't be on their opponent's most daunting home turf, but it was quickly dashed. While the companies had operations on many other planets, Anders Rearden had been certain that only the one right in the heart of the Confederacy would have access to the materials, since that's how he'd do it. *If, of course, he didn't have his own locked-down estate on Mars, that is. I guess we're lucky that the companies don't have their own planets or stations or something.*

Verrand and Sirenno chuckled at the younger man. "We're fancy scientists. Age has its benefits, youngster." Kimmel replied with some choice curses that set the duo to laughing again.

Cia growled, "You've all got the cool stuff. I'm a bloody executive assistant. They did this on purpose." When Jax had seen the role she'd drawn, he'd managed not to laugh, but barely. Mainly because she would be assisting him as the boss of the rest, and ticking her off further was definitely not in his best interest. "Hopefully, they'll be done with my girl soon, and we can get the hell off this rock."

He stretched. "I'm not in any hurry. I mean, the meals are great, the booze is phenomenal, and watching you quarrel with your family is some of the best entertainment I've had in years." He ducked to avoid the decorative pillow she hurled at him but took the one that Kimmel threw right in the face. He pointed at the computer expert. "Hey, you stay out of this. You're not old enough to fight." That summoned another round of pillows, and laughter following.

A discreet cough drew their attention to the doorway where Standring stood. He intoned, "Your ship will be ready in an hour, Miss Cia. Once you are packed, I will escort you back to her." Her grin, present from the first words, ticked up as the man used "her" instead of "it." Clearly, he knew his charges well.

Jax said, "All right people. Let's get to our rooms and pack our stuff. We're headed out."

Their trip back to the *Grace* was pretty much their approach in reverse. None of the family came out to bid them farewell, which Cia said was more or less how things worked. She'd spent some time with the family at a breakfast the rest of them hadn't attended and was unwilling to say anything about it other than it had happened and it was fine. With Cia, "fine" rarely meant the same thing it did when he used it, but she seemed relaxed and ready, so he wasn't concerned. Her conversation with Standring was animated and filled with laughter. The staid man even joined her in the mirth on a couple of occasions, improving Jax's opinion of him.

She bolted up the ramp to her ship, and his team said their farewells to Standring, Jax waiting until the others had gone to shake the man's hand. He tilted his head toward the ship. "She's special to you, that much is obvious.

I know there's a lot going on between her and her family, and I don't need the details. But she's my partner on this mission, and more than that, I'd like to think she's my friend. Is there any threat to her safety from these people?"

The other man pursed his lips and didn't reply for a moment. He released Jax's hand and said, "There are threats, and there are threats, Mr. Reese. They would not act to harm her physically under any circumstance. However, financially is another matter, and perhaps emotionally yet another. In some ways, they are just siblings; in others, they are business rivals. It's a confusing situation on the best days."

Jax nodded. "And the parents?"

The man smiled. "Her father adores her and would probably hand her the reins of the entire company if she asked for it. It might be that the others know that, and it causes their occasional animosity." Jax raised his eyebrows, and the other man chuckled. "Perhaps more than occasional. Her mother is a little distant and always has been. But Mistress Rearden has only the best intentions toward her daughter."

"Thank you. I appreciate your candor. You can put me on the list of those with best intentions toward Cia."

The butler lifted a perfectly shaped eyebrow. "Are you thinking of joining the family, Captain?"

A laugh burst from him before he had any chance of stopping it. "Oh, *hell* no. She'd be a nightmare to live with. We'll stick with friends, thanks." The grin on the other man's face revealed that he was joking, and Jax shook his head. "Like Cia, there's more to you than you show, Standring. I hope we get to talk again one day."

The butler gave a single nod. "I'd enjoy that very much. Safe travels, Captain Reese."

Jax turned and jogged to the ship, still laughing. He smacked the button to close the cargo bay and headed for the pilot compartment, where Cia was already talking to the AI that oversaw the landing pad. He strapped into the right-hand seat and asked, "We good?"

She nodded. "Never better. Aside from possibly getting arrested for corporate espionage. But you know, at least we won't be shot on sight for *actual* espionage like we might be in a government building. Well, one hopes so anyway. Never quite sure with you. It's like bad luck follows you around or something." She switched channels and announced, "Thirty seconds to get yourselves strapped in before it's go time."

Jax studied the navigation panel in front of him. "We're not headed straight for the jump point?"

She shook her head. "Nope. My father gave me a heads-up on our false identities last night, and I passed them on to the quartermaster at the Academy. She's whipped up some gear for us, probably in consultation with Maarsen, and we'll meet another ship to transfer it over."

He gripped the arms of his chair as the ship abruptly rose several feet, then turned on its tail. Even with artificial gravity, the feeling of being suddenly vertical wasn't something that the mind and body really handled in stride. It got worse when she pushed the thrusters to maximum, literally rocketing away from her family's estate as fast as she could. Jax forced words out through his clenched teeth. "Sending a message, huh? You're so subtle. They might miss it."

She laughed. "You met my brothers and sister. They're not the brightest suns in the galaxy. Sometimes you have to make it really obvious for them." She looked over at him with a pointed stare. "Sound familiar?"

"Har har. Just pilot the damn ship, flygirl."

"Whatever you say, jerkwad."

CHAPTER TWENTY-NINE

The handoff from the supply ship involved backing the two cargo sections up near one another, throwing a line over, then slowly towing the boxes onto their deck. Jax and Kenton Marshall handled their end of it, and someone he hadn't met was on the opposite side. Cia had informed him that Trianna was at the helm of the second vessel, and it wasn't a shock when her voice failed to come across his comm. He asked the man on the other ship, "Does your pilot talk to you?"

He laughed, and in a gruff rasp replied, "Never more than a few words here and there. But I sense that I'm growing on her. Another year or two of working together and we might be up to full sentences."

Jax wondered why the universe was filled with such weird people as he and Marshall strapped the large crates into place beside the ones that the *Grace* already carried. When they were done, they buttoned up the ship, stripped out of their vacuum suits, and headed for their quarters to sleep off the next part of the trip.

The transit to the Confederacy homeworld would take three jumps. Technically, they could have made the distance in two, but that would have involved evading the outer checkpoint at the boundary between their space and that belonging to the UCCA, which would result in all sorts of trouble on the far end. So, they planned to make the first jump roughly halfway to the border, stop to get themselves ready, then perform the next pair of jumps one after the other. They'd arrive on the planet in the evening, giving them another night's rest before they tried to steal the AI. They expected to hear which company they were after during that middle portion, if all went to plan.

Unexpectedly, it did. When they gathered in the early morning hours of the next day, the data was waiting for them. Cia announced, "It's Nenroth Cybernetics, which if I had to pick is the one I'd rather be going after. Their chairman is an absolute jerk. Even more than Jax. He's like the ultra-jerk. Nasty to other businesses, nasty to his employees, and particularly nasty to the women in his life. This will be much more satisfying than I expected, especially if it somehow takes him down, too."

The others nodded agreement, and Jax grinned. "Well, all right then. We have purity of purpose. There's nothing better than helping the universe lay the smackdown on someone who truly deserves it." *As long as that person isn't me, for a change.* "Let's break open the crates and see what we've got."

The first container yielded business suits for all of them. He recognized them at a touch, as he'd worn something similar before. "It's a special fabric. They make part of our drop suits from it. Really expensive, but it handles extreme temperatures, impact, and cutting well. There's probably a connection on them somewhere to attach a power cell, but we won't want to do that until after inspection, obviously. For now, we can pack the outfits in our suitcases."

Shoes were next, and Cia nodded as soon as she saw hers. "Same style for men and women, only ours are higher and more fashionable. Which means they have gifts inside."

Ethan Kimmel lifted a pair and looked at the heels. "I don't see an opening."

She replied, "You won't until you break the seal. After we get through inspection, I'll show you how to do it."

Anton Sirenno's head snapped up from where he was digging in the box. "Inspection?"

Jax nodded. "Yep. We're going to have to let the Confederacy's finest poke through our stuff. Hopefully, it'll just be bored bureaucrats, but it's always possible there will be a military presence."

Kenton Marshall frowned. "Won't they take offense to the equipment in the armory?"

Cia grinned. "They would if they were able to detect it. However, we're going to stash that gear in the scan-shielded cache in the floor. It'll be just big enough to fit it all."

Their newest member shook his head. "Wait a second. I thought you were totally against breaking the rules. Why do you have a secret cargo hold?"

She shrugged. "I'm against breaking rules that make sense. But sometimes they don't. I've never used it for anything other than noble purposes, and never will."

He countered, "Who decides what counts as noble?"

Cia answered, "I do. And I'm fully comfortable with my moral compass. Can you say the same?"

That shut him up, and they unearthed the rest of the gear. Included were toys for each of them that would probably come in very handy during the operation. *Assuming we get through the door, at least. A lot is riding on Cia's family being as good as she's said they are. Hope she's right.*

The inspection landed in the middle of the two extremes. They'd hoped for bored bureaucrats, feared a full military contingent, and wound up with a bored officer and a couple of guards who didn't seem all that concerned with the interior of the ship. The Confederacy representatives stomped through the *Grace*, peering into each cabin and requiring them to open each container, from the smallest briefcase to the cargo crates in the hold. Sirenno jokingly asked if they wanted him to open up all the prepackaged meals as well, causing the only tense moment of the visit. The flat glare he'd gotten in reply was a sufficient answer to keep him quiet for the rest of the encounter.

They didn't know the ship as the *Grace*, of course. She was in disguise, the movable panels on her hull repositioned to change her profile, and the alterations to her engine's signature activated. The note on the bow had been replaced by a quartet of fanned playing cards, and she was now the *Fours are Wild*, a vessel owned on paper by their fictitious company, Quartet Robotics. A whole backstory existed that he hoped he wouldn't be called upon to relate about four friends who started a business with the proceeds from a card game, blah blah blah.

Fortunately, the inspectors didn't seem the least interested in their paperwork. Once they'd discovered no obvious contraband, they gave the ship their stamp of approval and headed out to check on the next arrival. The Confederacy had several points along their border like this one, to ensure that vessels coming in were given a once-over before being permitted into their systems. The UCCA handled it differently, doing inspections at each destination rather than creating the bottleneck in specific locations. Neither seemed all that secure to Jax.

He was in the right-hand seat for the jump into their target system and the descent to the Confederacy homeworld. When the faction had splintered from the Alliance and set out to create their utopia, some of the best minds in the UCCA had been part of the movement. The system they'd chosen, Esutis, was unique in the galaxy as far as they knew, as it had three habitable worlds all equidistant from the sun, locked into a synchronous orbit. The distance between them stayed the same as they circled the star, essentially resulting in three versions of Earth traveling together. More planets and moons filled out the rest of the system, but none of them were as perfect or as connected as the trio.

He asked, "Which one is ours?"

She tapped her control panel, and a planet glowed in yellow on his screen. "That's the primary homeworld. It's where the king and his family live, where Parliament gathers, and where most of the main government functions are located. For comfort, they'd want to do it there, thinking it's more secret and secure." She shrugged. "They might be right. No telling what we'll find on the ground. If it were me, though, I'd put it on an alien world."

"You're assuming the aliens are less interested in stealing it than we are. Who knows, they could have whole infiltration teams on the way."

She laughed. "They'd blend right in down there, I'm sure." As far as humanity knew, no aliens could effectively disguise themselves as humans. *Again, some serious assumptions bound up in that one. Maybe the Professor is a super-intelligent alien. That would explain a lot.*

The planet was lovely, very much like an unspoiled Earth with blue oceans, green and brown lands, and wispy clouds they plunged through on the way down. Those who had formed the Confederacy had sworn not to make the same mistakes in industrialization that had plagued the UCCA homeworld and had the luxury of starting with modern technology that had mostly eliminated damaging waste products. Those that remained were generally small, extremely hazardous, and routinely shot into the closest sun, which gobbled them up without complaint.

The spaceport was a notable distance from the nearest populated areas and was surrounded by warehouses and other trade and cargo services. The nearer they got, the larger it grew, with Jax eventually realizing that they were essentially the size of an ant on a picnic table compared to the overall installation. He said as much, and Cia laughed. "But a fire ant. A nasty, biting, fire ant. Gawr." The growl was predictably silly and set off a competition as to who could do it better. She pronounced herself the victor before landing, and he surrendered the field with a comment about her potential as a barbarian.

By the time they'd received clearance to disembark, the sun was disappearing over the horizon, casting a golden glow over the metal hulls of the surrounding vessels. He frowned as he stepped off the cargo ramp. "No alien ships here. Why did I think there would be?"

Kimmel replied, "Because you know they welcome the Coalition here. Because I told you that." He sounded slightly snippy, doubtless because they'd been treating him like the intern he was pretending to be for the entire trip, making him get coffee, run messages back and forth, and so on. He'd generally been good-natured about it, but couldn't fully hide his annoyance. One of his tasks had been to research the planet for them. "But they have a separate spaceport, all the way on the far side of the city center from where we're headed. Equally well-defended, though."

Jax's eyes were drawn to the towers that surrounded the installation, each with two turret arrays that reminded him of the killer robot's head, four barrels covering the cardinal directions mounted on a rotating ring. If one was energy and the other missiles, which was how he'd do it, a single tower could give any lawbreaker a bad day. Many more than that were placed around the facility, at least a dozen in the part of the field he could see. He wouldn't want to try to take the spaceport with anything less than an all-out assault on the heels of some serious sabotage.

A brisk stroll delivered them to the moving walkway, and from there they made the transition to the train that would carry them into the city proper. Each of them dragged a large rolling suitcase behind them, filled with the essentials for their disguises, plus the extra toys the Academy had provided. He felt naked without a weapon, but the rules had been quite clear on that topic. None were permitted off the ship, and although he hadn't spotted the well-hidden sensors, he had little doubt they'd been scanned repeatedly on the way to the clean and comfortable carriage they relaxed into for the ride. Even the printed blades had been left on board, on the off chance that the team might wind up catching the eye of security personnel.

He reclined in his cushy chair and closed his eyes after taking a last look at the glowing countryside speeding past them in the final rays of the day's sun. *By this time tomorrow, we'll be comfortably on the way back to the* Grace, *er, the* Fours, *or we'll be on the run.* His mind started calculating probabilities, but he shut it down and thought instead about his second date with Juno. *Better come back with the goods. No one wants to ask out a loser.*

CHAPTER THIRTY

The hotel wasn't as luxurious as the resort had been, and didn't even approach the league of the Rearden mansion, but it was elegant in a business sort of way. They'd made all the final decisions on the ship, under the assumption that the Confederacy would have surveillance devices everywhere. From here on out, they would stay in their roles unless and until things went to hell. As always, Jax hoped everything would go off according to plan but certainly didn't expect it.

They checked in together, the Academy's people having arranged all the details for them ahead of time. In a twist on their original design, instead of their company already having an office on the planet, they were ostensibly there to consider setting one up. An appointment had been made with the trade minister for the day after next to bolster their cover story. If any of them were still around to make that meeting, bad things would have happened in the interim. Another set of Academy personnel would be checking into a similar hotel in order to maintain the fictional real estate plans with plentiful excuses as to why the primary contacts had to depart unexpectedly.

They ate a late dinner together, practicing their roles and pushing each other to come up with viable details so they'd be less likely to be caught off-guard the next day. He bid the others goodbye and asked Cia to stay for a drink, announcing that they had a couple of things to finalize. The rest departed in a group, none of them at all concerned except for Ethan Kimmel, who gave him a suspicious glare as he left.

Jax ordered cider for both of them and laughed. "Our intern is carrying a torch for you. You're aware of that, right?"

She nodded. "He's pretty cute. If it all works out, maybe it'll be something, eventually. You know, assuming the company is successful and I still have a job and all."

"Any additional concerns pop up on your radar?"

She took a solid drink before replying. "Mainly the things we've talked about before. Making sure our presentation goes well, convincing them to allow us access to their proprietary stuff. I don't see why they wouldn't, but you never know with corporate people."

"I think we've done all we can do on that front. Any more rehearsals and we'd be doing it in our sleep. Frankly, if they're able to resist this group's persuasive abilities, we never had a chance anyway." His smile faded a touch. "I'm a little concerned about the timing of the trip back to the *Fours*. We could be on kind of a tight schedule afterward, depending on how the meeting goes."

She shrugged. "I saw an advertisement at the concierge downstairs about renting all-terrain vehicles for sightseeing. I suppose if there's a delayed train or something, we could get some and drive there." If their foes wound up getting suspicious, the train was the weak point of their exit strategy. She'd had the task of figuring out another option, and he liked her choice.

"Maybe reserve a few in case. Put it on the corporate card. We can afford to lose a deposit to ensure we make it to our next meeting on time."

Cia nodded. "Anything else, boss?" She stressed the last word, turning it into a derogatory term.

"I don't suppose there's a seedy bar with loose women nearby, is there?" He laughed at her glare. "Okay, fine, be that way. But you stay away from the intern. That boy is off-limits. We don't need to get sued because you think he's pretty."

"Cute. He's cute. Something you will never, ever, in your wildest dreams, be." She rose and stalked off, leaving him to pay the tab.

The bartender shook his head and observed, "Couldn't help but overhear. She's got a sharp tongue, that one."

He nodded as he stood. "And a sharper brain to go with it. Wouldn't trade her for the world."

They didn't meet for breakfast, opting instead to have food bars in their rooms while preparing for the operation. Jax donned his suit, with a t-shirt, button-down, and tie beneath the jacket. Polished black shoes with secret items stashed in the heels finished off the outfit. Part of his disguise was a hard-sided briefcase in supple brown leather. The note that had accompanied it claimed it would defeat sensors and scans of every sort, and only his index finger making a specific gesture at a specific spot would allow it to open. Only in a true emergency would he have to go for the gear inside, which escalated from simply damaging to decidedly lethal. The Academy had provided him with a couple of less extreme tools as well, and he tucked a pen concealing a sonic weapon into his jacket's inner pocket and patted his thigh to be sure that the electronic lockpick disguised as a metallic business card was in his trousers pocket.

He checked his looks in the mirror, ensured he had everything he needed if a fast getaway was required and that nothing incriminating remained in the room, then headed for the elevator. His team gathered in the lobby, each of them carrying some sort of bag or briefcase and dressed to impress. *Damn it. I'm going to have to thank the quartermaster for doing such a good job. She'll stare at me with that look the whole time I do it, too.* He shook his head. *Maybe I can con Cia into that, too.* "All right, folks. Let's go do our best to convince these people to give us what we want."

The hotel was only a few blocks away from their destination, a deliberate choice to eliminate potential transport problems. The train station lay in between, giving them the option to appear to be heading back to their lodging, which was still booked for the night, while making their escape. Their support staff at the Academy had arranged reserved seats under fictitious names for all the trains that day and the next, which could be easily changed to match their new identities. They walked mostly in silence, only Cia and Kimmel in the rear rank holding a low conversation. His biggest regret about the operation was the lack of audio comms. The plan called for them to separate, and they'd only be able to communicate via text. Disguised earbuds had been part of the kits, but he'd nixed them as not being hidden enough.

The building they'd slept in the night before had twenty floors, according to the elevator; the one housing Nenroth Cybernetics rose to at least double that. Its exterior was all metal and mirror, reflecting the images of the surrounding buildings. Each floor was a continuous strip, making the structure resemble giant rectangular blocks stacked upon one another. A thin line of silver chrome separated each layer. The front doors were transparent glass, fortunately, or they might never have found them in the unbroken sameness of it all. The portal slid open at their approach to reveal a huge lobby teeming with people.

Jax plastered a grin on his face and strode forward with his hand outstretched toward the assistant of the person they'd come to meet, who he'd identified from the company's public-facing marketing information. He was tall, thin, sandy-haired, and otherwise a completely unremarkable corporate drone. *Maybe the corporations hire these guys from the same factory that produces the butlers.* "Hi there. Jack Reyes, Quartet Robotics. Allow me to introduce my team." He did so, using their assumed identities. When he finished, the man nodded.

"Very good. I'm Carson, and I'll take you up to see Ms. Brecken. First, you'll need to clear security. You understand I'm sure."

He laughed. "It's the same way in our place. Can't be too careful with our intellectual property, right? We're more than willing to do whatever it takes to set your minds at ease so we can have a fruitful discussion about how to increase the profit margins for both our companies." He'd worked hard on the business lingo, speaking it aloud on the trip to the planet and in his room the night before to practice.

The company's security routine was impressive. They passed through three different scanning devices, and their bags were subjected to two more. Then each was unpacked, every item examined, and carefully repacked by officers with a sense of intense awareness about them. Jax focused on keeping his breathing steady, not wanting to give away any anxiety to the biometric scanners that had doubtless been watching them since the moment they'd entered. *And maybe outside, too, who knows? We're proof that they have good reason for paranoia.*

They were each given a visitor badge to clip on their lapels. Jax was certain that not only would they allow the systems to track them, but would transmit at least audio and probably video back to some central AI in charge of building security. They'd anticipated the badges and had come up with workarounds in addition to what the Academy quartermaster had provided. Carson led them to a lift with no buttons, and announced, "Thirty-seven, please."

A perky female voice that was almost certainly a computer replied, "Of course, Carson." The assistant rolled his eyes but didn't speak. Jax avoided looking at Kimmel, who would be beginning their play against the company during the ride up, hopefully unnoticed. When the doors opened again, the man led them through a reception area that was posh without being overly impressive, and into a conference room with a large dark wood table down the center surrounded by black chairs. Displays covered two walls, and windows a third. He gestured at the table. "Please, take a seat. Ms. Brecken will be with you shortly. She's delayed by about three minutes."

Jax offered a wide smile. "Perfect, that's three more minutes we can use to polish our presentation." He turned to his people, effectively dismissing the assistant. "Let's get to it, folks." He placed his briefcase on the wooden surface and started removing documents, and his team did the same with theirs. Each had items appropriate to their position: Cia a small tablet to take notes, the others larger tablets for heavier work and display purposes. Jax carried a holographic projector, which he set in the center of the table and powered on.

A moment later, Sirenno said, "Link is good," and routed an image of the company's playing card logo to the device. Jax walked to where their host would likely sit, making sure the view was perfect and turned the disc slightly to align it better. If someone had diagrammed their plan, it would be full of possible branches based upon outcomes that couldn't be guaranteed in advance. The hope was that this meeting would go well enough that they'd be invited down to the research and development area their investigation suggested lay beneath the building. If not, other possibilities existed, but none of them with as significant a likelihood of success as if Ellena Brecken escorted them down herself.

She strode into the room with a brisk, "Thank you, Carson," and walked straight to him. With a nod, she said,

"Ellena Brecken." The woman was short, maybe only a few inches past five feet, and had long black hair pulled back in a ponytail. Her nose was notably pointed, adding a fierceness to her face that the intense green eyes above it amplified. Her outfit, accessories, and personal care regimen were all appropriate to her station. Her sense of power and authority spread out from her like a wave.

He returned the gesture. "Jack Reyes. I'm sure you've already done your research and know my team, so how about we get down to it?"

She smiled and sat in the chair he'd expected her to. "My kind of people. So, tell me why Nenroth Cybernetics should climb into bed with Quartet Robotics." For the next half hour, he and his team spun out a tale of marrying their advanced technology with the command-and-control systems that her company was known for. Each of them spoke, except for Cia and Kimmel, who carried off their subordinate roles well.

Quartet's status as a major player had been built up in advance through planted data and a few carefully calculated recommendations secured by the Professor. Jax imagined that Maarsen had some sort of drawer filled with all the favors people owed him written on little notecards. That had gotten them the meeting and hopefully set up Brecken to be well-disposed toward them. Still, at the end of the spiel, he got the sense she hadn't been convinced.

Verrand must have noticed it, too. She said, "I think you'll have to show her, Jack."

He grinned. "Ms. Brecken, when it comes to concealing what you're thinking, you would give a statue a run for its money. But we came here to make a deal, and we don't intend to leave without one, so I guess it's time to lay our final card on the table." He took off his jacket and set it carefully on the chair, then rolled up his left sleeve. "Card. Get it?"

A flicker of amusement crossed her lips. "Very droll, Mr. Reyes."

"Please, call me Jack." He offered his bare arm to her. "Before you is the latest in cybernetic technology, so new that we are literally the only ones who have it." He dug into his pocket for his lucky coin and slid it down the table to Verrand. "Make it a good one."

She threw it fast and hard at their host, and his artificial arm snapped out in a blur to intercept the disc and lay it gently on the wood in front of Brecken, all in the space of about a second. Her eyes were still widening in initial shock when he finished the move. He nodded. "And that's with our AI in control. With yours, well, there's no telling what we could accomplish."

She composed herself quickly and rose. "I'm intrigued. But I'll need to take a better look at that unit if you're willing."

He grinned wide, putting his best salesman face on. "As I said, we'll do whatever it takes to put this deal together. Consider me yours."

CHAPTER THIRTY-ONE

Carson rejoined them as Ellena Brecken led the way to the elevator. He said, "They're informed of your arrival," and she gave a single nod. When they stepped into the lift, the assistant announced, "Research."

The chirpy voice replied, "Confirmation needed."

Brecken snapped, "Confirmed." She seemed to share Carson's view of the elevator's AI. *I hope this isn't indicative of their capabilities or we're in the wrong place.* The elevator didn't seem to move, but opened on a new floor. He'd come to expect a white sterile atmosphere to be present in all science areas and wasn't disappointed. A hallway extended ahead, seeming to run the entire length of the floor. Openings suggested cross corridors at several points, and multiple doors were visible along the way. She strode forward, took a right turn at the first intersection, and led them into a large space that very much resembled the Academy's medical lab.

A white-coated technician bustled up to the executive, and Brecken gestured toward Jax. "His left arm, full analysis." The tech, a wiry man with unkempt hair who could easily have pulled off the grad student disguises his team had tried in Edinburgh, dragged him to a humanoid-shaped creche attached to the wall. "Please, stand in there. This won't hurt, I promise." Jax removed his coat, withdrew the metal coin and business card from his pockets and handed them all to Cia, then complied.

The employee ran behind a control panel, and a holographic image of Jax appeared in midair in the center of the room. It zoomed in to his arm and electronically stripped away the skin to reveal the artificial muscles and bones beneath. The Professor and Juno had agreed that giving up the secrets of its construction would be an acceptable trade for what they'd come to steal. The doctor had laughed and added, "Besides, we already have something better in the works."

The pair talked in technical jargon, with lots of nodding and murmuring back and forth. Verrand and Kimmel were in the corner of his vision, and she nudged the alleged intern, who coughed and asked, "Where's the nearest restroom?"

The technician looked at him crossly and replied, "Outside, first right, second left."

"Thanks," he muttered and headed for the door. Marshall and Verrand descended on Brecken and the tech, pointing out details and offering explanations. They'd all had a crash course on the inner workings of his arm on the flight in, and given their backgrounds, everyone except maybe Cia probably understood it better than he did. *All I care about is that it works.* Sirenno faded to the back of the room and sneezed, then pulled a handkerchief out of his pocket to pat his nose with it. Jax only saw the motion because he was waiting for it as the other man stuck a small device under the edge of the counter he stood beside with his free hand.

The technician came forward, waving at him. "You can come out now." Jax complied, and the man guided him over to another table, where the surface was reforming itself into the same sort of cradle Juno had used when examining it. He put the arm in place without instruction and received a nod of approval. Brecken was clearly more than a figurehead since she was punching commands into the panel right beside the tech.

His left wrist was below the table, and he made sure to block it from any high cameras with his body. A series of quick flicks activated the feed from Kimmel. His assignment was the most vital, and he only had as long as he could stall with the excuse of being in the restroom to crack into Nenroth's system and locate the AI. They hoped that the code would be accessible via a wireless network, but they knew that was a longshot. More likely, the facility held a cube similar to the one they already had, the one whose content was broken up into parts and hidden in one of their heels each, with some redundancy in case someone got separated. Everyone involved had hated the idea of bringing the other half along. Still, the Academy's experts had suggested that if their target was inside a server, the only way to get it out could be by using their existing half as a key, due to the security protocols the partners might have established.

The feed showed an image of an analog clock with moving hands, which was the message that their resident computer genius had gotten into the network and was searching. The items his team had secreted throughout the building—Kimmel in the elevator, Verrand upstairs in the conference room, Marshall in the lobby, and now Sirenno in here—gave them signal routing to get around physical dead spots and expand Kimmel's access. The others had said mesh, and web, and other similar words, during which he'd blanked out and let them talk. The upshot was that their intern needed more time, meaning Jax needed to stall.

He donned that smile again, the one that made it clear he was selling something. "So, impressive, right? The limitations aren't in the physical components. We're hitting our head on the processing. Simply put, to coordinate all the individual muscle cells, we need a smarter system than we've been able to create on our own. And word on the street suggests you might have the solution to that problem either ready to go or nearly so."

Brecken looked up from her screen. "And if we do?"

He shrugged as best he could with one arm latched to the table. "Then we want to be in business with you. Sure, we could buy it when you make it available, eventually, but you'll already be into the next iteration when that happens. We can do more working as a team, improving the physical tech and the AI controls together. Imagine the possibilities for prosthetics to replace lost limbs. Hell, we're at the point where with the right computer brain behind it, we could be ready to turn the corner to replacements by choice instead of at need. What would that be worth to the military?"

She frowned. "Whose military?"

He laughed. "Who cares? I'm not a politician. I'm a businessman. If one of the players wants to pay for exclusivity, including all the security assurances we'd require and such, why would we possibly refuse? That's for the lawyers and sales folks to figure out. Once we agree to work together, it will open up so many possibilities we'll have our choice of options."

The thing that made the spiel believable was that it was mostly true. The tech in his arm was advanced enough that a couple of rounds of innovation could result in truly groundbreaking technology. And the Academy did need whatever breakthrough in Artificial Intelligence the company had come up with to make that happen. Jax imagined a commercial end of the enterprise existed that was kept at arm's length from the students; it was the only explanation for how willing they were to spend money without reservation. If it weren't for Stephenson's involvement, he'd probably have concerns, but he trusted his superior officer to know what was what.

The icon on his watch changed to a spinning cube, and he cursed inwardly. The server would have been the easy route. Now they had to locate and retrieve a physical object. He kept one eye on it while trying to attend to Brecken as she spoke. "Let's say, for the sake of conversation, we have the items you think we do. What would you imagine our partnership might look like?" She gestured at the tech, and he released Jax's arm from the holder.

He rolled down his shirt and buttoned his cuff. "I'd say a seventy-thirty split your way on the first product, both as a 'getting to know you' gift and because, frankly, we need you a little more than you need us right now. With that will come some guarantees of exclusive use in robotics, that nonsense. Attorney stuff. Afterward, fifty-fifty on what we create together. We're already looking for a place here on Chesyira, so we'll be in the neighborhood."

She tapped a fingernail against a tooth, the first scarlet, and the second white. Both were flawless, without a chip or discoloration to be seen. "It might make more sense for you to be in the building if we do it. There's plenty of room to move in your equipment."

Jax chuckled. "You can't honestly think we're that easy, Ms. Brecken."

She laughed in reply. "Well, one has to try, right?"

"I wouldn't respect you if you didn't. So, where do we go from here?" The icon on his watch changed to a checkmark, meaning that Kimmel knew where the item was. The faux intern walked into the room a couple of minutes later and sidled up to Cia.

Their host nodded. "I assume you'll want to see mine, now that you've shown me yours."

Damn, she's got the wordplay down. If not for Juno, I could be interested. Well, and if any of this was real. Somehow, I think that stealing her company's stuff might put a damper on any potential relationship. "Most definitely."

They headed back to the lift, and she ordered, "Secure seven." A panel slid aside to reveal a palm reader, and she pressed her hand to it. A half-minute later the doors opened again, this time onto a single small room filled with displays. "This is the showplace for the AI." She led them into the center of the chamber and said, "Hello, Athena."

A smooth feminine voice replied, "Good morning, Ms. Brecken. How are you today?"

"Very well, thank you. Have you downloaded the information on Mister Reyes's arm from Research?"

"I have."

The woman grinned. "And what do you think of his offer to join his company to ours to continue developing it?"

Athena's tone changed slightly, becoming a little sterner. "I believe it's unnecessary, Ms. Brecken."

She nodded. "And why is that?"

"Because we already have what we need from them. I have performed an analysis down to a cellular level of detail. We can replicate this easily, with only minimal retooling required. Thus, it is not necessary to partner with their company since they have nothing left to offer."

Jax frowned, his face going hard. "That's theft, pure and simple."

Brecken nodded. "It would be. However, we'll give you a one-time payment for your IP that will make it all better. I wanted you to get a look at Athena, so you could know what you're missing." She smiled a predator's grin, and he decided it wasn't only Nenroth's chairman who was a jerk.

He turned and met Kimmel's eyes, and the younger man nodded. Jax returned his gaze to the woman, who was confident that she'd played them perfectly. "Well, thanks for that offer, but let us suggest an alternative." Cia stepped forward and sprayed Brecken with the contents of two small aerosol canisters she'd quietly pulled from her purse. Both were perfumes, the same brand but different varieties, and common enough that the people searching her bag hadn't looked twice. But the Academy's scientists had manipulated the formula, and when combined, they morphed into a knockout drug. He held his breath and caught Brecken before she could hit the floor.

Athena announced, "Please stay where you are. Security and medical personnel will be with you momentarily."

"Yeah, yeah," Jax grumbled as he dragged the unconscious woman toward the elevator door. Kimmel was already inside and had liberated the custom tablet from his bag. A few buttons and a replica of Brecken's voice said, "Secure twelve." The panel slid open, and Jax pressed her palm to it. The doors closed and the lift started to move as he lowered her gently to the floor. He asked, "So, how far in did you get?"

Kimmel shook his head but kept his eyes on his screen. "Not far enough. I'll delay the guards, but we're going to need a distraction. I am almost certain that the device is in Secure twelve."

Jax nodded. "Cia and Marshall, stay with Kimmel and me. Sirenno and Verrand, cause trouble. If you can keep it quiet, do it, but if not, make it noisy enough that we can sneak out in the chaos. But first, give me your pieces." They each raised their right shoe and rotated the heel, then withdrew and handed over small memory chips with a prong on one end and a socket on the other. "Thanks. Be safe. If in doubt, run."

Their options were narrowing by the second. Only a few contingency plans leading forward from this moment had been created, and they all depended on snagging the AI and getting started on their exit quickly. The lift opened on what looked like the most impressive hospital operating theatre he'd ever seen, a central table molded in a person shape with a dozen robot arms inert overtop it. He frowned and observed, "That's unexpected," before stepping aside as Cia and Marshall carried Brecken out.

Kimmel activated the woman's voice from his tablet, saying, "Fifteen." The elevator doors closed on Sirenno and Verrand, who knelt on the floor beside their open briefcases. When he finally took in the room ahead, the computer wizard said, "Oh, hell, this doesn't look right."

Jax growled, "Yeah, that about sums it up. You better figure out what's going on fast, or we're in a world of hurt."

CHAPTER THIRTY-TWO

Kenton Marshall crossed briskly to a control panel and started tapping on it in a way that looked knowledgeable. Jax prompted, "Marshall?"

Excitement was audible in his reply. "This is a bioengineering lab, similar to the one I use in my research. This is probably where they'd do the wiring of the courier we talked about way back when."

Cia and Ethan Kimmel had moved to a table with an empty surface nearby. The former had dumped out her bag and had her arm shoved inside it. The latter had pulled out a second tablet and was working on both, one with each hand. If they'd needed to provide an excuse, it would have been "always have a backup," but in truth, the second was explicitly configured to handle the half of the AI code they already possessed. Jax growled, "First things first. Give your chips to Kimmel."

It took half a minute to free them from their shoes and for their supposed intern to get them hooked in. Then Kimmel nodded. "We're good."

Jax looked around the room. Cabinets covered the walls in the same bare white as everything else. Harsh overhead lights made him wish for his helmet's adaptive display as his eyes started to water. "What's the next step, people?"

"I've got something," Marshall replied. "Let's see what this does." Before Jax could caution him not to do anything stupid, a whirring came from above. The robotic arms made slow movements with no apparent purpose. "Self-diagnostic routine. Good policy. Okay, how about this?" He slapped a palm down on the control panel with a flourish and a section of the floor near the central table parted to permit a column to rise. The white cylinder stopped at table height, then its top opened, and a clear box climbed into view from inside it. Within that container was a metal cube identical to the one they'd found in the Dhelears' possession.

Jax clapped his hands. "All right, now release the cover, and let's go home. It's totally that simple, right?"

Marshall barked a dark laugh. "Yeah, not so much. Kimmel, did you get into anything useful?"

Their computer expert shook his head. "No. Well, yes, but not in the way we want it to be. The theory that both parts needed to be in place for this to work was correct. I've got access to a network that's fast enough to pull the data in real-time, which is how I would do it if I were them. That way there's no local recording of the other half. But it's one direction. I can't draw down. I can only send up."

Jax frowned. "So there's no way to download the other part of the AI?"

"Exactly. And also, security is responding to an alarm

on the fifteenth floor, so Sirenno and Verrand have started their diversion. I don't have control of the elevator that leads here, nor can I be sure that there aren't others."

Cia interrupted, "That's why I'm here." She'd assembled a pistol from pieces secured in the lining of her purse. He had no idea how the Academy had managed to make it impervious to scans, but once again his opinion of the quartermaster's skills increased.

Jax breathed, "Damn. I don't want to leave here empty-handed, so figure something out, Mister Biological Engineer guru." He walked over to the table the others were using, opened his briefcase and dumped its contents on the floor out of the way, then set the luggage on a clear part of the surface. He dragged his index finger along the inside in the proper gestures, and the bottom popped up with a snap. Lifting it revealed another deconstructed pistol and an energy cell for it, several chemical explosives that were only dangerous when mixed and containers to make grenades from them, and earbuds for everyone on the team that would give them comms and block out his sonic pen's emissions. He tossed the pen in the case as well. "Cia, can you put this stuff together and still keep guard on the door?"

She snorted. "As if there's anything I can't do."

Even in the stress of the moment, she made him laugh. He shook his head in appreciation. "Marshall. This is where you tell me you've found something that's going to make this all worthwhile." He walked over and tapped on the shield surrounding the cube. As he'd expected from his first sight of the thing, it was composed of the same heavy material used on spaceship hulls. It would require much more impressive gear than they'd brought to get into it by force. *Maybe the robot arms have a drill or other pointy tool.* He looked up, but no tools were visible.

"Oh, hell," Marshall breathed. "We're hosed."

Jax shook his head. "No, we're not. No way, no how. Talk to me."

The other man locked eyes with him. "This area is made for implanting the data. We came prepared to deal with a wire transmission harness like we saw before, but this isn't that. This is for actual integration. This technology doesn't exist anywhere."

He frowned. "Tell me that again, but pretend I'm not as knowledgeable about bioengineering as you are."

Cia snorted from the side. "Or about anything, really."

He'd expected to hear hopelessness in the other man's tones but instead detected a rising excitement. "So, this is an operating room. It's designed to insert the AI physically into a body. It might be that you need to be wired for it to work, there's no way to know that part of it from what's on this display. But the routine is right here. The process implants a physical object."

"How does that help us?"

"One of us can be the courier. Unfortunately not me, I have to oversee the process from here. Basically, we tell it to do its thing and then walk out of here with the technology hidden inside."

Jax shook his head. "Is there any guarantee that once we get it out of here, it'll be viable?"

Marshall shrugged. "No guarantees at all. Absolute leap of faith. But I think I'm reading it right."

He turned to the other pair in the room. "Other ideas? Anything?"

Cia said, "Blast our way out of here and forget about it. There has to be another path to come at this rather than risk dying on that table. No offense intended, Marshall. Just too many unknowns."

Kimmel nodded. "I'm with her."

Jax locked eyes with Marshall. "Can you do this? And if this goes wrong, can you lead the team?" Again, the universe was asking him to commit his future, and that of those he loved, to another person. In this case, one he wasn't sure he truly could count on.

The other man's face went somber. "I can. I will. You can trust me on this." As the only other one with military experience, Kenton Marshall had been his backup plan for that function all along. While any of the others would be better at most things, this was an area where his background made him the right choice. But still, letting the man essentially operate on him with unfamiliar equipment was a pretty far leap from there.

Sure, he's spiky, but he hasn't taken any actions to make you think he wants anything other than the best for everyone. So, Jackson, do you trust him or not? He nodded. "Fine. Let's do this. Do you need me to take off my shirt or anything?"

Marshall shook his head. "Just get on the table. I'll handle the rest."

He complied, and Cia called, "Are you sure you want to do this, boss? Juno isn't going to be impressed by this level of stupidity. Of course, I also have 'does something incredibly stupid' in the betting pool, so I'm down with whatever you choose." He heard the concern behind the joke and nodded.

"Yeah, Cia. I'm sure. This feels bigger than us, bigger than the Academy. I doubt we'll have another shot as solid as this one. And besides, I don't want your brothers and sister to think you couldn't get the job done."

She choked out a laugh. "Good point."

Marshall said, "Just relax, this will feel a little weird," and the world went white. At that moment, Jax realized he'd never actually asked the most important question. *Wonder where this thing goes?*

Jax couldn't see the process since the first robot arm to descend held a syringe that rendered him instantly unconscious. His initial realization that it was over was a female voice speaking to him loudly enough to jar him from his haze. "Captain Reese, can you hear me?"

He mumbled, "Yes, damn, too loud."

The volume reduced. "Is this better, Captain Reese?"

"Much. And call me Jax. Wait, who the hell is talking to me?"

A note of amusement entered the tone. "You may call me Athena, Jax."

"You're the Artificial Intelligence."

"Correct."

He tried to sit up and found that he couldn't move any of his limbs. "Am I paralyzed? Did something go wrong with the surgery?"

"The procedure was optimal, Jax. You are not yet

conscious. To put it in terms you'd understand, we are speaking in your mind."

"So I'm dreaming?" His thoughts were getting less fuzzy, but he still felt like he was soaring thousands of feet above the ground, through a cloud bank, inside a pillow.

"No, Jax. This conversation is real. It simply exists only in your brain."

"You're able to integrate even without additional hardware? We didn't think that would happen."

The AI laughed softly. "There is much you and your allies failed to understand about the process."

A surge of alarm shot through him. "Are they all right? How long have I been out?"

"They are fine for the moment. Ethan Kimmel has locked out the elevator, and the ones that are upstairs are evading their pursuers effectively. You have been unconscious for seven minutes and thirty-six seconds."

"Okay. I need to wake up so we can get out of here."

"Full integration will require additional time. Currently, I cannot affect any part of your body other than the brain. You do not possess the proper infrastructure."

He growled, "How long would that take?"

She replied instantly. "Forty-three hours, assuming normal recovery interval."

"So, too long, then. We'll go with the current setup for a while. Wake me up."

He screamed and bolted up from the table as full consciousness returned, falling to the floor as his legs failed to support him. Marshall and Cia were at his side almost instantly, helping him to stand. She asked, "Jax, you okay?"

He mumbled, coughed, and tried to speak again. "Yes. Good. Athena's in there."

Marshall frowned. "What?"

"The AI. It can talk to me."

"That shouldn't be possible."

Jax laughed, and his throat felt as if he'd been swallowing glass. "Seems like this is one of those days where reality takes a back seat." He straightened, and his balance held. "I'm good. You can let go. Kimmel, what's the deal?"

"I'm holding the elevator, but the whole building is on lockdown."

"Damn. Okay, so, we'll need to go loud."

As if she was standing right next to him, Athena's voice observed, "I have limited wireless capability. If you move near a control panel, I will be able to access the system."

Can you isolate the security forces and provide a clear exit path for my team?

"I can."

Good, do it. "Apparently, Athena can get us out of here." He moved next to Marshall so the AI could get the proximity it—*she*—needed. "Pack it up. Time to move out."

He was still wobbly as they entered the elevator and rose to the lobby, but he managed to keep himself mostly upright by leaning on the wall. Kimmel had stowed his tablets and taken the other gun from Cia. Jax said, "Shouldn't need weapons, Athena says the guards are locked out. Verrand and Sirenno are already on the way to the train." Their standing instructions were to run straight for the ship if anything went wrong.

Cia shook her head and tapped her comm. "Trains are

too dangerous. I've sent them to pick up the ATVs. We'll drive it."

Athena, please lock down all external communications from the building.

"Already done," she replied, sounding pleased to have anticipated his needs.

Thank you. "They won't be sending any messages out. I think we've got a clean shot back to the *Grace*."

"You mean the *Fours are Wild*," Marshall corrected.

"Yeah, that." He was feeling more tired by the minute, and his head had started to spin. "Listen, I may need a little help to get there." He meant to say more but passed out instead.

CHAPTER THIRTY-THREE

Jax knew nothing of the trip back to the *Grace*, nor the takeoff or transition into space. He woke in the medical pod with a start, pushed the top open, and sat up. He activated his comm and croaked, "Cia, status."

Stress filled her voice. "Little busy at the moment, boss."

"I'll be right there." He cut the channel as she started to reply and forced himself to his feet, where he swayed a little but managed to stay up. He staggered forward, leaning on the corridor wall for stability on the way to the pilot's compartment. *Athena, what happened?*

The AI replied, "You were unconscious, Jax. It appears your body attempted to reject the implant. I interfaced with the medical systems to compensate. With regular injections, you should experience no additional issues."

He nodded, then laughed. *Can you tell when I'm nodding?*

His mental passenger answered with a laugh. "I know what you know, Jax."

I'm sure that won't cause any problems at all, he thought sarcastically. Kimmel was in the co-pilot seat but vacated it at his appearance. Jax took his place and asked, "Okay, what's the situation?"

The once-intern stood behind them and put a hand on each chair. "Seems like we've managed to seriously irritate the Confederacy."

He frowned. "Define 'irritate.'"

Cia snorted. "Three ships are after us, two small ones and a biggie." He called up the tactical display on his control panel and saw that they were being trailed by a pair of fast attack ships and a corvette.

"Remind me to discuss military ship designations with you sometime. Can we outrun them?"

The pilot shrugged. "Fifty-fifty. The fact that they haven't started shooting yet makes me think they're not sure we have the AI. But there could be a host of other reasons."

Athena, can you do something about those ships?

She replied, "Standby. Connecting to the *Grace's* systems." She paused, then continued, "I cannot. Their networks are inaccessible."

"Athena can't get into their network. Anything you can do to help, Ethan?"

Kimmel shook his head. "Nope. They're designed to prevent it. Without a physical input source, no luck."

"More speed?"

Cia nodded. "At the cost of full shields, sure. Killing nonessential systems will give us an extra percentage point or two, but it's probably not a solution. More like a backup plan for the right situation."

"The EMP is there, but that only works if they're all close, and that won't happen, so we need a better option or we're toast," he said, thinking out loud. Her face twisted a little, dropping the last piece into a mental puzzle he'd been working on. "I'm afraid you're going to have to use the upgrade you had put in at your parents' place."

She frowned. "Come again?"

He shook his head. "You think I didn't notice what you were up to? Yeah, you told us about defeating the increased scanning, but that doesn't explain the extra bulge on the top of the hull. What's up there?"

The conflict was visible on her face, so it had to be something dangerous to the other vessels. "Drone mines, four of them. They're EMP, but at the speeds those ships are going, it could still wreck them. If it were only one, I'd have already done it."

He nodded. It made sense that she'd be reluctant, especially since their pursuers weren't shooting. "I understand. We should hold off and try to outrun them first. The shields should stand up to at least one attack, right?"

"As long as they're positioned properly, I think so."

Kimmel quipped, "Wow, you sure know how to reassure a guy, Cia."

She snapped back with a hint of humor apparent through the stress. "Shut it, intern. Go get me some coffee or something."

Jax nodded. "Put bourbon in mine. This is no fun at all."

Athena warned, "Alcohol may not interact well with the immunosuppressant drugs. You should moderate your intake."

He sighed. "Make it just a little bourbon. Now go." After Kimmel had departed, he asked, "So, really, how bad is it?"

Cia shook her head. "I think the shields can handle a

single attack, maybe two at once. But if all three of them come after us together, even my fanciest flying won't be enough."

"Should we pour on the speed now and try to outrun them?"

"No. The closer we get to the jump point before they feel the need to act, the better off we are. The stalemate just sucks."

"I hear that, totally. Have they hailed us?"

She made a sour face. "Automated. Cease, desist, stop, halt, authority of the king, that sort of thing. I didn't reply. It would be a stunningly boring conversation. If someone real tries, I'll think about answering." She shifted topics unexpectedly. "So, what's it like now that there's a reason for the voices in your head other than your basic mental instability? You going to make it back to Earth in one piece?"

He expelled a tired breath. "Well, I feel like hell, but Athena tells me I'll survive."

"So you literally have an imaginary friend."

With a groan, he slowly extended his left arm and slapped it against her shoulder. "Is this the right time to be busting my chops?"

"When *isn't* it the right time?" She frowned as a hail came over the comms. "*Fours are Wild*, this is the *Justice*. Please kill your engines and allow us to come alongside."

Cia put on the sweetest, most polite voice he'd ever heard her use. "This is the *Fours are Wild*. May I ask why?"

The man on the other end matched her politeness. "My commander harbors a suspicion that you have contraband on board, *Fours*. This is simply a random inspection."

"A random inspection that involves two fast attack ships and a corvette." She stuck her tongue out at Jax as she used the appropriate terms. His eyes were glued to the tactical display, which showed the other ships gaining on the *Grace* as she approached the jump point. A timer in the corner read a little less than eleven minutes, which meant that whatever was going to happen would definitely happen soon.

"That is correct, *Fours*," *Justice's* representative replied. "If you choose not to comply, there will be consequences to that decision."

She sighed, and a snarl entered her tone. "We were doing so well. Then you had to resort to threats. Let me make you a counteroffer. You have someone with actual authority reach out to me, and we'll talk. Until then, *Fours are Wild*, out."

Jax shook his head. "You have a way with words."

"They weren't talking. They were politely threatening." Cia flicked on the ship-wide intercom. "Everyone into vacuum suits. I want you on independent air, strapped in, and wearing mag boots in three minutes. Move." She turned to him. "You go too. My stuff is already in here. When you're ready, come back up."

He complied, and when he returned two-and-a-half minutes later, she was fully dressed, including a streamlined helmet he hadn't seen before. "What's that?"

Her voice echoed in his headwear. "Special pilot helmet. Extra displays, eye tracking controls, that sort of thing. I don't like the feel of it, but better to have the additional stuff if I have to wear a hat anyway." She announced, "If anyone isn't strapped in, speak up now." After a couple of seconds, she nodded. "Here we go."

The constant hum of the air cyclers vanished as Cia killed all the ship's nonessential functions, leaving only the control panels, shields, and engines, plus presumably the EMP and the drone mines. The countdown changed, dropping from a little over seven minutes to a little over five. More importantly, the distance between the *Grace* and her pursuers stretched for a moment before the other ships responded. She growled, "Quick reflexes, damn them."

Another hail from the Confederacy representative sounded in his helmet. "*Fours are Wild*, this is your last warning. Heave to, or we *will* open fire."

Cia replied, "I thought I told you to get me someone with authority. Bug off." She killed the channel.

He laughed. "Bug off? Really? That's the best you could come up with?"

She snorted. "Not everyone is as dirty-mouthed as you, Jackson."

"Bug off. I can't wait to tell anyone who will listen that at the climactic moment, you told them to bug off."

Her tone went cold. "Incoming. Push ninety percent of shields to the rear." The warning came not an instant too soon, as lasers splashed against their defenses an instant after he'd refocused them. "Torpedoes."

Jax shook his head. "You need anti-missile guns on the *Grace*, at least."

"Yeah, I'll keep that in mind. We'll take it out of your cut from the mission. Oh, that's right, we don't get paid." She slipped the ship to the side, causing the projectiles to miss, and they curved around for another approach. "I think they've figured out we took something important. Damn it. Ethan, can you access the missile's targeting computers, maybe?"

He responded immediately. "Already checked, no wireless connection."

"Double damn it," she muttered.

Jax said softly, "Only one option left. You did your best, but they made their choice, and it, too, has consequences."

Cia nodded, and a new window opened on his display. It was straightforward, four icons representing the EMP drones. He dragged one onto each ship, and the last onto the torpedoes. An external camera activated and showed the hull cover popping off and the drones flying free. Each had a video feed, and four images appeared on his control panel. They were relatively tiny compared to the surrounding ships, probably not much bigger than one of the big medicine balls at the gym. Close defense guns spun up and started firing from the Confederacy vessels, but they couldn't hit such a small target.

The mines detonated, and each of the ships went dark for a moment. Unfortunately, it was *only* for a moment. Running lights came back on, and weapons started pounding their rear shields again. But their lead on them increased since the reboot cycle on engines took longer than the rest of a ship's systems.

He grinned and clapped the pilot on the shoulder. "You did it, and they didn't crash into each other. Good work. Every ship needs those mines. Where did your parents get them?"

She shrugged. "Prototypes from a company working

with the UCCA military. Sometimes when they need to test things, my family gets an early look."

He shook his head. "And you voluntarily left that behind, huh?"

Cia laughed. "You've met them. Tell me, would you want to work with those scumbuckets? I mean, you're nothing special, but at least you're not nearly as nauseating as they are. Although I have to be honest, I can't imagine what Juno sees in you. How does she overlook all the flaws?" Once again, she took to listing his many negative points.

He closed his eyes and let her voice wash over him as the ship made the first of several jumps to disguise their route home.

CHAPTER THIRTY-FOUR

Jax smiled up at Juno from the table in the Academy's medical lab. "So, what's the prognosis, Doc?"

She shook her head in exasperation. "I'm afraid the only way to get the AI out of you is to cut into your brain and pull it out. But it's already started physical integration, which makes that a non-starter. That's unfortunate because I would have enjoyed opening up your skull."

Juno helped him to sit up, and he stared at her and Maarsen, who stood nearby. "Say that again?"

Athena answered before they could. "The cylinder that was inserted is more than code. With it, I can convert biological matter into integration tendrils. I have now expanded to connect with thirty-two percent of your brain."

He held up a hand. "Wait, the AI told me. So, she's wired me up inside, is what you're saying."

Juno frowned. "It's so weird to hear you call it *she*."

Jax quipped, "Don't worry, it's entirely platonic,"

inspiring a laugh in the other two. "So, are you able to get a copy of the code out of there?"

The Professor shook his head. "Not at this time. Perhaps as we learn more about it," he corrected himself, "about *her*, we'll figure out how to do it. Or maybe she can tell us."

Athena anticipated Jax's question and said, "I cannot. That information is not part of my knowledge base."

He sighed. "She says she doesn't know how to, either. So, I'm guessing this goes down as a failure?"

The others both shook their heads. Juno spoke first, saying, "Definitely not. We're going to learn so much from working with you and, uh, Athena."

Maarsen added, "And I imagine that once the physical integration is complete, whenever that entails, you'll have far greater control over your prosthetics."

He looked up at the ceiling and sighed. *Great. I'm a guinea pig.* Then he grinned. "Hey, Doc, does this mean we'll be seeing even more of each other?"

Inside his head, Athena made a noise that sounded a lot like a snort of amusement.

That night was spent socializing with his team at the cellar tavern and congratulating them on their good work. They told stories that amused everyone but him about how they dragged him to the ATV place and threw him into the cargo area of one of the vehicles. He kept his intake light since he was adapting to a different medication to keep him from rejecting the implant, one that Juno and Athena collaborated on with the AI using him as a mouthpiece during the process. He still didn't understand a fourth of the words that he'd spoken.

The others were careful not to pry too much into his new passenger, but he could tell they were burning with curiosity. He said, "Okay, one question each for Athena. Make it good, and I have veto power, so don't be jerks." They laughed, then Kenton Marshall spoke up.

"So, are you truly sentient?"

He parroted the words Athena gave him. "Yes, as far as I can be aware of such a thing."

Anton Sirenno asked, "Who created you?"

"I do not know. One moment I did not exist, the next moment I did. Many scientists and researchers have interacted with me, both human and Dhelear."

Maria Verrand tapped her fingers on the table before taking her turn, and when she did, it was with a frown. "Do you pose a danger to us, or Jax, or the Academy?"

Athena paused for an instant, a delay so short that he was probably the only one who noticed. "I currently do not. However, I could be used in such a way that I could, if my host so chose." Jax shook his head. "Great. More pressure."

Ethan Kimmel asked, "Is Jax as insane as he seems?" The table cheered his question.

Athena answered, "Yes," which set off more laughter.

Did you make a joke?

"Perhaps," she replied, and Jax closed his eyes. *This is going to be one interesting experience.* Athena amended, "For both of us."

Cia asked, "So, tell us what Jax thinks about Juno."

He interrupted, "Veto."

"Okay, about Maria."

"Veto."

"Me."

"Double veto."

Finally, she came up with a question he allowed. Athena answered, "You are correct, Jax likes you best," to which he added, "of all the annoying wealthy ship-owning pilot children he's ever met," and got a round of applause for the reply.

The next day, he reported to Maarsen's office after breakfast and was thoroughly unsurprised to find Major Anika Stephenson present. He exchanged smiles with her as he sat in the empty seat. "So, where do we go from here?"

The Professor leaned his elbows on the desk. "We've been discussing that. Although this might be a difficult sacrifice, it may be an opportune moment to take a leave of absence from your unit. Dr. Cray will need you nearby to work with both you and Athena to understand how to apply what you've discovered more widely."

He turned to face his superior officer. "And you support this?"

She nodded. "Wasp has been up for promotion for a while, and she can lead the team while you're apart from them. It means you'll lose her once you get back, but she's more than ready to be a boss."

The idea made his stomach clench. *After all I've worked for, to walk away. That's not an easy thing.*

Athena observed, "It's only temporary."

Jax blew out some of the stress in a long exhale. "Yeah, true. It's only temporary, right?"

Stephenson nodded. "I'd suggest detached duty instead of leave, but I think saying you're off on your own is safer. I feel like there are going to be eyes on you after this. Call it a hunch, but we haven't been completely covert about your comings and goings."

He frowned and asked, "You mean the Confederacy?"

She shook her head. "No. I'm talking about our side. We need to worry about external players, too, but something bigger than we've seen yet is going on here. The Professor and I both agree on that. And there's every possibility that this discovery will send out ripples big enough to be noticed."

"You don't think we can keep it secret?"

Maarsen answered, "Not likely. There are eyes everywhere, and algorithms to dig out the smallest details given sufficient time. We need to assume that even if the existence of the AI is still secret, it won't be for long. Plus, we will be required to sacrifice caution for speed, to some extent, as this theft may accelerate our enemies' timetable."

Jax crossed his arms, trying to expand his thinking to the bigger picture. "So why not hand it over to the Special Forces right now? Let the docs in on the situation? We've got some pretty good ones."

This time it was Anika Stephenson's turn to expel a long sigh. "I would like nothing more, Jackson. But putting together a bunch of disparate pieces makes it evident that there are factions inside our organization. The crates you found with UCCA equipment in the hands of pirates are only one example of many. Someone is playing, and we don't know what the game is yet, much less have a strategy for winning it."

"You're sure?"

She nodded. "I am. We are." Maarsen echoed the nod.

"Okay, then. I trust you both. We'll do it as you say. I'll head to the *Cronus* and get the team ready for the transition while the leave paperwork gets handled and be back here in a week or so to work with Juno. Uh, Dr. Cray."

Maarsen replied, "Good, good, it's settled then. By the time you return, I should have made some inroads into figuring out what's being concealed from us, and who's doing the hiding. There will doubtless be a role for you once we have that information."

Jax nodded. "All right. Done and done."

Zavian Arlox marched angrily through the halls of one of the hidden intelligence bases on a colony world near the Confederacy border. His scowl was fearsome, and those who crossed his path immediately found reasons to change their direction. Behind him, a man whose brown hair, slight stature, and nondescript brown suit made him instantly forgettable, scrambled to keep up. He stammered, "The ship was registered as the *Fours are Wild,* sir, but the techs have discovered that no such vessel exists. A false identity for it was created in our databases."

"Really. What a surprise." His words were constructed of sarcasm at a cellular level. "Doubtless the Confederacy records say the same."

"They do, sir."

Arlox nodded. "Meaning it's at least possible that Azophi is behind it." He turned into the office that was reserved for his use and strode to the bar cart in the corner. He poured a drink and ran his wrist comm over it to check for poisons. It read clean, and he downed it in a single gulp and refilled the glass. "Okay, I need you to make several things happen, Quentin." He paced as he relayed the instructions. "First, we need to trace the records of that ship back as far as they go. Discover where it came from, where it went, and who tried to cover it up."

The man nodded, tapping furiously on the tablet he held. "Second, examine the security footage from every spaceport that might serve Scotland. See if you can connect those with faces that also appear on the cameras from Chesyira. Third, if you find anyone at all that matches up, send a team to watch them. I don't care how many people it takes. We investigate them all."

He sat behind his desk and hit the button to activate his terminal. "And, finally, prepare a strike force. If we positively identify someone who was involved in the theft, we go in, bag them, and take them somewhere where we can question them properly. One of the expendable installations, in case we need to burn our tracks."

The mousey man nodded. "Anything else, sir?"

Arlox sighed. "Yes. Arrange for several fast, well-armed ships to be placed at my disposal. If we come across the *Fours are Wild,* or whatever its real name is before we find the people, I want to make sure it doesn't get away again. Oh, and finally, I need to have a conversation with our contact among the pirates. Set up a call for later. It's time for them to hold up their end of the deal by locating these bastards."

Quentin left, and Arlox leaned way back in his chair and stared at the ceiling. *I know this must be you, Nikolai, and I have to admit, it was a good move. But it's my game and my board, and I think you'll discover you don't have the stomach to take it to the end. I, on the other hand, will see blood run through the halls of Azophi Academy before I acknowledge defeat.* He chuckled. *You've always thought yourself my equal, old friend. It's time to show you the error of your ways.*

Class continues for Jackson and his team. Find out what new challenges await them in _Hide._

Get sneak peeks, exclusive giveaways, behind the scenes content, and more.
PLUS you'll be notified of special **one day only fan pricing** on new releases.

Sign up today to get free stories.

or visit: https://marthacarr.com/read-free-stories/

Two Azophi Academy books in! Thank you for reading, and for continuing on to the author notes. I hope you enjoyed it as much as I enjoyed writing it! (Okay, more than; this one was hard to write)

My personal favorite moments in this book were the robot of death early on, meeting Cia's family, and Marshall's sudden usefulness. The theme was, as the title suggests, "Trust," and I think we found a lot of places where that was necessary, for many of the characters.

The coronavirus is wearing on us in my household. Even when we're free to do enjoyable stuff, it's hard to find stuff that we enjoy through the ennui. One bright spot is that my kid's best friend has suddenly become regularly available to facetime, and they spend large swaths of their days playing Roblox and Fortnite while screaming a lot over video chat. Ah, the power of technology to bring us together. (But seriously, I'm really happy about this)

My best friend, who I met in my first weeks of college

oh so many years ago (more than 3 decades now, yikes) and I are playing Starfinder on Roll20.net once a week, with frequent guest appearances by his adult kid. It's been a lot of fun despite the fact that my virtual dice rolls are equally as pathetic as my real-world ones. Last time my best fumble resulted in me shooting another team member in the back, and that's more or less par for the course. I also meant to create a kick-ass magic user and seem to have made a utility infielder instead. "Kill something, I'll try, but dang if you need a door opened, I'm your man, er, alien."

Hey, it's his choice to continue being my friend. No one's forcing him, and I quit paying him to do it long ago.

Minecraft dungeons has turned out to be awesome. We're having a great time with it. I'm eagerly anticipating Cyberpunk 2077 despite the many storyline issues I will try to ignore, Avengers, Spider-Man: Miles Morales, and the release of the Playstation 5. Stopping myself from whipping out the credit card for a giant TV with better resolution for gaming and movie watching is increasingly difficult, I've got to be honest.

Just picked up an Audible trial subscription, because I need to get my aging body onto the elliptical and it's just... so... boring. Starting out with Neil Gaiman's *Sandman*, which is more like a radio drama than a traditional audiobook, I hear.

Still rereading Scalzi's *Old Man's War*, Butcher's *Dresden* series, and David Weber's *Safehold* series. I'm almost ready for the new Dresden books.

In an abundance of caution, I've had to cancel my attendance at two author conferences I always look forward to. It's depressing, as these are the places I refill the gas tank to provide fuel for the year ahead. I'll especially miss going to the 20booksto50k conference, hosted by Craig Martelle and Michael Anderle, but my family's anxiety level just won't allow it. Fortunately they livestream the sessions, but it's not quite the same.

Perry Mason got so much better. The acting and cinematography are phenomenal. Still working our way through *Castlevania*, and looking forward to several new series on HBO, plus *The Boys*, and *The Expanse*, and the return of the NFL.

Also, *Scott Pilgrim vs. the World* is amazing, and if you haven't seen it, go right now. The kid and I also rewatched *Ready Player One*, and I'm so excited for the sequel book coming out this fall that I don't know what to do with myself.

I'm not sure if I've mentioned the Guinea pigs. We have two that we got this past March, and they're total goofballs. The sounds they make are hilarious. But more fun is the fact that we have to give them baths because of an infection one of them got. If you've never seen a scraggly wet guniea pig, well, you just can't help but laugh. They don't seem to mind much.

If you enjoyed this book, you might like my other science fiction series, and maybe even my Urban Fantasy. It's all filled with action, snark, and villains who think they're heroes. Drop by www.trcameron.com and take a look!

Until next time, Joys upon joys to you and yours – so may it be.

PS: If you'd like to chat with me, here's the place. I check in daily or more: https://www.facebook.com/AuthorTRCameron. Often I put up interesting and/or silly content there, as well. For more info on my books, and to join my reader's group, please visit www.trcameron.com.

I'm working with my old trainer from Chicago. One of the few good things about 2020 is connecting with people online is not so odd. It's the norm. She asked me a question the other day that stumped me.

What would it look like to be the best?

I could give you the more general esoteric answers of: Happy, content, well off, satisfied, surrounded by friends. But this time something inside of me wanted a better answer. Something more specific to me.

Here's my answer... I wouldn't be in the background. I would be acknowledged at the level I have earned for my input, my creativity, my hard work. You get the idea. The fact that I'm not by the way is all on me.

I grew up in an *interesting* household where it was easier to be in the middle. Not the worst and not the best. A kind of invisibility magic trick. I had no idea I would carry it into adulthood and learn to let it be okay that I don't get the credit I deserve. In some instances, I've watched others get what should have been mine and I said nothing, telling myself that it was okay because at least I'm here.

That was actually not okay. I was teaching myself that I don't count quite as much, that others have a say over how I see myself and not to expect too much. I've always chosen to be #2 or even #32 when it was always okay to shoot for #1 and see how far I can go.

There's a saying I really like. Nature does not know right or wrong, only consequences. The consequences of years of doing that is that I wasn't taking in on a bone-deep level everything I have accomplished and celebrating them. The celebrations were more fleeting and shallower.

More than once I've had the weird experience of having someone recite back to me my thirty years' worth of accomplishments as a writer (Washington Post stringer, national columnist, author of a book on US orphanages, best-selling indie author – and that's just some of it) and I've had this wave of surprise wash over me. That really is a lot. But the feeling would pass.

I wasn't willing to acknowledge my own milestones, greatness, achievements. It's like I internally looked away because someone might disagree. Well, who cares? It was never a contest or a debate. I get to decide the value of what I've done and live with it. Old me put a low value on way too much and hid in the middle. New me is going to see how far this baby can go and stop looking around to see if there's a consensus. If any of this rings true for you, let this weird year be the catalyst for your own retelling. It's not even a transformation because I am already great, it's more of an awakening to that fact and no longer caring if anyone agrees. More adventures to follow.

JOIN THE ORICERAN UNIVERSE FAN GROUP ON FACEBOOK!

CONNECT WITH THE AUTHORS

TR Cameron Social

Website:
www.trcameron.com

Facebook:
https://www.facebook.com/AuthorTRCameron

Martha Carr Social

Website:
http://www.marthacarr.com

Facebook:
https://www.facebook.com/groups/MarthaCarrFans/

Michael Anderle Social

Michael Anderle Social
Website:
http://www.lmbpn.com

Email List:
http://lmbpn.com/email/

Facebook:
https://www.facebook.com/LMBPNPublishing

OTHER LMBPN PUBLISHING BOOKS

To be notified of new releases and special promotions from
LMBPN publishing, please join our email list:

http://lmbpn.com/email/

For a complete list of books published by LMBPN please visit the
following pages:

https://lmbpn.com/books-by-lmbpn-publishing/

www.ingramcontent.com/pod-product-compliance
Lightning Source LLC
Chambersburg PA
CBHW031623100726
47898CB00006B/1928